Glancing Through the Glimmer

The Glimmer Books

Book One

PAT McDERMOTT

FOR BEVIN

Also in This Series

Autumn Glimmer
A Pot of Glimmer

PREFACE

In 1002 A.D., the chieftain of an obscure Irish clan became High King of Ireland. Brian Boru united Ireland's warring tribes under one leader for the first and only time in Irish history. A scholar as well as a warrior, King Brian rebuilt churches, encouraged education, repaired roads and bridges, and roused the country to rise against the Norse invaders who had ravaged Ireland for centuries.

On Good Friday in 1014 A.D., Brian's army challenged a host of Vikings and their allies on the plains of Clontarf. Though his troops were victorious, Brian's son and grandson perished in the battle. Brian himself died as he prayed in his tent, murdered by fleeing Vikings who stumbled upon his camp.

Many historians have said that Ireland would be a different place today if Brian Boru and his heirs had survived the Battle of Clontarf. The Glimmer Books offer one possible scenario.

CHAPTER ONE

The horses screamed. Their galloping hooves thundered over the moonlit plains of Galway. Jewels embedded in their foreheads reflected the flames they breathed. The riders' capes flew wide behind them in an even green array. No hint of a winner yet.

The finish line, a sloping stream, appeared in the night like a ribbon of sparkling stars. Finvarra roared with joy and spurred his stallion hard. Bracing its mighty quarters, the black beast leapt high and hurtled ahead of the others.

Finvarra won every race, yet he exulted in each victory as if it were his first—at least until the competition ended. Quickly bored yet again, the King of the Connaught Fairies wished himself home to the crystal palace beneath the hill the mortals called Knock Ma.

He climbed the steps from the stables thinking that home was looking tired these days. When the glimmer slipped, as it did when the troop diverted their magical muscle to dancing or racing their horses, the wear and tear of the centuries glared. Cracks had appeared in the ivory stairs, and the flickering golden sconces ought to have emitted a more pleasant perfume. Little holes dotted the rock crystal walls: misfortune had forced Finvarra to sell the decorative gemstones.

He swept through the arched entrance to the bustling, music-filled banquet hall. Decked out in their tattered party attire, the laughing fairies whirled and reeled around marble pillars. Those taking their turn as liveried servants carried ale to the dancers. In *wooden* cups!

What would they eat tonight? Bad luck to the Munster fairies who owned the bottomless cauldron that never ran out of food. Perhaps one day Finvarra would lead his troop on a raid to steal the vessel from them. In the past, when the mortals believed in the fairies, the peasants left milk and butter on their windowsills every night. The wealthier mortals offered kegs of good wine and tasty oat cakes. Now the troop had to pilfer what they could, though they didn't seem worried as long as they could dance.

They spun around couches covered with matted, mangy furs. Half the candles in the chandeliers had burned out. Cobwebs covered the tapestries.

Finvarra stomped into the room. "Have a care for the glimmer, my friends!"

The startled fairies stopped in their tracks. Turning their heads like addled owls, they squeaked and tsked as if they'd only just noticed the deterioration around them. Once they'd boosted their glimmer and cloaked the hall in its former glory, Finvarra cheerily retired to the private rooms he shared with Oona.

With the glimmer in full force, all was as it should be. Gems adorned the furniture. Silk brocade trimmed with gold covered the bed. Seated before the smokeless hearth, he sipped a goblet of so-so wine and watched his stunning queen prepare for her next outing. Oona primped before a gilded mirror, changing the color of her big, round eyes. She finally selected periwinkle.

Whatever color she chose, her eyes beguiled Finvarra. He adored her. "Where are you going, Oona?"

"To Gort, to catch a hurling match. You know how much I appreciate the mortal players' skill." Her voice trilled as it always did when a rollicking good time chanced her way.

"I know how much you appreciate the mortal players' physiques." Finvarra grew jealous, not of the players, but that Oona had something to do and he didn't. "Ah well. Have your fun. I'll find some means to amuse myself." He drummed his fingers on the arm of his chair. "Perhaps I'll order a formal ball."

Yes, that would do it. How brilliant he was! Though he joined in an occasional polka or jig downstairs, ages had passed since he'd spent an entire night dancing. A proper ball would occupy him for a good long stretch, but he must find a mortal woman. The female fairies might be nimble, but a mortal woman had more grip to her—and Finvarra enjoyed his gripping.

Oona tossed her head. Her thick blond hair cascaded over her shimmering curves and swept the gilded floor of their boudoir. "I heard the mortal king is having a ball soon. Such a shame his clan no longer invites us to their parties."

Finvarra considered her words. "It has been some time, hasn't it?" Wounded by the perceived insult, he punched the palm of his hand. "I should have let him die in that battle! We rode with the Irish and fought bravely. I doubt they would have succeeded in trouncing the Vikings without our magic. King Brian himself would be dead if I hadn't personally saved him from assassination. Then where would Ireland be? They'd have presidents and prime ministers instead of kings. Why does Brian spurn us? Why, Oona? We've been good friends to him."

Oona's reflection smiled at him from the mirror, her aging face still heart-shaped and lovely. "How often must I tell you, sweet? You saved Brian Boru nearly a thousand mortal years ago. Ireland has a different King Brian today. Same lineage, same name, but generations have passed for the mortals since the Battle of Clontarf."

Finvarra often forgot such tedious details. "Ah yes. Modern, they call themselves now. Building, always building. They used to know better than to violate our homes, but they've damaged several of our forts and hawthorn trees lately. I can't abide the noise, and our coffers won't bear the strain of paying for repairs much longer. Why, the mortals have made a golf course out of Cousin Donn's sand hills down in County Clare! Ripped one of his finest hawthorn trees right out of the ground. I would have blinded the thieves, for all the good it would do. They don't believe in us anymore, Oona."

A tiny pout appeared on Oona's mulberry lips. "That is a concern, but we have lots more forts and palaces. Why don't you have the troop keep a closer watch on them? Tell them to wield our old mischief when the builders approach. Nothing too extreme. Make their machinery stall. Untie their shoelaces so they trip. They'll believe in us then."

Oona applied her glimmer. A burst of youthful beauty masked her true appearance. Decay had crept into more than the palace: the fairies were growing old. They needed the mortals' belief to keep them young and maintain their magic at adequate levels, but if the mortals no longer believed in them, what would become of Finvarra and his troop? Of all the fairy folk in Ireland, for that matter?

"I'll give it some thought," he said. "Right now, I want to dance. I must obtain a mortal dancing partner."

"Have Becula help you. She has a knack for finding suitable partners from Out There. But remember, sweet. We promised the mortal kings we wouldn't keep the girls anymore. Just borrow them for a dance or two and send them back."

Finvarra sighed. He hated rules, but maintaining the mortal women had proved more trouble than they were worth. The troop had to feed them, and they eventually aged and died, even in the fairy realm, where they lived much longer than they would Out There. They were down to three mortals now, ancient women far too old to dance. Now they spun cloth and helped serve food at special parties. In their youth, they'd favored Finvarra with many hours of dancing and other delights. He would miss them when they were gone.

"The same goes for you and your hurling lads, Oona. Don't be bringing them back here."

She shot him a lusty smile. "Of course not."

"And don't be away too long. I may enjoy dancing with mortals, but I prefer your company."

"Oh, Fin, you say the loveliest things." She patted his face, studying him as she did. "Be sure to spruce up your glimmer before you meet your mortal dancer. You wouldn't want to frighten her." She kissed him and vanished.

Lips still tingling, Finvarra glanced in the mirror. The handsome youth he'd been for ages no longer stared back at him. He'd grown shorter, and his golden locks had faded to lifeless silver strings. And his face! Grizzly stubble blotched his once smooth cheeks. Webs of lines rimmed shrunken eyes whose brilliant azure had dulled to gray.

Peeved that his regal good looks had melted away, he let out a roar that would reach every corner of Ireland: "Becula!"

CHAPTER TWO

The far-off grumble of motorcycles drew Janet to the windows. The Presidential Suite had three of them, monstrous gobs of glass set in the outer curve of the oval room, the biggest guest suite in the sprawling mansion. She slipped by the antique desk and drew the flowery curtain back.

Beneath her, the dreary gardens of Deerfield House, the official home of the American Ambassador to Ireland, sat soaking up the rain. She thought an ambassador's garden should have more flowers, more color, look more like Boston's Public Garden. But this was Dublin, not Boston. She would never forgive her grandparents for dragging her here.

Beyond the gardens and rolling lawns that Gramp said would make a good golf course, Phoenix Park stretched green and boring. At the far end of the forever driveway that wound through the shrubs and grass, the motorcade crawled toward Deerfield House like a swarm of hungry bugs.

Janet tried to guess how long it would take them to reach the mansion. No more than a few minutes, she thought. They'd already passed the security gate. "They're coming, Matti. As soon as my grandparents leave, we can go into town."

Matti slapped her e-book reader shut and set it on the coffee table. "About time. I can't wait to see more of Dublin, and the places I've been reading about will be crowded on a Saturday." She pulled off her glasses, rose from the couch, and stretched. "What do you want to do first?"

The blue and white sofa in front of the fireplace had become Matti's favorite spot in the suite, the only guest quarters in Deerfield House with twin beds. She'd arrived four days ago for a ten-day visit, and the girls would share the space until the following Thursday, when Matti would return to Boston to start her junior year of high school.

Janet should be starting with her. She glanced down at the gardens again and pictured herself back in Boston. "How about a walk through Boston Common?"

"Come on, Jan. You're not giving Dublin a chance. I think it's great. At least what I've seen of it so far." Matti cleaned her glasses on the hem of her shirt and slipped them back on.

"I still don't see why I couldn't have stayed with you," Janet said. "Your parents offered. I'm going to ask Gram again. I can't stand this place."

She'd only been in the Kingdom of Ireland a little over a month, and already she missed her Drama Club friends. Was it so unreasonable to want to finish her last two years of high school with them? Not only was she lonely, but Mr. Bates had promised her a big part in the Christmas play.

"Yeah," Matti said in a teasing tone, "it's horrible. A big mansion with a cook and a maid, and a bedroom you can get lost in. Don't expect any sympathy from me." Her face brightened the way it did when she tried to act. "Hey, want to trade places?"

Janet beamed at her friend. "I'd trade places in a minute if it didn't mean we'd have an ocean between us."

The hardest part about leaving Boston had been leaving Matti behind. They'd met two years ago, two nervous freshmen trying out for the Drama Club's first play of the year. Mr. Bates had asked Janet to read for three of the one-act mystery's roles. She breezed through the audition and landed the juicy part of the damsel in distress.

The stage quickly became her second home. She loved being anyone but herself. In the magical cloak of a false persona, her confidence soared, at least for a while. Her slim blond looks made her perfect for ingénue parts, but her flair for drama had won her a wide assortment of roles. Mr. Bates even thought she might win the next regional drama competition—but then she'd moved to Ireland.

Matti couldn't act for beans. At that first audition, Mr. Bates had asked her to read for the spinster aunt's role. She'd fumbled the lines and ended up crying. Janet felt sorry for the plump, nearsighted girl and tried to cheer her up by encouraging her to work with the scenery and props. Matti found her niche painting backdrops, and the girls became best friends. They loved the rehearsals, the makeup, the costumes and cast parties. For the first time since her parents died, Janet had felt she fit in.

Whenever she thought of her parents, she touched the last gift she'd ever received from them: the heart-shaped locket they'd given her for her twelfth birthday. The locket hung from a delicate chain she wore around her neck. They'd put a miniature picture of themselves inside, almost as if they'd known they'd soon be gone. She touched the locket now. Her parents wouldn't have made her leave her friends and move to Ireland.

"I mean it, Matt, about talking to Gram. If I catch her and Gramp just right, I'm sure they'll let me live with you until Gramp's term ends. Or at least until the Class of 2012 graduates. Maybe longer. Gramp said the colleges here are great, but I don't want to go to college in Ireland. High school is bad enough!"

Matti had gone to the bureau to comb her hair. "How long is he here for? My mom thought three years."

Janet sighed. "Yes, but if the president gets re-elected, it could be seven. I'll be twenty-three. I'll be so old, I could die over here!"

"Can we see more of Dublin before you do, Drama Queen? Let's go to the zoo. It's right here in Phoenix Park, and I heard on the news they have a two-week-old baby giraffe."

Before Janet could answer, someone knocked on the door. "Come in," she said.

Gram blew into the room dressed in the full-skirted navy blue suit she'd had specially made for meeting the Irish king and queen. The lambswool coat she'd bought the first day they arrived in Dublin hung over her arm. Her manicured hand held a small blue envelope and a brochure. As usual, she wore lots of jewelry, and her stylist had perfectly curled and heavily sprayed her short white hair. Gram had declared war on the Irish humidity the day they'd moved into Deerfield House.

She snapped a greeting at both girls before her familiar wooden smile appeared and zoomed in on Janet. "I have two surprises for you, dear," she said, waving the blue envelope and the brochure. "You know that next Friday night, your grandfather and I are attending the Ambassadors' Ball at Clontarf Castle. Well, the royal family has invited you too."

"Me?" Janet gripped the flowery curtain. "It must be a mistake. I'm not old enough to go to a ball!"

Gram had attended lots of upper-crust parties when she and Gramp lived in all those foreign countries. They'd left their lavish lifestyle behind when Gramp retired from the State Department so he and Gram could raise Janet. She'd hardly known her grandparents when she first met them, but she couldn't say they hadn't taken good care of her. Too good, in fact.

Janet's father had been their only child. Losing him was undoubtedly what caused them to smother her to death. They kept her from school activities they considered risky and monitored every move she made. She hated it, hated that Gram had let her know more than once how much she'd given up to look after her. At least they'd let her join the Drama Club.

When Gramp had received the president's invitation to serve as Ambassador to Ireland, he'd accepted. Not because he missed the job, he said, or because Ireland had great golf courses, but because Janet could attend school in Europe and see some of the world. If she heard one more time what a wonderful opportunity they'd given her, she'd scream. The opportunity seemed more for Gram, who'd clearly been ecstatic to reclaim her former lifestyle—a lifestyle it seemed she was trying to foist upon Janet.

Except for the junior prom, Janet had never attended a formal event, and she never wanted to attend another. The prom had ended in disaster. Ricky Gagnon, the school's handsome basketball captain, had asked mere sophomore Janet to be his date. She'd jumped at the chance, and her grandparents had approved. She and Gram went shopping together and selected a lacy lavender gown. Gram treated her to an afternoon at a salon for the works, and Gramp hired a sleek white limousine.

With Ricky as her prince, Janet easily assumed the role of a glamorous fairytale princess. She'd never worn spiked heels, however. While freestyle dancing with Ricky, she stabbed dozens of defenseless feet, and that wasn't the worst. The evil shoes caught the edge of a long white tablecloth. She'd tripped and knocked over the entire dessert buffet.

She still had nightmares about it, of the whole junior class, including that jackass Ricky, laughing at her. The chance to escape the taunts of the snooty new seniors had been the only good thing about moving to Ireland.

"Of course you're old enough, dear." Gram fixed her carefully made-up face into one of those *looks*, the one with the tiny twist in her lips that said that she knew best and that Janet was only a silly girl. "You're already sixteen. Queen Eileen herself called me this morning. We had a lovely chat, and she insisted we bring you along."

"But I'll have no one to talk to. Everyone will be so"—Janet caught herself before "old" slipped out—"grown up."

"Not so, dear. The queen said Princess Talty and Prince Liam can't wait to meet you. They're not much older than you, you know. We'll have a wonderful time. The Boru clan may be one of the oldest royal dynasties in the world, but they're far from stuffy. They all love to dance."

Dance! Afraid she'd pull the curtain down, Janet released it and clutched at her jean pockets. "But I have nothing to wear!" she cried, knowing she sounded pathetic. Why did Gram always make her feel like such a little girl? As she suspected, her protest proved futile.

Gram had already made an appointment with a Dublin dressmaker. "Louise is a prominent designer, the same couturier who dresses Queen Eileen and Princess Talty. You're seeing her today at two o'clock. We were lucky to get you in so soon. The queen put in a word for us." Gram held the blue envelope out to Janet. "Here's the address and some extra cash, dear. Take a taxi into town."

"Yes, Gram." Janet crossed the room and took the envelope. It would be full of those silly euros. The coins confused her, and the bills looked like they belonged in a board game.

"There's more than enough for you and Matti to have a proper lunch somewhere. Take your cell phones, and be sure to stay together. And Janet, I know you won't do anything to embarrass your grandfather."

"Like what? Run naked up Grafton Street?"

The face beneath the makeup turned white. "Janet Gleason! What sort of thing is that for a young lady to say?"

Janet bit her lip to keep from laughing. "Sorry, Gram."

"Oh, I nearly forgot. Here's the second surprise." Gram handed Janet the brochure. "Here's some information about that school we found for you. I know you'll love it. We've arranged to visit it next week. Matti is welcome to come along." Gram slipped into her coat. A quick shrug settled it on her shoulders. "We'll see you sometime tonight. Be good!"

Gram never hugged or kissed when she was dressed for a public event. She blew the girls kisses and opened the bedroom door. And she was gone. Off to Dublin's mysterious Tara Hall, where the Irish royal family worked, if worked was the right word for what royal people did. Today Gramp would formally introduce Gram and himself to King Brian. Relieved that she didn't have to go with them, Janet scanned the front of the brochure.

"Sweet!" Matti shouted. "My friend, Cinderella! Wait till everyone hears you danced with a real prince, Janikins!"

The school looked really posh. Janet already despised it. "I'm not dancing with anyone. I don't know those ballroom type dances. They're not like the dances we do in school."

"Do you think Ricky will be jealous? Maybe not. I read an article about Prince Liam. Saw his picture. He's a real nerd. Thick glasses, perfect haircut, only wears suits and ties, goes to school all year. All software, no hardware. A total geek."

Leave it to Matti to read up on everything. "Unlike you, only a half-geek. And who cares what Ricky thinks? He's not my boyfriend. He didn't even say good-bye before I left." Janet continued reading about the school, which was seven miles south of Dublin. One of Matti's breakneck statements, the one about the prince attending school all year, echoed back to her.

"Why does Prince Liam go to school all year? Nine months is bad enough."

"All the kids in the royal family do," Matti called from the walk-in closet. "They're seriously smart, and they have to have special training so they'll be ready to rule the country. They even have special tutors on top of school."

"Great. Just the kind of kids with whom I want to hang out," Janet said, mimicking her sophomore English teacher explaining the correct use of prepositions. "They'll know all the atomic numbers and think I'm a moron."

Matti emerged from the closet with their jackets. "What's gotten into you, Jan? You really need to cheer up. If anyone can pull this off, you can. You're an awesome actress. If you rehearse, you can come off like a Beacon Hill debutante. You're cute and skinny, and you're going to have a totally hot dress. So let's go. I'm hungry."

Janet opened the brochure. Her stomach dropped. "Wait a minute! This is a boarding school! They're sending me to a boarding school!"

Outside the house, the motorcycles coughed and roared. Janet ran back to the window in time to see her grandparents enter a black limousine. "Why are you doing this?" she called through the glass. "I hate you!"

The chauffeur closed the door. The car and its noisy escort turned in the circular drive and rolled away.

CHAPTER THREE

The sun broke through the clouds as a luxury sedan turned onto a south Dublin street with only one abode: the palatial King's Residence. Black security gates embellished with the royal lion of the Boru clan swung open. The car inched through and coasted to a stop in a flower-filled courtyard. His Royal Highness, Prince Liam Conor Boru, the second child and only son of King Brian and Queen Eileen, thanked the driver and breezed through the back entrance, taking the stairs two at a time to his rooms.

Liam had spent a delightful morning immersed in Ireland's wealth of legends and myths. Though only seventeen, his family had fondly dubbed him their unofficial *shanachie*, the Irish word for storyteller. His talent for telling the old tales had made the prince a popular visitor to schools, hospitals, and nursing homes. Today he'd cast his spell in a hospital ward filled with sick children.

Such visits were part of the royal duties that sometimes overwhelmed him, though they hadn't burdened him this fine summer day. He'd left the children smiling, and he still had the rest of the afternoon free. Eager to shed his constricting suit and tie, he entered his bedroom suite and found his cousin Kevin waiting, as they'd planned.

Kevin Boru, the younger son of the king's only brother, was also seventeen. He and Liam had grown up together as close friends and confidants. They attended the same schools, shared the same tutors, and played the same sports.

They played the same video games too. Shoeless and deceptively sleepy-eyed, Kevin lay sprawled on Liam's bed saving the world from rogue asteroids. He sat up when Liam came in and set the remote control on the night stand. "Hey, Li. How'd your recimitations go?"

"Easy cakes." Liam wriggled out of his jacket. "The kids loved the evil stepmother more than the children she turned into swans."

"Ah, King Lir and his brood. That one always makes me sad."

"It's one of Talty's favorites. She used to make my father tell it over twice in one night."

"Is she coming home for the Ambassadors' Ball? I haven't seen her for ages."

"Neither have I, and yes, she is. The whole clan is coming. Any excuse to dance." Liam couldn't wait to see his sister. He missed the ally who understood what being a child of the king entailed. The brunt of attention, both private and public, had fallen on Liam since she'd gone off to serve in the navy, and he hated it.

Liam's father wanted him to study law. Liam didn't mind, as his studies would include ancient Irish law. If he had his way, he'd be a historian, a keeper of tradition. He often felt out of place in the modern world. Talty had told him that she did too, that she identified more with the women warriors from Ireland's olden days than with her genteel female relatives.

Some of the clan's elders claimed that their noble bloodlines ran back so far that subconscious memories of such things trickled down to them like water melting from a vast sheet of ice. Others said the souls of their ancestors returned repeatedly to ensure that each new generation of Borus had the right balance of poets, warriors, lawmakers, and, Liam hoped, storytellers.

Kevin closed his eyes and groaned. "I can't wait. The dancing would be fine if I didn't have to listen to, 'Oh, you're so cute, Kevin! Look at those big blue eyes! Look at those dimples! Look how big and tall you've grown!'"

Laughing at Kevin's mimicry, Liam hung his suit on the valet rack beside his desk. His personal assistant, a persnickety tailor-cum-valet named Ross, would be back later that afternoon to see to the suit. For nearly ten years, Ross had looked after Liam's wardrobe, keeping the growing prince well-dressed and ensuring that he looked his best for public appearances, such as the one he'd attended that morning.

Liam often wondered what an old man approaching thirty could possibly know about style, yet he was content to let Ross keep his enormous closet in order. Each week, Ross received a copy of Liam's schedule and planned accordingly. Even without the schedule, Liam knew that everything from his knockabout duds to his finest formal attire would be ready to wear in seconds, no small achievement, as he'd shot up to six feet over the past year.

"I hope we'll have the dance at Clontarf," said equally tall Kevin.

"Why wouldn't we?" Liam pulled a pair of old jeans, worn sneakers, and a T-shirt from the well-stocked closet. A hooded gray sweatshirt completed the outfit.

"My father says there's a bad run of rats in the cellars now. Said all the rain this summer brought them inside."

Liam shuddered. He detested rats. One had skittered over his foot when he was a boy playing hide and seek in the secret passageways beneath Clontarf Castle. His sister and cousins had teased him when he screamed, but he didn't care. He'd rather meet ghosts than rats.

"I expect the exterminators are up there now," he said. "I hope so. We have the best dances at Clontarf. If not, they'll have this one at Tara Hall."

"Your parents are at the Hall today. What's going on?"

Liam removed his gold-rimmed glasses and pulled the T-shirt over his head. "The new American Ambassador is presenting his credentials. Some old fella the Yanks pulled out of retirement."

"I hadn't heard that. What happened to the last ambassador?"

"I don't know for sure. He spouted some diplomatic cleverality and went home. Probably had no sense of humor about our fine Irish weather."

While Liam mussed his hair and inserted his contact lenses, he told Kevin how his mother had invited the new ambassador's granddaughter to the ball. "She's only sixteen. Lost her parents in some sort of accident a few years ago. She's lived with her grandparents since."

"And they dragged the poor unsuspecting thing to Ireland with them?" A thoughtful look narrowed Kevin's eyes. "Either they're saving her from hordes of eager young males like us because she's gorgeous, or they're hoping someone here will feel sorry for her because she has a face like the back of a bus." He slipped into his sneakers and tied the laces. "I'll dance with her if she's pretty. You get her if she's ugly. Hurry up, will you? I'm ready to bite a baby's arse through the bars of a crib."

Dressed now as Kevin was, Liam checked his appearance in the mirror above his bureau. The dark red hair and brown eyes of the Borus marked him well. Kevin, on the other hand, had inherited his mother's jet black hair and light blue eyes. Both red and black hair were common in Ireland, however. The boys would blend in easily with the general population.

They often disguised themselves in this way so they might roam freely around Dublin without the hassle of bodyguards. There'd be the devil to pay if their parents found out, but they knew full well that their fathers had done the same thing when they were young. Stealing past the guards was a time-honored family tradition.

His dressed down reflection made Liam smile. "Our own mothers wouldn't know us."

"Change your watch," Kevin said, his attention still on his shoes. "And take off that ring."

Liam had already removed his Rolex, but the emerald pinky ring fit so comfortably, he'd nearly forgotten it. Emerald was his birthstone, and Talty had given him the ring for his birthday in May. As he twisted it from his finger, a familiar twinge of pity for his older sister saddened him. Less than three years separated them, but it might as well be a century. She led a complex life as Crown Princess, and one day, she'd be Queen of Ireland.

Liam thanked his ancestors yet again for passing the Act of Heritage that made Ireland one of the few constitutional monarchies in the world where the throne passed to the firstborn child, male or female. He wanted nothing to do with being the heir to the throne. After he finished university and law school, his royal duties would increase, but not to the degree his sister's would. He hoped she'd enjoy the Ambassadors' Ball.

The thought of the ball set him wondering about the American girl his mother had asked to the party. What did she look like? Tall and scrawny? Fat and mousy with braces? The few American girls he'd met were overly painted and fancied themselves a step above the buttermilk. Fur coats with no knickers. This one would be the same, he thought, though he hoped she'd be pretty and somewhat intelligent. His mother had made it clear he'd be keeping her company for the better part of the evening.

Kevin grabbed his jacket from the back of a chair. "I want to try that new Mexican restaurant in Temple Bar. I'm in the mood for nachos. "

"Sounds great. Today's Saturday. Temple Bar will be running their outdoor book sale. We can give it a gander after we eat."

"Looking for more stories?"

"Always, Kev. You never know what treasures you'll find when you're out and about in Dublin. Let's go!"

CHAPTER FOUR

The taxi driver stopped at the curving intersection of Nassau and St. Andrew's streets, opposite Trinity College. "Wicklow Street's just up Grafton there, miss," he said, pointing vaguely. "Mind your purses, now."

Janet thanked the driver and paid the fare. He'd been polite, as were all the cabbies who'd picked her up at Deerfield House. That wasn't a bad thing, but sometimes she wished no one knew who she was. If not for the appointment at the dressmaker's shop, she would have tried taking the bus into town. She never had, but some day before Matti left, she would. When Matti was with her, Janet would try anything.

"What did he say?" Matti asked when they'd closed the taxi door. "I couldn't understand a word."

When they'd first gotten into the cab, Janet hadn't understood the driver either. But she'd learned that once you caught the rhythm of Dublin speech, the words cleared up. "Like tuning a radio dial," she told Matti after translating the cabbie's warning.

Janet had nearly cheered when she'd learned the dressmaker's shop was near Grafton Street, a part of Dublin she'd come to love in the last few weeks. She and Matti had spent the previous day there, bouncing through the crowds like ping-pong balls. They'd loved the street performers: the singers, the musicians with their fiddles and bagpipes, the painted human statues, even a juggler on a unicycle. Carts of fresh flowers perfumed the air, offsetting the odors of garbage and age.

August in Ireland wasn't nearly as warm as in Boston. The girls wore light jackets, each with a hood. Rain popped up quickly here, even when the sun shone.

"That's why they have so many rainbows," Matti had said.

Janet had seen several. They appeared in the clouds like magic breaking through holes in heaven. She glanced up hoping to see one now, but the sky was blue—for the moment.

The taxi pulled away, leaving a clear view of the "tart with the cart," as the locals fondly called the statue of Molly Malone. Milling about in a makeshift line, a dozen tourists waited to have their pictures taken in front of the famous black sculpture.

Matti started singing *Cockles and mussels, alive alive-o.* Janet laughed and started up Grafton Street. Swarms of people bustled over Dublin's famous pedestrian thoroughfare. Restaurants and upscale stores lined the brick street. One store had a doorman dressed in a top hat and tails who reminded Janet of the Mad Hatter from *Alice in Wonderland.*

"I wish we could skip the dressmaker and watch the buskers," said Matti. "Hey, aren't you supposed to get what you wish for in Ireland?"

"If you are," Janet said, "then I wish I could dance. My grandfather tried to teach me to waltz, but I kept getting confused. If I try to waltz with Prince Liam at the ball, I'm sure I'll step on his feet. Or cause a disaster, like at the prom."

"You had the wrong shoes at the prom. I'll bet that dressmaker knows the right ones to wear. Come on, let's find the dress shop."

Zigging and zagging through tourists who jabbered in scads of odd languages, Janet and Matti made their way to a side street on their right. They paused to get their bearings, moving close to a store to escape the mob.

Hand shading her eyes, Matti looked all around. "Is this Wicklow Street? I don't see any street signs."

"They're on the sides of the buildings." Janet pointed to the second floor of the store opposite them. "Look."

A blue sign with white letters in two rows clung to the concrete. The top row's italicized letters spelled *Sráid Chill Mhantáin.* Beneath the foreign words, Janet read "Wicklow Street."

Matti squinted up at the sign. "What the heck does *Srade Chill Manhattan* mean?" She spoke as if the words were strangling her tongue. "It doesn't even look like 'Wicklow Street.'"

"It's Irish," Janet said. "They pronounce the first word *shrawd.* It means 'street.' I have no idea what the rest says."

She stepped away from the building, her attention on the sign. She didn't see the white-haired woman until they'd collided.

"Mind your step," the woman said, though she didn't sound angry. In fact, she smiled, and her pouchy cheeks jumped up in a mass of wrinkles that nearly hid her blue-gray doll eyes.

Janet's hand flew to her mouth. Horrified that she'd been so clumsy, she gawked at the woman. "I'm so sorry. Are you all right?"

"No better or worse than before, love, and wasn't I goin' too fast? No harm."

"I was trying to read the street sign. I really am sorry." Janet thought the woman was older than Gram, though she couldn't be sure. Gram took such good care of herself.

This spry lady wore no makeup. She'd pinned her hair in an old-fashioned twist. Her dress looked old-fashioned too, a flowery frock with buttons up the front and a collar of lacy triangles. She looked ancient. It wasn't fair. Janet's parents had both died at thirty-eight. She stroked the locket around her neck.

"What about the street sign?" the woman asked. "You're on Wicklow Street, love."

Matti stood beside Janet. "But what does the Irish mean? How do you pronounce it?"

The woman's smile grew. "Ah, you Americans. It's *Shrawd Kill Mantan.* The Street of Mantan's Church. I've got to run, love. Late for work. Enjoy your visit."

She hurried up Wicklow Street, whose name still mystified Janet. She checked her watch. "It's almost one. We'd better find that dress shop fast."

Resuming the game of dodging pedestrians, they searched the numbers on the doors until they found the sign for Kincora Designs beside a jewelry store. According to the fancy gold letters, the dress shop was on the first floor.

Matti opened the door and peeked inside. "I don't see any dress shop."

"They call the second floor the first floor here." Tension had thinned Janet's voice. "The first floor is the ground floor."

Why was she so nervous? She'd visited dress shops often with Gram. Still, she'd only gone once for herself, to pick that awful prom dress from a rack of mostly grotesque gowns. That must be why her mouth was so dry.

With Matti's footsteps tapping reassuringly behind her, she climbed a narrow staircase. The palms of her hands felt hot and sticky on the carved wooden railing.

The steps turned at a landing with an oval stained-glass window depicting a mermaid. Mottled sunshine streamed through her scaly green tail to the stairway, which was clean and in good repair. Still, the place smelled musty.

"Everything is so old here," Matti said in a near-whisper. "I'll bet this place is haunted."

Janet tripped on the last step. Scowling at Matti, she opened the door to Kincora Designs.

They entered a shop so sleek and new it seemed out of place in such an antiquated building. Big windows with sheer silvery drapes let in tons of bright light, though the sun had disappeared again. Raindrops suddenly spattered the glass. Janet looked away from the depressing sight, taking in the potted trees and the black-and-white photo gallery covering two of the walls.

Several women dressed in black slacks and blouses scurried in and out of doors around the shop. Another, young and very thin, came from behind a glass reception desk. She had short choppy hair dyed pink and white, and she approached Janet with her right hand extended. "Hi, I'm Louise. Which one of you is Janet Gleason?"

"I am," Janet said. "This is my friend, Matti." Loving the lilt in Louise's voice, Janet shook hands.

"Pretty cool place," said Matti. "Does the queen really come here?"

Louise smiled and waved the girls to the sitting area. "She only came once, to wish me luck when we first opened. I go to her when she needs me. She called this morning about you, Janet. Asked me to look after you personally. So how do you like Ireland?"

After a moment of polite chitchat, Louise summoned an assistant to fetch refreshments. Janet declined. Matti accepted a fruity soft drink, and Louise got straight to work.

Feeling like a peasant, Janet paged through a sketchbook of formal gowns. "It's hard to tell how a dress will look from drawings."

Louise said she was working on the gowns for no one in particular. "They're in the back room. Most are nearly done. Let's see if you like any of them. We have costume jewelry to help clients imagine how the finished dress will look. I'll have someone bring in some necklaces."

Enjoying herself now, Janet followed the designer to a dressing room. Louise issued orders to a nearby aide, wished Janet luck, and returned to the sitting area.

The assistant hung a rainbow of gowns in the mirrored cubicle and set a box of costume jewelry on the bench. Saying she'd be right outside if Janet needed anything, she closed the curtain.

The gowns were gorgeous, much nicer than the semi-formals Janet had tried on in Boston. Admiring the different colors, she touched each dress, savoring the silky feel of the cloth. Carefully placing her locket in her purse, she pulled off her shirt and jeans and tried on the dresses, rejecting each in turn until she saw herself in the last. It was THE dress.

The sapphire blue color enhanced her golden hair and perfectly matched her eyes. Most of the seams weren't fully sewn, and the beaded strip that went around the waist was only tacked on, yet she easily pictured the end result. She loved the tiers of mesh on the skirt and the sheer cap sleeves. The wide square neck would definitely require a necklace. She rummaged through the box and selected a silver chain with white beads.

Amazed at how stunning she looked, she opened the curtain and called the assistant. "Can I show it to my friend?"

The aide eyed the dress and smiled. "Of course. Careful with the length. We haven't hemmed it yet."

Pestered by flashbacks of the prom fiasco, Janet lifted the skirt and tiptoed in her stocking feet to the sitting area. "Well, what do you think?"

Matti whistled. "Wow, Jan, that's gorgeous!"

Louise clapped her hands in delighted approval. "It's brilliant!" Grinning broadly, she scampered to Janet and inspected the gown. "It's the one I envisioned you in. The blue. Your eyes, right? Let's see. You don't have any figure flaws we'd need to disguise, and the dress is nearly done. One more fitting to adjust the length should do it. Do you like it?"

"I love it! But…do you think…can I wear it without big heels?"

"I'll tell you a secret," said Louise, lowering her voice. "Queen Eileen and Princess Talty never wear big heels. None of the royal ladies do. In fact, they change into dancing shoes right after dinner. I'll give you the names of a few special shoe stores along with a sample of the dress material. Get the shoes you like—be sure they're comfortable—and bring them when you come back for your next fitting. We'll fix the dress so no one will notice your feet."

It sounded so simple, until Janet thought of dancing with Prince Liam. "Do you think I should get dancing shoes too?"

"Why?" Matti asked with a smirk. "You can't dance."

"I can learn!" Janet and her new dress swirled back into the dressing room. She unfastened the hook, tugged at the zipper, and stared at her mirror image. "Who am I kidding? I'll never learn to dance."

A tiny knock, and the curtain parted. "You might like to try this necklace with that dress."

Janet looked in the mirror and gasped. The reflection of the old woman she'd nearly knocked down on the street smiled back at her. She turned around. "Hello. I didn't realize you worked here. I'm Janet."

"Yes, I know, love. You can call me Nora." The old-fashioned dress was gone. Nora wore the same black slacks and blouse that seemed to be the uniform of Kincora Designs. She opened her hand.

The golden necklace she held enchanted Janet. It's old, she thought, so very old. Whoever had made it had woven tiny gold beads into the links. The pendant, three interwoven Celtic triangles, enclosed a glittering blue stone, the same sky blue as the gown she wore—and she'd seen enough of Gram's jewelry to suspect that the gem was real.

"Is it a sapphire?"

"It is." Nora entered the cubicle. "Turn and I'll fix it so you can get an idea how it looks."

Janet obeyed, lifting her hair from her neck, bracing herself for the metal's chill against her skin. Its heat surprised her. No doubt it had grown warm in Nora's hand.

"They say this necklace is magic." Nora stepped back to the cubicle's entrance. "If you make a wish while wearing it close to your heart, your wish will come true."

"Ireland is full of stories like that."

A chuckle prefaced Nora's reply. "Yes, I know. It's only a legend, but it wouldn't hurt to try. Who knows? You just might get your wish. I'll be back in a few minutes."

The curtain closed. Janet gazed in the mirror. The sapphire had fallen to just the right spot on her chest. If only it really were magic! She'd try anything to avoid looking lame at the ball. Maybe she should wish she didn't have to go. That she could go back to Boston. That her parents were still alive.

You're sixteen, not six. She sighed at her reflection. Then she smiled. Pushing the pendant to the left, she pressed it hard against her skin and squeezed her eyes shut. "I wish I could dance," she whispered. "I wish I could two-step. I wish I could one-step. I wish I could waltz like a princess! I wish Wish WISH I could dance!"

Feeling ditsy, she opened her eyes and glanced around the dressing room. No one could have heard her. No one but the necklace. She was fumbling with the clasp when Nora returned.

"I'll get that, love. Just pick up your hair. Such lovely hair."

A few little twists and the woman departed, wishing Janet good luck with her dress.

Five minutes later, Janet returned to the sitting room. She thanked Louise for her help and made an appointment to come back the following Tuesday for the final fitting. "I think a sapphire necklace would look great with the dress," she said, hoping Louise agreed.

She did. "A sapphire necklace would be perfect. And maybe earrings and a bracelet to match."

"My grandmother has lots of things like that. I'm sure she'd let me borrow them."

"Ask her later," Matti said. "I'm starving. Louise says there's a pizza place five minutes away. She gave me directions."

Janet tucked a plastic bag with the swatch of material and the addresses of the shoe stores into her purse. Mission accomplished, she and Matti left the shop in a bubbly mood the rain couldn't dampen. They raised their hoods and hurried along, dodging puddles and chatting away. The sun reappeared before they reached the end of Wicklow Street.

Matti stopped and stared at the sky. "Look, Jan!"

A rainbow arced through the clouds. Janet admired the magical sight. "It's a good omen."

"Yeah. We're going to have great pizza!"

Laughing in the drizzly sun shower, they continued down a narrow lane, turning left on Trinity Street. A short walk brought them to Dame Street's busy traffic. They waited at a crosswalk, where the "Look Left" warning painted on the street reminded tourists that the Irish drove on the left side of the road. When the beeping pedestrian light came on, Janet and Matti raced across Dame Street and entered the Temple Bar district.

CHAPTER FIVE

Liam didn't mind the drizzle. The people he and Kevin passed were too preoccupied keeping themselves dry to notice other strollers, especially two scruffy young fellas wearing American baseball caps. And when the sun eventually took its turn in the sky, they had sunglasses to augment their camouflage.

They'd escaped the King's Residence at noon and rambled north, crossing St. Stephen's Green to the southern end of Grafton Street. Taking their time, they navigated the crowds, enjoying the buskers and mimes who amused or annoyed the shoppers darting in and out of the stores.

Halfway down the street, the rain shower ended. The breaking sunlight drew street musicians from various improvised shelters. Guitarists, fiddlers, and even an uilleann piper all staked their claims on the walkways just beyond each other's hearing.

Chatting about football, Liam and Kevin slowed their pace to enjoy the show. They stopped altogether to watch a young Asian cellist. They'd heard bits of her classical repertoire before and stayed until she finished a lively Mozart divertimento.

"Brilliant," Kevin said, pitching a coin into her open cello case.

Liam did the same. The smiling cellist nodded her thanks and launched right into another piece.

The cousins moved on. Near the end of the street, Trinity College came into view.

"Ah, there it is, Kev," Liam said with a theatrical flourish. "Our home from home for the next few years. As Finn MacCool went off to study with the Druid Finegas, so too will we be off learning our trade. It falls to us to preserve the ancient traditions of our forebears."

"You can preserve them. Your father asked me to consider studying corporate law when it's time for law school. A little more practical than druids and poets and fairies. That codology is for storytellers. Entertaining but useless."

The words hit Liam like a punch. Scathing retorts popped into his head. So did the children's smiling faces in the hospital that morning. In true Boru fashion, his temper cooled as quickly as it had flared. How could anyone quibble on a perfect summer day on Grafton Street?

Opting for humor, he slapped a hand against his chest. "I'm wounded, Kev. Here I am endeavoring to safeguard our ancient ways to protect the likes of cynics such as yourself from repeating the sins of the past, and what do I get? Codology. Corporate law or no, you'll have to study the old Brehon Laws. It's a prerequisite."

"One you could probably teach." They'd reached the crosswalk at Nassau and St. Andrew's streets. Kevin pushed the button for the pedestrian light. "Whoever wrongs another pays a fine. The higher the injured party's rank, the higher the fine. Be said and led by me, Li. That stuff's all codology. Even the criminal court thinks so. Let it go. Make yourself useful. Learn how the family's companies run."

Liam already had a fair idea how the royal corporate holdings helped keep the Boru clan solvent without having to rely on the Exchequer for support. Self-sufficiency was a matter of pride for the family. He would end up knowing as much if not more about business matters than Kevin, but while he could, he intended to study the old ways, and not just the myths. The Boru lineage was more than a thousand years old. Someone had to remember.

He grinned at his somber cousin. "You're cranky when you're hungry, Kev. We'd best get you fed, and fast."

The light changed. Amiably shifting the conversation back to football, Liam hurried past the "tart with the cart" to Dame Street. Anonymous in a herd of human cattle, he and Kevin crossed the street near the former Bank of Ireland building and turned down Crown Alley.

The medieval cobblestones added bounce to Liam's step. He inhaled a meld of rain, fresh coffee, and stale beer. The delivery trucks would have rolled their beer kegs into the pubs at dawn. Pedestrians had the run of

Temple Bar now. Packs of them explored the open air shops and restaurants that occupied the ground floors of countless brick buildings.

Flowers cascaded from windows and terraces. Fanciful murals adorned several walls. Traditional music oozed from brightly painted pubs and flew from the fingers of street musicians.

"There's at least six guards in the crowd," Kevin said.

Liam had already spotted the yellow jackets and visored black hats of the Dublin police. If anyone recognized him, the sharp-eyed *gardaí* would. Seeking to avoid them, the cousins crossed the street that led to the square.

They stopped at the corner near the ice cream shop. Before them, in the center of the bustling square, scores of bibliomaniacs rummaged though boxes of books set on tables. Liam couldn't wait to join them. "Which way is the Mexican restaurant, Kev?"

Kevin tilted his head to the left. "Over there. I've been craving their nachos all morning." He raised his eyes in ecstasy. "And they have the best chicken chili!"

Liam hopped over a puddle and turned—straight into a warm, solid object.

The crash knocked the breath from him. He didn't see who'd clobbered him. He only knew his royal arse was on the cobblestones.

"Li!" Kevin dropped beside him, inspecting him like a fussing mother hen. "Li, are you all right?"

Thankful he hadn't landed in the puddle, Liam heaved himself up on his elbows. He wanted to get away before a crowd gathered. "I'm fine," he said, raising his arm. "Give us a hand, Kev."

As Kevin pulled him to his feet, he noticed a girl his age sprawled on the ground nearby. Blond. Ponytail. Extremely good-looking, with high round cheeks that tapered to a charming chin. Before he could help her to her feet, a dark-haired miss did just that.

The second girl was clearly a friend. Pretty enough. A tad overweight. Glasses. Backpack. "Nice going, Jan," she said. "You did it again."

"I'm so sorry!" the blonde named Jan blurted out. "Are you okay?"

Yanks, for sure. The brunette seemed amused, but the blonde sounded desperate. Terrified. In need of immediate consolation.

Liam hatched his best smile. "I'm sure I'll survive. Are you all right yourself?"

"Here, Li." The slap of a sodden baseball cap at his arm fortified

Kevin's warning tone.

Ignoring his cousin, Liam took the hat, which had apparently fallen from his head and landed in the puddle. He also took the girl's arm and steered her onto the sidewalk. "Let's get out of the way, shall we? Jan. Is that short for Janice?"

"No, Janet."

"Ah, Janet. The fair Scottish maiden who plucked an enchanted rose and saved the mortal knight, Tam Lin, from the clutches of the fairies."

The girls stared dumbstruck at Liam. Kevin rolled his eyes.

"I'm Matti," said the brunette. "Short for Martha. Not such a great name."

"Martha is a lovely name," said Liam. "Martha, the Flower of Sweet Strabane. Cheeks like the roses, hair lovely brown."

Matti giggled. "You guys are Irish, right?"

"What gave us away?" Kevin peered accusingly at Liam. "The blarney?"

Liam grinned. "It's fine to meet the two of you. I'm Liam. This is Kevin, and yes, we're Irish. We'll be struggling new students at Trinity soon, and we came to town to map the lay of the land."

"Do you live in Dublin?" Janet straightened a locket that hung from a chain around her neck. Or was she touching it for comfort? The design on the gold looked old-fashioned, probably some sort of keepsake.

Intrigued, Liam contrived a change in the afternoon's plans. "We live nearby, but I'm thinking that you young ladies are a long way from home. You seem a trifle lost. Can we help you find your way?"

A tiny kick at his heel nearly made him laugh out loud. For a moment, he thought Kevin was right: they should be on their way, and unencumbered.

But then the Goddess Janet smiled.

"We're visiting from Boston," she said. "We were looking for a pizza place called Manetto's, but it's hard to see the signs with all these people."

Her gossamer voice, velvety soft despite its American accent, charmed Liam. He pitched the wet baseball hat into a trash bin. "Why, we're going there ourselves. Kevin was just saying he's been craving pizza all morning. Weren't you, Kev?"

"But, Li—"

"Come on, we'll treat you."

Janet's smile dissolved in dismay. "We should treat you. I knocked you down."

"I believe the knocking was mutual. In any case, it's all done and dusted, my fine new friend. The treat is ours. I insist."

He touched her shoulder, shepherding her through the throng, sensing Kevin and Matti right behind them. They passed by the book sale, but Liam had forgotten all about it.

CHAPTER SIX

"I think they're drug dealers."

Janet spun from the sink frantically searching the stark white ladies' room to see if anyone else had heard Matti's outrageous pronouncement. They were the only occupants of Manetto's "jacks" at the moment. She snapped a paper towel from the wall dispenser and dried her hands. "That's ridiculous, Matti. You read too many spy stories."

Finished primping, Matti returned her comb and lip gloss to the front compartment of her backpack. "If I'm going to be a good lawyer, I have to know how to read people, and these guys are easy to read. They're real urbane. Way too smooth. Did you see Kevin checking his messages? He has one of those smart phones that does everything. They cost a bundle."

"So what?" Janet pulled the tie from her ponytail. Her hair was one of her best features. She brushed it out and left it flowing to her shoulders. Her black jersey had been a good choice today, but why hadn't she done her eyes? Fortunately, she had her powder blush with her. She tinted her cheeks, smoothed her eyebrows, and straightened her locket.

Matti was still yakking about the smart phone. "Drug dealers need the right tools to keep in touch with their clients."

"Get serious, Matti."

"I am! That Liam talks like he samples the goods himself, and Kevin is one moody dude. Like he needs a fix or something. He's cute, though."

Their accents did sound different from other Irish accents Janet had heard. More proper than the cab drivers or people in stores. She supposed it had something to do with the part of Dublin they came from. People from different parts of Boston had different accents, after all.

"Liam knows something about Irish culture," she said. "What's wrong with that? And Kevin is hungry. He said so. Since when did you become an expert on drug dealers?"

"I read, Janikins. Did you notice how they steered us away from the cops?"

Janet had wondered about that. "They steered us around a lot of people. Temple Bar is a crowded place."

"Yeah, maybe. They have really awesome haircuts. And did you catch Liam's fingernails?"

"No. What about them?"

"They're buffed." Matti zipped up her backpack.

"That doesn't make him a drug dealer."

"How does a struggling young student find extra cash for manicures?" Matti appeared thoughtful for a moment. "Maybe he's gay."

Janet huffed in annoyance. "Billy and Josh in the Drama Club are gay. Liam is *not* gay."

"Maybe not, but I think he's one bad boy." She grinned sideways at Janet. "And we all know how good girls like bad boys."

"Will you stop? I crashed into him! He's trying to be nice about it. You're just not used to Irish guys."

"I'm not used to *any* guys. Do you think their names are fake? They sound fake to me."

Satisfied that she looked her best, Janet closed her purse. "Why on earth would you think that? Liam and Kevin are common Irish names. The cab driver's name was Liam. The gardener at Deerfield House is a Kevin. The prince is Liam. There's lots of Mikes and Tims around too."

"Yeah, maybe you're right." Matti opened the rest room door.

Janet followed her back to the table, where Liam and Kevin sat chatting. Liam spotted them and smiled. He and Kevin stood and waited for her and Matti to take their seats. Were these guys for real?

Liam's hummingbird gaze skimmed over Janet, hovering in all the right places. Definitely not gay. Secure in her role as a young American tourist, she stared back at him. As Matti had said, his dark red hair was movie star perfect.

Eyeing his well-toned physique, Janet thought he must play sports. Almost every young guy in Ireland played sports. It was like the national religion. Kevin had a similar build, tight and hard if not quite muscular. Ricky Gagnon played basketball, but next to these guys, he was jiggling jelly set in a man-boy mold.

Liam's eyes, cinnamon brown and lively, seemed to laugh at everyone and everything, as if he were constantly enjoying some private joke. His cryptic half-smile reappeared often, adding to the effect. He was a good-looking guy, and he knew it.

Was he a "bad boy?" As she doubted she'd ever see him again after today, Janet didn't care. For now, she meant to relax and have fun. Act the temptress. Practice the facial expressions she'd learned in her acting workshops.

Matti claimed the seat beside Kevin. Fixing her lips in what she hoped was a foxy smile, Janet sat next to Liam. The sodas they'd ordered, called minerals here, had already arrived.

Janet sipped her cola and shuffled her thoughts for something to talk about. "So. Temple Bar. Is there a temple here, or is that the name of a pub?"

"There is a pub called Temple Bar," said Liam, "but the area isn't named after it. It's the other way around. A fella named Temple bought the area in the eighteenth century and set up his home here. Good location, close to the River Liffey. His part of the river had a sandbar. The sailors called it Temple's Bar."

Matti sampled her soda and twisted toward Liam. "You seem like a smart guy, Liam. Do you know why the sign for Wicklow Street says the Street of St. Mantan's Church instead of Wicklow Street?"

Liam leaned back in his chair as if he were going to tell a story. "Ah, Saint Mantan," he said, his voice lilting beautifully. "The name means 'toothless.' Mantan was a disciple of Saint Patrick. Some of those rascally pagan folk didn't want Patrick visiting Wicklow, so they grabbed a rock and knocked out Mantan's teeth. The priests built a church for the poor gap-toothed fella and called it Killmantan."

The recitation impressed Janet. "Where does the name Wicklow come from?"

"From the Viking word *Wykynglo*. It means the Viking meadow."

The soda and the prospect of food seemed to have cured Kevin's bad humor. "Liam is a wonder at such things," he said, "useless as the information may be."

The sparkle in Liam's eyes vanished, though only for a moment. "Kevin, of course, is a world of practicality. All facts and business. A dull lad indeed."

Matti's head pivoted toward Kevin. "What will you study at Trinity?" The blinking brown eyes behind her glasses were riveted to him. Her unusually goofy grin betrayed a developing crush. "I'm going to be a lawyer," she said.

What might have been interest flashed across Kevin's face and quickly disappeared. "Is that a fact? So am I. Liam too." He smirked at Liam. "At least that's the plan."

Janet peered suspiciously at Kevin. Was he lying? Flattering Matti to gain her trust? Suddenly feeling protective of her friend, she stirred her straw through the ice in her drink and decided to poke. "Do you guys have last names?"

An angelic grin appeared on Liam's face. "Murphy," he said without skipping a beat. "We're cousins. Liam and Kevin Murphy."

Kevin nodded. "That's right. Fine old stock." His head snapped toward the approaching waitress.

She set a scrumptious pizza loaded with cheese and pepperoni on the table and asked if anyone needed anything else. Heads shook, Liam thanked her, and she left them to their lunch. Kevin seized his knife and fork and attacked the food, distributing fragrant, steaming slices to everyone's plates before slapping one on his own.

How polite of him, Janet thought, glancing from Kevin to Liam and back. They couldn't be cousins. They looked nothing alike. Was Matti right about their criminal activity? Maybe. Still, they could be "bad" without being drug dealers.

Kevin and Matti devoured their pizza. Feeling Liam's gaze on her, Janet folded her slice and took a dainty bite.

Liam seemed in no hurry to eat. He used his fork to break the point from the slice on his plate. "How about yourself, Janet?"

She swallowed and said, "I'm definitely not going to be a lawyer."

His gentle chuckle rippled through her, prickling her skin and making her giddy. "Good on you, love. You're smarter than the rest of us, I think, but that's not what I meant. Do you have a last name?"

Two can play your game, Mr. Liam Murphy. "Smith. Janet Smith. Matti's name is Jones."

His mouth stretched in a knowing grin that showcased straight white teeth. Even as she realized they each knew the other had fibbed, she wondered what it might be like to kiss him. Cheeks burning, she focused on her pizza to avoid his piercing gaze.

Between bites, the foursome discussed what the girls had seen and should see in Dublin. Kevin suggested the Hop-On Hop-Off bus tour. Liam said they should venture outside the city to view Ireland's spectacular scenery.

The waitress left the bill and a ballpoint pen and hurried off to her other tables. Kevin kicked his chair back and stood. "This one's yours, Li. I'm going to wash up."

Matti stared at her greasy hands. "That sounds like a good idea." She returned to the ladies' room.

Liam drew his wallet from a pocket in his jeans and left some cash on the bill. He asked Janet for her cell phone number. "I could show you around a bit."

She shouldn't. She didn't know him. What if Matti was right? What would her grandparents say?

He reached over and tapped her wrist. "I'm a wonderful tour guide, Janet. I don't bite, and I'm housebroken. How long will you be in Ireland?"

His playful tap left her arm tingling. She liked him. A lot. But what would he do if he learned she was Ambassador Broderick Gleason's granddaughter? Run away, most likely.

"About another week," she said, thinking that was when Matti would be leaving.

Leaving Janet all alone.

"You can see a lot in a week," he said. "I'm serious about the scenery. The countryside is packed with things to see and do. Do you ever go hill walking?"

"Hill walking? Oh, you mean hiking." She didn't like to think about hiking. Her parents had loved to hike. When she was a child, they'd taken her on the easy trails in the Blue Hills and the Berkshires, even to the mountains in northern New Hampshire. She suddenly recalled how much she'd loved the pine trees and birds, the chipmunks and waterfalls—until a rockslide killed her parents on a mountain in Maine.

Her fingers brushed the locket. "I haven't hiked for ages, but I'd love to go." She had to open her cell phone to find the number. "I don't call myself very often," she said sheepishly. He smiled, and she read the number to him. Using the pen the waitress had left, he jotted it on the back of the bill for the pizza and slipped it into his wallet.

"What about Matti?" she asked. "I can't go without her. We're best friends."

He slanted his head to one side. His eyes sharpened as he studied her, and his little half-smile reappeared. "Matti is welcome to come along. I have a feeling she wouldn't object to spending some time with Kevin." Liam lifted Janet's jacket from the back of her chair and held it for her.

Feeling treasured, she turned and slipped her arms into the sleeves. As she did, she spotted Nora, the woman from the dress shop, sitting at a table near the door. She must be on a late lunch break, Janet thought. Nora smiled at her. She smiled back. She'd stop and say hello on her way out.

Matti returned to the table. Kevin followed right behind her. His grumpy mood had vanished. "The pizza was great," he said, smiling at Janet. "Fine food, fine company." He turned his smile on Matti then, though it seemed more of a polite afterthought.

"Thanks for lunch," Matti said. "We still have time to check out that book sale, Jan."

Liam started to speak. Janet felt sure he wanted to join them, but Kevin cut him off and nudged him toward the door. "We have to go, Li. Things to do. It's been grand, girls. Cheers."

"After you, ladies." Liam waved his arm. He winked at Janet as she passed.

She smiled and turned toward the table where she'd seen Nora.

The woman had vanished.

CHAPTER SEVEN

The added bounce in Liam's step no longer came from the cobblestones. Secure in his sunglasses and Kevin's baseball hat, he maneuvered through crowded Temple Bar toward the narrow alley of boutique shops leading to Merchants' Arch.

The arch in turn led to the River Liffey. Once they'd crossed the Ha'penny Bridge, the cousins would saunter along vibrant O'Connell Street, Dublin's historic main thoroughfare. Liam planned to browse in the city's largest bookstore, and Kevin wanted to visit the sports shops.

The boys passed under the old stone arch, built in the days when ships docked there to trade with local merchants. Foot traffic dwindled inside the short tunnel, whose gray brick walls displayed senseless swirls of graffiti. Urban art, some called it, though in Liam's opinion, the gaudy doodles merited only a good hosing down.

Kevin waved his hand before his face. "This place really stinks today. Worse than usual."

Liam wrinkled his nose at the fetid fug, but he didn't mind it. Nor did he mind missing the Temple Bar book sale. He could come any weekend, and Kevin had clearly been keen to escape Miss Matti's increasing adoration. But Kevin would keep her company if Liam asked, and Liam intended to ask. Maybe tomorrow, if Janet agreed. He had no commitments tomorrow. If the weather cooperated, he'd take her to Newgrange to see the tombs, or perhaps they'd walk in the Wicklow hills. He had all sorts of ideas where they might go.

Wherever they went, Kevin and Matti would lag behind, enjoying—at least in Matti's case—an easy Sunday stroll while Liam escorted Janet the Fair on a private tour of his father's kingdom.

A scruffy guitarist performed in the alley. The cousins passed by him.

"That fella must have snorted his nose away to play in that stench so long," Kevin said.

The same thought had crossed Liam's mind, yet he said, "A perfume we should breathe in more often, Kev. It's good to get out of the house now and then."

At the crosswalk on Wellington Quay, they stood in a throng of mostly young people waiting for the lights to change. Directly across the street, the clean white pickets of the Ha'penny Bridge glistened in the sunlight, a gateway inviting further adventure.

"Would you two Casanovas like a ride home?"

The growling voice had come from behind them. Liam winced. Kevin's shoulders slumped. They'd been busted.

The lights changed. Trucks and buses braked to a stop. The crowd crossed to the bridge, leaving Liam and Kevin behind. As they backed against the wall to escape the endless stream of pedestrians, Liam scanned the cars parked along the curb until he spotted the blue Mercedes. No driver today. No one to shield them from Kieran's wrath.

Liam scowled at his hulking gorilla kinsman. "Thanks, but we'd rather walk."

Eyes blazing, Kieran Dacey closed in on the boys. His three-piece suit— perfectly tailored, Liam knew, to conceal the gun he wore—suggested he'd come from a formal affair, most likely the ambassador's luncheon at the Hall.

The ultimate responsibility for the royal family's safety fell on Kieran, the Ard Shivail, or High Protector. He was first cousin to both Liam's and Kevin's fathers. His fine-boned face, a mature version of Liam's, looked much older than that of a man in his mid-forties. As a young soldier, Kieran had served with the international peacekeepers, and the African sun had left his skin leathered and deeply lined. Silver shone in his chestnut hair. Despite these signs of age, he moved with the grace of a much younger man.

A jagged scar, another memento of his time in Africa, zigzagged down his left cheek to his jaw. The scar usually blended well with his skin, but fury whitened it now, like a bolt of lightning signaling an ominous storm.

"Get in the car," he said.

Bristling with resentment, Liam stretched to his full height and crossed his arms. "I said we'd rather walk."

A firestorm flashed over Kieran's cheeks. "Get in the car now and I won't tell your fathers what a pair of bollocks the two of yez are!"

Several passersby glanced their way. That wouldn't do.

Kevin surrendered. "Don't get your knickers in a twist, Kieran. We're coming."

Kieran opened the car's rear door for them, slamming it shut after they settled themselves on the leather seats. Liam gazed wistfully at the Ha'penny Bridge. He might as well be in a prison van.

"How did you find us?" Kevin asked as the car eased into the Dublin traffic.

Kieran glanced in the rearview mirror. "I'll let you boyos wonder about that. You put the heart crosswise in me, pulling a stunt like this."

"Don't be a maggot," Liam said. "We were fine. No one could have known us. No harm."

"No harm? Did either of you two geniuses ever stop to think you could be kidnapped, or worse?" Kieran's mood had improved: he'd caught his fish. "You were lucky this time, Li. You only got reefed by a slip of a girl." Evil infused his throaty chuckle.

Liam resented the slight to his manhood. Did everyone think him a useless weakling? "That's how you found us? You saw her crash into me?"

"No, but I'd love to have seen it. One of my lads picked you out in Stephen's Green. So much for no one could have known you. The fella called me. If he wasn't enjoying a day off, he'd have kept after you. As it was, he followed you until I could slip out of the Hall." Kieran chuckled again. "At least you got me away from a boring lunch."

"We never noticed him," said Kevin.

"Keep that in mind, lads. And keep in mind that I know more about being seventeen than you do about being forty-five. I remember sneaking out. Your fathers did the same. Next time you're planning a jailbreak, let me know. I promise you'll never see the guard I assign. Just let me know. That's all I ask."

The car turned left, though Liam neither knew nor cared where they were. He slumped into the seat thinking of the outing he'd promised Janet, an outing planned for privacy so he could steal a kiss or two. Not even the most skilled of guards could remain unseen in the places he wanted to show her.

Kieran was right. Liam should tell him what he had in mind. Yet if he did, the old foxhound would want to know all about Janet. Before he was done with her, he'd know what sort of nappies she'd worn as a baby.

Liam wanted to enjoy her company unfettered by rigid security rules. Kevin would help him. If they planned it carefully, Kieran would never know.

Confident that he could work something out, Liam pulled the baseball cap over his eyes and schemed.

CHAPTER EIGHT

In the land the mortals called the Emerald Isle, even the rocks were green. At least they were in Connemara, a wild, remote district of western Galway touched on three sides by the mighty Atlantic Ocean. For thousands of years, both mortals and gods had quarried the marble found in the hills there. The diversity of greenish hues in the 600-million-year-old stone matched the countless tones in Ireland's scenery: the forests and carpets of moss, the checkerboard pastures and bogs, the mountains and grasslands and glens.

Mortal men may have hewn the fine-grained marble into goods ranging from spearheads to jewelry, but the Tuatha Dé Danann, the divine tribe to which Finvarra belonged, got the best of the stone. They could reach depths the mortals couldn't, accessing wondrous places beneath the earth where the marble's colors were more intense and the stone retained more of the land's vital energy. The Dananns transformed that energy into powerful magic.

The enchanted stone in Finvarra's private chamber had been part of Oona's dowry, bestowed upon her by the Goddess Danu herself. The seven-foot slab helped keep Finvarra in touch with his Danann kin and provided an eye to Out There.

He hadn't always needed the eye. The Dananns had lived Out There themselves, before the mighty Celts had landed on Ireland's shores nearly three thousand mortal years ago.

Finvarra recalled the day the forebears of the modern Irish sailed in from Danu knows where and claimed the bountiful island. Equally determined to defend their homeland, the Dananns engaged the invaders in combat.

Both sides suffered heavy losses in battles fraught with sorcery. Their leaders wisely called for a truce and agreed to divide Ireland between them. The Celts would dwell above the ground, the Dananns below.

Those Dananns displeased by the treaty left Ireland. Finvarra and several others opted to stay. They became known as the *Daoine Sídhe (Deena Shee)*, the People of the Mounds. The *sídhe* promised to dwell in their underground world and behave themselves.

For the most part, they'd honored the bargain.

The marble slab hummed. Finvarra had been in the banquet hall winning a game of chess when the stone's tingling energy summoned him. Standing before it now, he admired the fine beaten gold adorning its edges. Black veins of dolomite threaded the deep sea-green of its polished surface. Specks of mica glinted in mottled shadows of gray and brown that usually slumbered within the stone. The veins and shadows rippled now, pulsing to life to bring Finvarra a message.

About time, he thought, watching the swirl of light expand until Becula's wiry gray hair and hideous face appeared in the marble. Accustomed to her bulbous nose, rheumy eyes, and broken teeth, he eyed her in a detached and businesslike manner. The hags had their uses.

"You have news for me, Becula?"

A shrewish cackle nickered from the stone. At her end, she'd be gazing into a basin of water, seeing Finvarra's face as clearly as he saw hers. "I do, sire. I've found a perfect dancing partner for you. Something new. An American girl."

"American? Oh, the Yanks. Will I have difficulty understanding her?"

"Not at all, sire. She's perfect for our purposes. Comely and blithe, and she wishes to learn to dance." Becula cackled again. "She wished it on my bridling necklace, she did. Tried it on with the dress she's going to wear to the mortal king's ball."

King Brian had invited an uncivilized Yank to his ball and spurned the *sídhe*? Finvarra scowled at the marble stone. The girl would attend a ball, all right, but not Brian's. "Well done, Becula. Show her to me."

The smiling face of a lovely young blonde with even features and bright blue eyes replaced Becula's misshapen visage. Enticingly innocent, the girl gazed around her in wonder. Finvarra smiled. He'd teach her to dance all right—and he'd teach the mortals to slight the King of the Fairies. Oona's reminder to give the girl back sprang to mind, but Finvarra thought he might keep her. He could dance gazing into such a face for ages.

"What is her name, Becula?"

"She calls herself Janet."

The hag's face returned, supplanting that of the winsome young lady whose name Finvarra mouthed as if he were tasting a delicate morsel of pastry. He wanted her image back, and now. A sudden urge to dance with her nearly overwhelmed him.

"Where is she?" he asked. "How soon can we obtain her?"

"Tomorrow, perhaps. She's in Dublin. Met a boy who wants to take her walking."

"Oh?" No mortal youth would take her from Finvarra. She was his. "Walking where?"

"I don't know yet, sire."

He would lead his troop to County Dublin, a tricky feat. The Dublin fairies, not to mention Manannan MacLir, the King of the Sea, weren't fond of Finvarra and his Connaught fairies. He couldn't recall exactly why. Something about a faction fight that had started as great sport and ended with Finvarra's troop trouncing the Dublin fairies. Oh yes, he remembered now. He'd stolen someone's wife. How was he to know she turned back into a mermaid every third day?

Manannan MacLir had taken the side of the Dublin fairies. He'd not only made Finvarra give the woman back, he'd forbidden the Connaught troop to return to Dublin until Danu's Comet reappeared. Threatened to launch a raid on Knock Ma if they dared to come near. No sense of humor! But Dublin's grudges mattered not. Finvarra knew of several outposts around County Dublin where he and his troop could not only camp undetected, they could hold an impromptu party. MacLir would never know they were there. All they required was glimmer.

"Let me know the instant you learn where she's going," Finvarra said. "I'll rouse an eastbound wind and order the troop to prepare to ride."

"As you wish, sire." Cackling softly, Becula faded away.

CHAPTER NINE

When Gram and Gramp had no evening commitments, they liked to enjoy a glass of wine before dinner. Janet had found this "happy hour" the best time to strike when she wanted to talk about something important. Tonight she would try to persuade them to let her go back to Boston.

Leaving Matti happily reading one of the half-dozen books she'd picked up at the Temple Bar book sale, she stepped from the warmth of the Presidential Suite to the gloom of the second-floor landing. Ordinarily, she'd go down the backstairs and cut through the kitchen to Gramp's study, but Rosemary would be preparing dinner now, and Janet didn't want to get in her way.

Daydreaming about Liam Murphy, she crossed the balcony that overlooked the formal entrance of Deerfield House. Liam had made her laugh, and he'd asked for her cell phone number. He probably wouldn't call, though she hoped he would. She thought she'd like to see him again before she went back to Boston. But what if she didn't go? Maybe he'd be a real boyfriend—if her grandparents didn't lock her away in Hazelwood College. They'd told her the Irish called high school "college." She didn't care what they called it. They might not let her go back to Boston, but she wasn't going to let them chuck her into a snobby rich kids' school. Determined to stand up for herself, she passed the upstairs den where everyone watched movies on the big screen television. She placed her hand on the cold oak railing and started down the grand staircase. The curving banister sat on ugly black stair rails that looked like the bars of a big twisting jail cell swooping down to the front hall.

No guests were expected tonight. The enormous crystal chandelier was off, the stairway lights dimmed. When Janet had the stairs to herself, she liked to pretend she was someone famous. Tonight, she assumed the role of a princess descending the stairs in her castle.

As she reached the bottom step, she wondered if coming this way had been a good idea. When all the lights were on, the foyer looked like a museum, all artwork and antique furniture. Tonight, only the lights over the paintings and the lamp on the hall's lone table were lit. The hall resembled a scene from a haunted house, and she half-expected a ghost to pop through the walls.

She hurried past the brass cane stand that displayed Gramp's collection of walking sticks. Between skittish glances at gloomy corners, she monitored every squeak her sneakers made on the marble floor to ensure that she only heard one set of footsteps. Once she crossed the foyer, she raced down the hall to the study.

She fingered her locket and knocked. "It's Janet," she called through the door.

Gramp's mellow voice invited her in. He met her halfway across the room, his open arms clad in his favorite burgundy golf sweater. His merrily wrinkling forehead stretched to a balding head fringed with thick silvery hair. His blueberry eyes, his caterpillar eyebrows, his toothy smile—the real one, not the one he used in public—all of him welcomed her. She grinned and hugged him, and he kissed her cheek.

"Look who's here, Henrietta," he said. "Sit down, Ladybug. Tell us about your day. Grab a soda." He jerked his thumb toward the well-stocked mini-refrigerator beneath the wet bar.

"No, thanks." Janet stepped onto the oriental carpet and exchanged hellos with her grandmother, seated before the flickering gas fireplace.

Lined with wood paneling and books, the study had been the inner sanctum of several American ambassadors. Now it belonged to Gramp. The scent of his aftershave had staked its claim amid the subtler scents of tobacco and whiskey. Family photos personalized the monstrous oak desk. His diplomas and awards hung on the wall behind it. Across the room, the Roman numeral wall clock he'd brought from Boston chimed on the hour. He'd even laid out a putting mat to practice his golf game.

Gramp had returned to his seat. He and Gram sat facing each other on small leather couches. An open bottle of champagne sat on the glass coffee table between them. Two half-full glasses, one with a lipstick stain, suggested they'd had a successful day. Perfect.

"We just watched the news," Gram said, nodding toward the open doors to the built-in flat-screen television. "They featured our visit to Tara Hall. Your grandfather looked so handsome on TV." Her smile left no doubt that she liked the way she'd looked too. She patted the couch, inviting Janet to join her.

Janet sat. She listened politely, and not without interest, while her grandparents took turns describing Tara Hall's grandeur, the king's hearty laugh, and the queen's classic dress.

"Speaking of dresses," said Gram, "did you choose one, dear?"

"Yes. It's great." She told her grandparents about Louise and the dress shop, describing the blue gown and the shoes and jewelry she'd need.

Gramp beamed at her. "You'll have those Irish boys fighting to dance with you, Ladybug."

Janet shuddered. "We'd better practice some more, Gramp."

"You bet we will."

She shifted to face her grandmother. "Louise thought a sapphire necklace would be perfect. Maybe a bracelet to match. Do you have something I could borrow?"

"Sapphires?" Gram frowned the way she did when she was going to say no. "My sapphires are priceless. I seldom take them out of the safe. Anyway, they're much too old for you, dear. Why don't you wear your locket? It's lovely."

Confused and hurt, Janet touched her locket. "Yes, but it's a little girl necklace. Could I please try the sapphires? I promise I'll take good care of them."

Gram's head shook. "I don't think so. If you don't want to wear your locket, we'll get you something else when we shop for your shoes. Aquamarine would flatter your eyes and match the dress. Blue topaz would do as well, or perhaps tourmaline."

"But Louise thought—"

"Louise is used to dealing with royalty and older ladies like me. You need something appropriate for a girl your age."

"What about the necklace you wore to the prom?" Gramp asked, the diplomat in him scrambling to defuse a critical situation. Janet had often thought he'd make a wonderful actor.

"Gram let me borrow her pearls for that." She didn't try to disguise the resentment in her voice. Gram hadn't said a thing about the pearls being too old for her. Why was she being so difficult? She was the one who'd insisted that Janet attend the ball.

"Where did you have lunch, dear?" Gram's question signaled an end to the discussion.

Janet wished her grandmother wouldn't dismiss her like that. She wasn't a child. If she were, she'd have stormed out by now.

Her report on Temple Bar and the pizza excluded Liam and Kevin. That would be her secret. By the time she told them about all the books she'd talked Matti out of buying, her anger over the sapphires had dwindled. She began to look forward to shopping with Gram for a necklace of her own. She was almost an adult, after all, and should have something more grown-up than a locket. The stores were open on Sunday, weren't they? But she seemed to recall her grandparents were going somewhere the next day.

"I know you won't be home tomorrow. I forgot where you're going."

"We're visiting Kilkenny," Gramp said. "It's my—our—ancestral home, Ladybug. Maybe you and Matti would like to come along."

Gram squinted at him. "Don't be ridiculous, Brody. They'd be bored to death." She conjured up her "I know best" smile and explained. "We'll be meeting business leaders and local officials. Hardly something you'd enjoy. Do you and Matti have plans for tomorrow?"

"Not yet. Maybe we'll go to the zoo."

"That's lovely, dear. Go and change those jeans. We'll see you and Matti at dinner."

Janet clenched her teeth. Gram had dismissed her again. She started for the door and stopped, remembering why she'd come downstairs in the first place. Fingers curled tight, she spun toward her grandparents. "I want to go back to Boston and live with Matti. Do the same stuff other kids do. Go to my own school instead of being locked up in a boarding school." Her voice rose to a frenzied shriek. "How could you do this to me?"

Gramp looked like she'd slapped him. Gram's mouth fell open. "Now see here, young lady," she said. "We can't allow you to live across the ocean with strangers. We're responsible for you. You're all the family we have left!"

"It's all right, Henrietta," Gramp said in that gentle voice that made everyone like him. He hurried toward Janet as he spoke. "Janet has a right to be upset." He smiled—sort of—and regained his considerable dignity. "No one is locking you up, Ladybug. We chose Hazelwood because of the drama programs it offers. We know how much you love theater arts. You're only staying there because it's too far for a daily commute. You'll be home on weekends."

Was she whimpering? "But no one will want to be friends with me. I'm a foreigner!"

Gramp's arm encircled her shoulder, giving her quick little hugs. "Nonsense, Ladybug. You won't be the only American there, or even the only non-Irish student. We've already checked. You'll be fine. We'd never place you in an impossible situation."

Tears blurred her vision. She bit her lip to keep from crying. They'd done so much for her, and she'd behaved like a two-year-old throwing a temper tantrum. She'd said mean things, and Gramp was being so nice.

Even Gram had calmed down, though she still seemed peeved. "I know going to a new school is scary, dear. Your father reminded us every time we moved." She smiled sadly.

Gramp chuckled. "He sure did, but he found he enjoyed learning about new places. You will too, Jan. You said you'd have no friends because we live in a big house in the middle of nowhere. Well, the boarding school will fix that. You'll make lots of friends there. And once you do, you can invite as many as you like here on weekends and holidays. Can't she, Henrietta?"

"Of course you can. Now go and change. We'll see you and Matti in the little dining room in half an hour."

Janet mumbled that she was sorry and left the study. Once she'd closed the door, she ran down the hall to the busy kitchen, raced past the startled housekeeper, and took the back stairs two at a time. When she opened the door to her room, she was sobbing.

Matti looked up from her book. "Hey, what's wrong?"

"I don't know. I'm…it's just…" Janet felt like a rubber band being pulled tight and then loosened, over and over again. She wiped her sleeve over her eyes. "My grandmother won't let me borrow her sapphires. She's taking me shopping next week for something else."

"And?"

"And what?"

"That's it? That's why you're bawling like a freshman the seniors locked in the bathroom?"

Laughing at the image, Janet plucked a tissue from the box on her bureau. She dabbed her eyes and blew her nose. "No. I don't know. I'm just being stupid."

Matti set her bookmark and sat up straight. "So what happened with Boston and the boarding school?"

Janet joined her on the couch. "No way on Boston." She sighed heavily. "And they made the school sound really great."

"Maybe it *is* really great, Jan. Your grandmother said they're taking you to see it next week, so you'll know soon enough."

"You'll come and see it with me, won't you?"

"Sure, rub it in. Stick me with the Ricky Gagnons of the world and go off with all those hunky Irish guys." Matti nodded toward the bureau. "By the way, your phone vibrated while you were downstairs."

Janet had only given her new cell phone number to one person. Trying to appear nonchalant, she strolled over and checked the screen.

"New Text Message" appeared above the image of an envelope. Below that were the words "Unverified Sender."

Why wouldn't he want her to know who he was? It was probably a wrong number.

She viewed the message: *Can I c u tomorrow? L*

"Are you trying to air-dry your teeth," Matti asked, "or is that message from Liam?"

Suddenly oblivious to Matti, Janet sat on her bed and texted him back. Maybe living in Ireland wouldn't be so bad after all.

CHAPTER TEN

Ten miles north of the City of Dublin, the fishing village of Howth occupies a neck of land that juts into the Irish Sea. The rugged southern side of this peninsula overlooks Dublin Bay. On the gentler northern side, Howth Harbor provides shelter for fishing trawlers and private yachts. Beyond the small lighthouse on the East Pier, Ireland's Eye and Lambay Island loom in the distance like sleeping sea monsters.

Fancy boutiques and trendy restaurants line Howth's main street. Splendid homes dot the rolling hillsides right to the top of Howth Head. Foremost among these grand abodes is Garrymuir, a majestic estate that had been in the Boru family for generations.

Prince Peadar Boru lived there now with his wife and their two sons, Neil and Kevin. Kieran Dacey might be in charge of the royal family's personal safety, but Prince Peadar supervised the security of the kingdom itself. He was the leader of the elite Fianna, the warriors sworn to protect Ireland, and Howth was his home. He and his family were safe there.

Peadar's agents weren't the only ones keeping watch over Howth and its royal residents. The locals who knew the Borus as neighbors protected them in their own way. They respected the family's privacy, greeting them with a discreet nod or a quiet "God bless you" when they visited the village and its scenic surrounds.

The Borus were a close-knit clan, and Liam knew Garrymuir as well as Kevin knew the King's Residence. Liam's request to spend Saturday night at Garrymuir watching movies with his cousin aroused no suspicion. While their parents dined together in Dublin, the boys settled into Garrymuir's comfortable den for a cozy, convivial evening.

"You owe me for this!" Kevin spat, sulking before the huge flat-screen TV flashing music videos. A hefty slug from a bottle of beer underscored his annoyance.

They'd helped themselves to the beer with Peadar's blessing, as long as they kept to one bottle apiece. Liam didn't even like the bitter stuff. He'd taken only a sip or two from the bottle and set it on the table beside his chair. "What's up, Kev? Don't have the neck for it? I'd do it for you. Janet won't come without her friend, and Howth is the only place I can think of to see her without having to get Kieran's preapproval in triplicate."

A sympathetic sigh prefaced Kevin's response. "Yer man's a right bowser for sure. So what'll I do with the girl? What would we talk about? I don't want her thinking I like her or anything."

"You're talking like she's a total dog, Kev. She isn't. She's bright and funny. Walk her out on the pier for a look at the islands. She wants to go to law school, remember? Have a chinwag with her about that. Impart your wisdom, such as it is."

"Eff off, Li." Kevin took another swig of beer. "And where will you be trick-acting with the blonde while I'm dazzling the woofin' brunette?"

"Up on the cliff walk. I'll show her the gulls' nests, impress her with my knowledge of the history of the place. Educate her Yank sensibilities to our fine Irish heritage."

Kevin shot him a look of pure disbelief. "Go 'way, will ye? If I know you, you'll be squeezing her through the tightest passes in the rocks. And you want to watch that storytelling, Li. More than one and she'll be shoving you over the edge."

Liam cringed at Kevin's tone as much as at the idea of falling from the cliffs. "When did the dark side overtake you, Kev?"

"Has it?" Kevin sighed again. "Sorry. It's been awful in the house with Neil gone off to the Military College. The parents are on me for every little thing."

"I feel the same with Talty away. Chin up, Kev. The brave man never loses. We'll have ourselves some proper diversion tomorrow."

"That's what you said about today."

"It was hardly a total loss. Now find us a film. Something funny to cheer you up."

Kevin exchanged his beer for the remote control. He clicked until he found a slapstick comedy, and the boys spent the rest of the evening laughing at nonsense.

At nine the next morning, Liam received a text message from Janet saying that she and Matti were on the train to Howth. Grateful that Kevin's parents weren't up yet, the boys had a quick bite to eat and left word with the cook that they were off for a breath of fresh air.

A guard opened Garrymuir's side gate for them. No doubt he'd alert someone in the village that the boys were on the loose, but Liam didn't mind. So what if the family learned that he and Kevin had gone walking with a pair of attractive young ladies? He simply wanted to do it without having to beg for permission first, without being under a microscope.

The sun was out for the moment. The boys sauntered down to the village enjoying a sparkling view of the harbor and islands. They passed the old abbey ruins and crossed the main road to the promenade.

Just past the yacht club, familiar whiffs of diesel and rotting marine life blew by on a sudden breeze. A blast of clean salt air quickly routed the stench, and Liam breathed in the glorious seaside morning. Shrieking seagulls drifted high overhead. In the shelter of the marina, boats bobbed at their moorings, their masts and lines clicking and clacking in the breeze, their gently chiming bells enhancing the maritime music.

Liam and Kevin ambled west to the station to meet the train. The few people they passed, mostly well-dressed villagers walking purebred dogs, paid no mind to two teenagers in jeans and baseball hats.

The one old gent who did spot Kevin nodded and wished him a fine good morning. A beatific grin burst over the man's withered face when he recognized Liam. "God bless you, Your Highness," he said.

Liam offered the standard response. "And you and yours, sir."

The old gent didn't stop to chat, and the boys, spurred by an approaching roar and the squeal of metal wheels on tracks, hurried on. Liam sprinted past a pub called The Bloody Stream and up the stairs to the station concourse. Out on the platform beyond the turnstiles, passengers spilled from the train's open doors. He spotted Janet right away.

Heart thumping, he worked his way through day-tripping families toting baby gear and cameras. "Janet!"

Her searching gaze homed in on him. Her smile melted him. What mortal man could resist those azure eyes? Lively and perceptive, they shone upon him, and he basked in their enticing light.

"Howya," he said, resisting the impulse to kiss her hand. She'd think him altogether daft. "Hey, Matti."

Blinking behind her brown-framed glasses, Matti grinned and said hello. Liam wondered why she didn't wear contacts, as he did. At least he did until they began to irritate his eyes. He had his glasses in his pocket, but he doubted he'd need them till after the girls went home.

Kevin adopted his public persona and graciously welcomed the girls. Good man yourself, Liam thought, admiring his cousin's sportsmanship. Plainly smitten, Matti edged closer to Kevin and coyly described the train ride. Yes, Liam owed him, but then he forgot him.

Feeling bold, he touched Janet's arm and led her out of the station. He'd advised her to dress for the fickle Irish weather. She'd followed his advice, sensibly selecting sturdy walking shoes and a hooded jacket over a dark sweater and jeans. The rugged ensemble somehow enhanced her fresh appeal—and she still wore the locket around her neck.

He liked that. It must mean something to her, and he knew instinctively that it wasn't a gift from a boyfriend. Thinking that he'd enjoy surprising her with a similar gift, he decided to ask her about it later, when they were alone.

Alone with Janet. He couldn't wait.

CHAPTER ELEVEN

Matti was eager to see the cliffs, but Kevin said he wanted to show her the lighthouse and Ireland's Eye first. Janet and Liam left them at the entrance to the East Pier, a long stone jetty that curved around the eastern half of Howth Harbor.

"We'll catch up to you," Kevin said.

Janet caught the sly glance that he and Liam exchanged. So did Matti, from the smile she shot Janet. The boys had clearly conspired so they each could be alone with their…what? Not girlfriends. They'd only just met.

Alone to get to know us better.

Hand cupping Janet's elbow, Liam led her toward a steep street. "We have great weather today," he said. "A little cool, but clear and calm. Perfect for the cliffs."

She loved the way she buzzed when he touched her. This had to be a dream. He was so handsome, so tall, so solid, so polite. And so smart. Trusting him to guide her, she walked with him to the edge of one of the loveliest little bays she'd ever seen.

Seagulls sat on rocks jutting up from the twinkling blue water, and the waves sounded so peaceful rolling in and out. A steep neck of hilly land stretched beyond the bay like one of Matti's stage settings.

"This is Balscadden Bay," Liam said when she asked. "The name comes from *Baile na Scadán,* Irish for the Town of the Herrings. The hill is Howth Head. That's where we're going. Right out to the nose."

Between craggy rocks and patches of green, a sparse smattering of houses had Janet wondering who lived there. The houses looked tiny from where she stood. They seemed so far away. So did the tip of the hill, which must be the nose Liam mentioned. "How long will it take to get there?"

He touched her arm again. His fingers lingered this time. "Not long at all. We'll be there in jig time."

Janet couldn't breathe. "Jig? That's a dance, right?" Common sense told her no one would be dancing here, and she relaxed. "A fast dance?"

"Fast and easy. Lots of fun. I'll teach you sometime, if you like."

And have him learn what a bumbling klutz she was? He'd never want to see her again, a notion that somehow worried her. She changed the subject. "I'll bet you know why the sign on the train said something besides Howth. Binn something."

His easy smile appeared, and he snickered. Was he laughing at her?

"I love a betting woman," he said. "Lucky for me you're asking the right questions. We can't have you thinking me devoid of brilliance."

The oddly amusing way he spoke delighted her, especially when she realized he'd been laughing at himself. Giggling with relief, she asked again, "So what's Binn?"

"*Binn Éadair*. The Ben of Edar. Ben means mountain or hill. According to the legend, Edar was a chieftain of the Tuatha Dé Danann, those mischievous fairy rascals who went to live underground when the Celts invaded Ireland. Edar is supposedly buried here somewhere."

"Where did the name 'Howth' come from? Another Viking word like Wicklow?"

His smile grew to a wide grin. "Give the lady ten points. The Norse word *hoved* means head. Now let's go before I run out of answers."

They resumed their walk in a genial silence that conversed in its own way. After greeting an older couple heading toward the pier, they climbed the street that would take them to the cliffs. In one spot, a clump of greenery extended over the sidewalk. Liam slipped an arm around Janet's shoulder and drew her away from the shrubs—drew her close to him. She leaned against him, and he pulled her even closer. Once they'd left the bushes behind, he let her go, and she felt lost.

I'm so sappy…

The road curved left to a pricey neighborhood. Plush homes lined both sides of the street. A dog barked somewhere. The air smelled smoky rather than salty here. Janet recognized the pungent odor of burning peat, called turf in Ireland. She supposed that even in summer, the people who lived here needed warmth, being so close to the sea.

The ground leveled out. Her step slowed as she scanned the upscale homes. "Lots of rich folks here. Lots of big houses."

Liam adjusted his pace to hers. "The biggest is near the top of the hill. The king's brother, Prince Peadar, lives there. I'll point it out when we get to the right spot."

"You almost sound like you know him. How do you know so much about Howth?"

"I grew up around here. All right, my turn for a question. Does that locket you wear mean something special? You had it on yesterday too. Not many girls wear such classic jewelry these days. It's a fine old thing. Is it gold?"

Instinctively, she reached for the locket. She fondled it and smiled. "Yes. My parents gave it to me for my twelfth birthday." She didn't tell him her parents had died soon after. His pity was the last thing she wanted, especially on such a perfect day. "It's my good luck charm."

"May it bring you all the luck in the world," he said.

At the end of the road, they reached a vacant car park. Liam seemed surprised. "I've never seen it empty on a Sunday morning. I'm sure tons of tourists will be here soon, but it looks like we'll have the place to ourselves for a while."

They crossed the lot and stepped onto a well-trodden path. No trace of peat remained in the air; the salty tang of the sea ruled here. Janet's hair whipped in the breeze, blinding her. She fumbled in her pocket for a band to tie it back. Ponytail set, she gazed around and gasped.

Mounds of heather in full bloom grew between bumpy outcrops of rock. The blossoms covered the gently rolling ground like a flowing purple carpet. Bright yellow flowers that Liam called gorse grew where the heather didn't. Green plants grew too, adding contrast to the colorful tapestry, as did the walking paths that wound through the flowers and rocks.

Janet had never seen anything like this back home. "What a beautiful sight!"

Liam pointed. "Look behind you."

She turned and gasped again. She couldn't believe they were up so high. Far below them, the village, the harbor, and the long curving pier that Kevin and Matti must be on by now all looked like miniature scenery.

Above the panorama, menacing swirls of charcoal clouds hurtled over the sky. Janet wished they'd go away. "I hope we don't get rained out after coming all this way."

"Those clouds are always coming and going. If we worried about the weather here, we'd never get anything done. We'll survive a shower or two. I have a hat, and you have a hood on your jacket. Come on, let's walk."

They tramped over the main walking trail to the cliffs. Fascinated by the view, the height, and Liam's comments about the terrain looking much the same as it had when the Vikings first raided Ireland, Janet knew she'd never forget this day. She hiked beside him on a path that often came close to the edge of the cliffs. At times, the trail narrowed, and she walked behind him, content to let him lead the way. He pointed out a pair of seals cavorting in the water. The sight thrilled her. She'd only seen seals in aquariums before.

As they twisted along the track, the charcoal clouds caught up to them. The sun vanished, and the wind picked up. A chilly raindrop spattered Janet's nose.

"Oh no!" she cried.

"Don't worry, it's only a shower." Liam grabbed her hand and quickened his pace.

The rain fell harder, and then they were running and laughing and dodging puddles. He stopped at a sheltered nook in the rocks and pulled her in beside him. The space was snug, and they had to turn sideways to fit. Sideways and face to face.

Thanks to her watchdog grandparents, Janet hadn't been alone with too many boys. Feeling awkward, she sought a role she could play to mask her meager boy/girl skills. Then the clean, woodsy smell of Liam jumbled her thoughts, and she found that she needed no role. Huddling with him felt natural, as right as the rain that suddenly burst from the clouds.

He slipped his arms around her and pulled her hood up over her head.

And then he lifted her face to his and kissed her.

It was nothing like when Ricky Gagnon kissed her after the prom. Ricky had tasted like beer and he'd slurped and tried to stick his tongue down her throat and she'd choked and shoved him away and called him a jerk and he'd never called her again, but Liam's kiss erased all that.

Boston was far away. She was here in Howth with Liam, kissing him back with the same neat pecks and long soft slides he was teaching her. The tingly butterscotch taste on her lips left her panting. Reeling.

One last kiss, and he sighed and bussed her forehead. His strong arms tightened around her. She rested her head on his chest. They watched the rain fall, and Janet knew that when she looked up, she'd see a rainbow.

She saw two, in fact, so vast was the sky. They shimmered and pulsed and vanished, stolen by clouds that blew away like galloping smoke.

"Off to Scotland," Liam murmured. The rain had stopped, yet he seemed in no hurry to leave their refuge.

Janet wondered where Scotland was from the Nose of Howth. Disengaging herself from Liam's embrace, she stepped onto the path, lowered her hood, and gazed out at the Irish Sea. After the few experiences she'd had with boys, she'd thought that kissing them would be something she'd have to pretend to like, simulating a phony smile to show that all was well.

Kissing Liam hadn't been like that at all. Sensing him close behind her, she turned and surprised herself by smiling for real.

He smiled back and took her hand again. "Come on, Jan. I'll show you the lighthouse."

The path was free of puddles. Either the soil had soaked them up, or they'd run off into the sea. Janet didn't care which. Still tasting the sweet, pleasant newness of Liam's kisses, she strolled hand in hand with him.

He stopped once, bringing her close to the edge to show her where the seagulls nested in the cliffs. They made their nests with seaweed, he said, and she thought they must be very special birds if Liam knew their ways.

He asked her about Boston and New England's seasons and said he'd like to see the autumn foliage sometime. She'd just realized he was hinting that he'd like to visit her when music wafted toward her. A radio, she thought. People were nearby. The droves of tourists Liam had mentioned. Intruders.

"Where's that music coming from?" she asked.

He stopped and listened. "I don't hear anything."

"I think it's a harp." She glanced around, focusing on the sound. "It's coming from up there." She pointed to the grassy rise above them. A narrow path led up the hill. "Where does that go?"

"To the summit, eventually. There's a knoll on the way. We can see the lighthouse from there."

The music grew louder. A harp for sure. Fast music. "It sounds lovely. Is that jig time?"

"Janet, I don't hear anything."

She wasn't looking at him, but she heard the frown in his voice. How could he not hear it? A sudden compulsion to climb the path made her release his hand. She scampered up the side of the hill, vaguely aware but unconcerned that he'd called her name.

Following the music, she reached an area she hadn't seen from where she'd stood with Liam. The cottage surprised her. Stone-walled and round, it looked like the pointed grass huts she'd seen in pictures of Africa. Liam hadn't mentioned it. Maybe he didn't know the area as well as he thought. She glanced behind her. He wasn't there.

A twinge of fear nibbled at her until she looked back at the cottage. An elderly woman stood smiling in the doorway. Janet blinked in disbelief at Nora, the woman from the dressmaker's shop.

"Hello, Janet," she called, waving. "Did you come to visit me?"

Janet seemed to float toward her. "I didn't know you lived here, Nora."

"Come in and have tea, love," Nora said, raising her suddenly crackly voice above the deafening music. "Look what I have for you."

She held up her hand. The sapphire necklace glittered in the sunlight.

CHAPTER TWELVE

The first time Liam slipped and fell, he cursed the rain-damp grass. He blamed his second tumble on his haste to catch up with Janet. What on earth had possessed the girl to run off like that? She couldn't possibly want to find music that badly.

Music only she could hear.

The third time he lost his balance, he'd swear someone had pushed him, but no one was there. He landed on his hands and knees and cursed again. He might not be a muscleman, but he was far from a clumsy dolt. A lifetime of sports and outdoor treks had surely left him fit enough to climb a scrubby little hillside.

Something strange was afoot.

I'm being ridiculous, he thought. The breeze must have kept him from hearing the music she heard. She'd likely gone after the owner of whatever was playing the tune to learn its name.

Yet the Nose of Howth seemed deserted. How odd for a sunny Sunday morning. Even if Janet had gone off seeking the source of the music, no amount of rationalizing could explain why she'd left so abruptly. The chilling sense that she was in danger had Liam's heart thumping high in his throat.

Should he call his cousin? If Kevin was still on the pier, it would take him a while to get here. And practical Kevin would surely think Liam astray in the head.

Maybe he was, but something told him he had to find Janet, and fast. Keeping close to the ground as if he were dodging radar, he clambered monkey-like up the hill. This time he reached the top of the rise. Lumps in the landscape surrounded him, clumps of rock and rolling masses of heather and gorse that encircled the level spot where he stood. He knew the place well. Except for the curious lack of weekend hill walkers, nothing seemed amiss.

"Janet!"

He listened hard. A seagull cried in the distance. Otherwise, all was silent. No, wait! Music drifted toward him, a plucky harp tune he might have enjoyed under different circumstances. Was that what Janet had heard?

Where was it? He turned in a circle, squinting in the sunlight, scanning, straining to hear. When he returned to the spot where he'd started, a jolt of fear set his pulse racing.

A round stone hut had appeared on the highest part of the clearing. Its low thatched roof rose to a ridiculously high point. It resembled a roundhouse, the sort of dwelling that belonged in a prehistoric ring fort.

Or a fairy fort.

Liam swallowed hard. He'd seen replicas of such huts in Ireland's folk parks. He'd also viewed ruins of the original ring forts, all that remained of the structures built by the mysterious peoples who'd lived and died in Ireland thousands of years ago.

Where had this one come from? Why was it on the Nose of Howth? Liam had never seen it before, nor had he heard of any gimmicky tourism plans for the cliff walk. Of course, he didn't know everything. Convincing himself that he'd failed to see the hut at first because the sun had blinded him, he ventured toward the structure.

He spotted a doorway and relaxed. Janet was there, speaking to a woman wearing a period costume, medieval or older. That's what it was, he thought: tourism come to tarnish Howth. How could Uncle Peadar have allowed such nonsense?

Liam called Janet's name again, but neither she nor the woman showed any sign that they'd heard him. The wind must have carried his voice away. He stalked toward the roundhouse. As he approached, the costumed woman placed a necklace over Janet's head.

The roundhouse flickered, faded, and reappeared. Alarmed, Liam stopped. This was no tourist gimmick. As his thoughts scrambled for an explanation, the woman grabbed Janet's arm and pulled her into the hut.

"Janet, no!" His ferocious roar proved useless. Unbelievably, the roundhouse began to dissolve. No longer doubting his horrified senses, he dove at the hut and charged through the disappearing door.

The world around him melted away.

***** *

Contented and pleasantly drowsy, Janet seemed to float across a carpet of fragrant grass. She followed Nora into an orchard of oddly shaped trees with colorful fruit that sparkled like jewels and bent the twisted branches low. Birds whose feathers glowed like neon rainbows whistled and trilled among the shiny green leaves. And all the while, the pleasant music played.

Violins and flutes joined the harp, rendering harmonies so soothing, Janet thought she might fall asleep. Her steps were out of time with the lively tune, yet its rhythm matched her heartbeat.

Nora's constant chatter sounded far away and made no sense, but her comforting voice drew Janet through the trees to a shimmering pond. Orange fish jumped from the water as if they were staging a show for her. At the end of the pond, the brilliant white flowers of a tree in full bloom perfumed the air with honey and musk. Beside the tree stood a tall flat stone.

Nora stopped before the stone and raised her arms. *"Tatther rura!"* she shouted. The stone hummed. A spot of light whirled in its center, spinning, growing.

Smiling amiably, Nora took Janet's arm. What a kind, lovely woman she was, Janet thought. Together they stepped through the stone.

***** *

A nightmare of jet black darkness enveloped Liam. He might have been wearing a blindfold. His racing pulse thundered in his ears. What had he done? Was he caught between two worlds, forever trapped beneath the Nose of Howth? No one would ever know he was here.

And where was Janet? Barraged by waves of shivers, he stretched his arms and tested the blackness around him. *The likes of me would never make a warrior.*

As his vision adjusted to the darkness, shadows emerged in the gloom. Specks of light outlined a hole in the floor near a wall. Feeling his way across the room—he found no furniture—he considered the purpose of the opening.

A souterrain? Most ring forts included some sort of manmade tunnel that led to chilly underground storage chambers connected by multiple passages. The tunnels had also served as emergency escape routes in case of attack. He doubted either purpose was at work here, or that any mortal had constructed this passage.

But that was impossible. Just because he knew the old stories didn't mean they were real. His overactive imagination had taken off on him, that's all. A logical explanation existed to explain all this, and he meant to find it.

The shaking in his knees eased. His heart no longer threatened to jump through his chest. With the light from below guiding him, he descended a rough stone stairway.

He found himself in an arched passageway with walls of dry-stacked stones. No mortar kept them in place. They fit together like the pieces of a jigsaw puzzle. His shoulder bumped the tapering wall once. After that, he took care to keep to the middle of the passage, where his head cleared the rocky roof by a scant few inches.

The old woman's voice echoed up ahead. He hurried down the curving tunnel, which grew brighter as he turned each bend. He found no chambers. Whoever had built the tunnel had meant it for passage, not storage.

As he turned the last curve, light streamed in from outside. After pausing briefly to let his eyes adapt, he stole into the grounds.

An orchard of peculiar trees covered the field before him, bizarre looking things with colored stones for fruit. He spotted Janet at the far end of the orchard. The old woman with her had grown even older and hulked over her now. Liam remained silent, fearing the woman would harm Janet if he called her name, but he ran as fast as he dared between the trees.

Each footstep released a burst of sickening fumes from the grass. The stench made him dizzy. Holding his breath, he passed a pond filled with leaping salmon and slipped behind a gnarled tree trunk, where he gulped down air now thick with a musky floral scent.

He peeked around the tree trunk. Janet and the woman approached a flowering hawthorn tree. But how could that be? Hawthorn bloomed in May, not August. Swallowing hard, Liam accepted at last, that in this place, whatever it was, the ivory blossoms on this particular tree were always in bloom. The legends claimed that a solitary hawthorn tree signaled an entrance to the Otherworld. The orchard must be an "in-between" place. He drew closer and noticed the standing stone beside the tree.

"Tatther rura!" the woman cried before he could think what the stone's purpose might be. She'd not only grown taller since he'd seen her in the doorway to the hut, she'd become hunchbacked and ugly too. He guessed the witchlike persona to be her true form. An old Irish verse sprang from the wealth of ancient poems he knew by heart:

> *A hag she was, a loathsome offense*
> *Broad of tooth and nose like a plowshare*
> *Paunchy belly and scabby black crown*
> *A hideous weight on every heart.*

"I couldn't have said it better myself," he muttered.

The bizarre words she'd spoken seemed to cause an expanding swirl of light to pulse from the rock. Liam ran. He had to get Janet away from that stone, yet he knew he'd never reach her in time. Still, he ran, shouting for her to stop.

But the hag had already seized her arm and pulled her through the stone.

CHAPTER THIRTEEN

Nora steered Janet around corner after corner in the dusky passageway. Light appeared, and the music swelled to its loudest yet. Laughter bubbled between each note, boosting the merry sound. Despite the din, the sputtering flames from the torches set in the corridor's walls crackled in Janet's ears. The gown she wore rustled with each step, its gold cloth twinkling in the firelight. Where had the dress come from? When had she put it on?

Nora wore a similar gown. "We're going to a party, love," she said.

A party. A blue dress drifted through Janet's thoughts like feathery milkweed pods gone off in the wind.

Ladybug, ladybug, fly away home…

Who had taught her that? Where had she been before she'd come to this place? And with whom?

Rain. Rainbows. A boy. A boy with a playful half-smile and laughing eyes. She couldn't recall his name, but his fleeting features set her lips tingling. Butterscotch. He'd kissed her, and she'd kissed him back. His elusive image joined a procession of snatches and snippets the music swept away.

Their departure from her memory saddened her, yet she was happy here, with Nora and the golden gown. Nora had promised her joy, an evening of feasting and dancing with loyal, loving friends.

Janet followed her around another corner, the last in their outing, it seemed. They entered a dazzling hall, the biggest room Janet had ever seen. She felt as if she'd walked on stage as part of a play, but she couldn't remember her lines.

She stared all around her. So much gold! Burning torches lined the walls. Marble pillars ran from the floor to the ceiling, where candles glittered in golden chandeliers. Beneath them, laughing people danced. Men and women dressed in gold raised circles of shimmering dust as they kicked and spun.

The music suddenly stopped. The dancers stared at Janet until "oohs" and "ahs" arose from their midst. In unison they parted, and a regal young man with pale flowing hair approached her.

Taller than the other men, he wore a crown of gold and jewels that made him appear taller still. Diamonds sparkled on the golden brooch at the neck of his long white cloak. He lifted his head and dipped his chin, a signal to Nora, it seemed.

"Go in, girl," she said.

Janet trembled, though she felt no fear. She stepped to the center of the hall, glancing left and right. Such beautiful people, she thought.

The man with the crown was the loveliest of all. She stopped before him, admiring his fine-boned face, his delicate nose and electric-blue eyes. He wasn't much older than she and her high school friends.

He inspected her, nodding as he did. At last, his lips curved in approval. "You've done well, Becula. The lady is even more comely than the marble stone depicted her."

"Nora," Janet tried to say, "her name is Nora," but her mouth wouldn't work.

The young man flashed Janet a pearly smile. "I am Finvarra, the King of the Fairies." He waved his hand over the crowd, presenting his subjects. "You may speak, girl. Tell the *Daoine Sídhe* your name."

His purring voice unhooked the latch on her tongue. "My name is Janet," she said, relieved that she could speak again. Her thoughts seemed to clear the tiniest bit, as if someone had cracked open a window in her soul.

"A lovely name." He held out his hand to her. "Dance with me, Janet."

"But I can't dance, sir."

His laughter sounded like muffled bells. "Of course you can. I have said so. Becula heard your wish to learn to dance. She allowed you to wish it upon a necklace that once belonged to the Goddess Danu. The necklace allowed me to hear your wish as well. I have found you pleasing, Janet, and so have granted your wish."

Janet stroked the sapphire necklace. She'd forgotten all about it. Touching it warmed her fingers, made her feel as if she were flying.

Something was caught beneath it. Something she should know. But Finvarra, the King of the Fairies waited to dance with her. She took his hand.

He called for a waltz, and the music restarted, slower this time. Secure in his arms, she whirled with him, gracefully gliding around the room. Tinkling cheers and dainty applause rose from the fairies, and then they were all waltzing. Glowing with pride and confidence, Janet could think of nothing but dancing.

The music picked up speed. Finvarra spun her through reels and jigs, hornpipes and polkas, slides and marches. She never tired, though she soon grew thirsty. When the next dance ended, she asked for a glass of water.

Her request seemed to please Finvarra. He clapped his hands. "We will have more than water. We will have food and drink!"

Janet gawked as banquet tables materialized in the room. Pink flower petals held together by delicate webs of silvery thread covered the tables. Everything on them, from plates to goblets to beverage pitchers, was made of gold. Bowls of fruit and boards of bread appeared, whetting Janet's appetite.

She hooked her arm around Finvarra's proffered elbow. "So much food," she said.

"More is on the way." His courtesy and constant smile enchanted her. "We must replenish your strength that you may keep dancing. But first, we will offer a toast to our new dancer. Come forth, good women, and serve us our wine!"

A trio of sad-eyed, gray-haired women entered the room. Their simple tops and long plain skirts, inferior to what the fairies wore, struck Janet as servants' attire. Neither smile nor frown broke the lines etched on their weary faces. They poured dark liquid from the pitchers into the goblets, placed them on trays, and distributed them.

While one woman served the king his drink, another leaned close to Janet and whispered in her ear, "Eat and drink nothing. Once you partake of Finvarra's fare, you can never return to your home. We know."

The words seeped through the crack in the window to Janet's soul. Her hands shook. Her knees quaked. For the first time since she'd seen Nora in the doorway to the hut, she was afraid.

Finvarra handed her a golden glass. "A dram of mead for you, dear Janet. Drink. Raise your glasses, my friends. A toast to Janet!"

The fairies toasted and drank, but Janet's glass remained in her unmoving hands. "I can't," she said. "I'm not old enough to drink."

A collective gasp filled the room. Grumbles rippled through the crowd: *She refuses the king's hospitality! Bad manners! Disgraceful! Shocking! An insult!*

The king grabbed her glass and squeezed her arm. "You will drink!" he roared. He pressed the glass to her lips.

She pushed it away and screamed.

CHAPTER FOURTEEN

Liam raced toward the standing stone. He reached it just as the swirling light began to fade. His wary touch met no resistance. He shot straight through the stone.

A fetid stink jerked him to a stop. He gagged at the stench, which smelled like old tires and rotten seaweed burning together. The passage was cold and dark, the rock walls beside him covered with soot. Breathing through his mouth, he zipped up his jacket and waited until his vision adapted to the gloom. Shadows moved in the tunnel before him, as if firelight flickered around a bend. What awaited him up ahead?

...you could be kidnapped, or worse...

Wishing that Kieran were with him now, Liam tiptoed toward the twitching light. When he turned a corner, the passage grew brighter. Torches flared from the walls at irregular intervals. Nothing else moved in the distant gloom, though he detected faint echoes of the old woman's babbling. Steeling himself, he jogged through the tunnel.

The stench swelled each time he passed a torch. He guessed that rancid oil rendered from animal fat fueled the putrid flames. Fairy magic wouldn't smell so bad.

Or would it?

Something ran across his path. He flattened himself against the wall. Cringing in revulsion, he watched a black rat scurry into a crevice. Its repulsive tail slithered after it. A fairy rat guarding the passage? Even now the flea-ridden thing might be on its way to report his intrusion. He hoped not. He hoped to surprise whoever had taken Janet.

The tunnel turned several more corners. As Liam ran, the woman's voice grew louder. So did the music. The gap between him and Janet was closing fast.

What would he do when he overtook them? He didn't know how to combat magic. At least he wasn't under a spell himself—not that he knew of—but Janet had to be, and he'd bet it had something to do with that necklace the old witch had fastened around her neck.

He tried to recall what the legends said about women the fairies had stolen. Some were new mothers taken to nurse fairy babies. Others, like Janet, were blooming young girls kidnapped by lecherous fairy kings.

A vague recollection about red-haired men being able to help mortals taken by fairies encouraged him. He had the red hair, dark as it was. Surprised that his baseball cap still sat on his head, he whipped it off and shoved it into his jacket pocket.

The fairies would see his hair right away. He might be only seventeen, but he'd make sure they thought him a man, not a boy. He had no doubt he could pull it off. If he was man enough to kiss the girl, he was man enough to save her. At least he hoped so.

The music stopped. A gritty-voiced man—gritty no doubt from breathing the fumes from the torches—asked Janet to dance. Liam ran faster, on guard for anything bigger than a rat, suspecting he was about to meet the biggest rat of all.

He turned the last corner and stopped. The entrance to a cavern bright with firelight yawned before him. Watching where he placed each step, he crept along the wall and peered inside. He could just make out the top of the cave.

Torches similar to those in the passage illuminated the chamber, as did candles set in a rusty chandelier. The ceiling wasn't much higher than Liam's head. He'd have to duck to keep from hitting the lights.

Inching closer, he scanned the bottom half of the cave. The absurd thought that his contact lenses were holding out well gave way to astonishment. Scores of people, dwarf men and women no more than two feet tall, stood around what appeared to be a small banquet hall. The people themselves were ancient, their faces withered, their hair, what there was of it, white. Their rustic clothing had clearly seen better days.

Still in her jeans and jacket, Janet stood with the ugly hag before a grizzle-bearded man about three feet tall. He'd just introduced himself as—

Finvarra? This was the King of the Fairies? If so, the old rogue had fallen on hard luck. Perhaps the Tuatha de Danann weren't immortal after all. Perhaps their kind, whatever that was, simply had a longer lifespan than humans. Liam didn't care how long the fairies lived. He only wanted to get Janet out of there.

Finvarra announced that he'd chosen her for his new dancing partner. The music started again, and he waltzed with her, a ludicrous sight. She loomed over him, though she didn't seem to notice. From her sleepy eyes and dreamy smile, Liam suspected she saw things that weren't there. The necklace had done something to her. The necklace and the hag.

While the fairies and Janet spun through the dust, Liam tried to think what to do. He eyed the cave, recalled the tunnel, wondered if there was another way out.

The dancing stopped. Janet asked for a glass of water. The king seemed eager to please her. He called for food and drink.

Tables and benches appeared. The magic, weakened though it might be, still worked. Liam counted three elderly serving women whose superior height and raggedy clothing suggested they were mortals. They brought trays of wooden cups when Finvarra called for a toast.

Janet mustn't touch whatever was in those cups! If she did, she'd be trapped, like these poor women. Mindful of the chandelier, Liam hurtled into the room to stop her, but she'd already refused the drink.

Good girl!

Finvarra snagged the cup from her and tried to force her to drink. She pushed him away and screamed.

Liam charged toward them. "Let her go, you thieving scut!"

Bubbles of fairy shrieks plinked through the cave. Finvarra puffed up in challenge. "Who in the name of Danu are you?"

Janet remained silent. Liam ached to speak to her, to see if she knew him, if she was all right, but he didn't dare unpin his gaze from the shifty-eyed fairy king. "My friends call me Liam," he said, striving to sound bolder than he felt. The storyteller in him came to his aid: his voice remained clear and steady. "I've come to reclaim the young woman you've stolen."

A venomous snarl twisted Finvarra's face. "How dare you violate our gathering! Remove this intruder from our midst!"

Braced for an attack he doubted he could handle, Liam stole a glance at Janet. She smiled at him. She knew him! But as fast as the light in her eyes had flashed, it dimmed again.

He planted his feet apart. "That's hardly hospitable, Finny. I'm only after arriving. And you're the one doing the violating. A little off your turf, aren't you? Don't you and your kind usually infest County Galway?"

Though his glare remained fixed on Liam, Finvarra addressed the hag, "You assured us no one followed you, Becula. I should strike him blind for spying upon us."

The woman cackled. "There's no need of that, sire. A red-haired man. I never would have seen him. This one has a true *shanachie*'s soul. You'd have a wealth of stories from him, but mind: he has the heart of a lion."

The king's glare eased to a calculating frown. "That red hair bestirs fond memories in me. I know you, *shanachie*. Or your lineage. How is your clan called?"

No longer caring if Janet knew his name, Liam summoned every drop of royal blood that flowed in his veins and puffed out his chest. "My clan is the Clan Boru. I am Liam Conor Boru, the son of the King of Ireland."

Finvarra's mouth fell open, though he quickly composed himself. "A most noble lineage. We have fought beside you when your battles were just."

"So I've heard. Thank you for that. You've done much good, but taking this young woman was wrong. You must give her back."

The fairy king appeared to consider Liam's demand. "She wished to learn to dance. I'm merely granting her wish."

"She knows nothing of you. You've taken advantage of her innocence."

"What of it? I required a new dancing partner, and Becula found one for me. It was well worth moving my troop from Galway to obtain her."

"You don't *obtain* young women so! Give her back, now!"

Finvarra peered at Liam as if he were preparing to step on a cockroach. A hooligan's smile crept over his face. "If I'm to return to Galway without her, you must recompense me for that trouble."

A bolt of icy fear zapped Liam's spine. "What sort of recompense?"

"I will have a story, noble *shanachie*." Finvarra clapped his hands. "Bring our guest a measure of wine, and another glass for me."

The mortal women brought more wooden cups. One woman approached Liam. Her piercing gaze cut into him. While the others served Finvarra and Becula, she warned Liam to bypass the wine.

"His silver tongue lies," she whispered. "He will never let you go. You must take the girl and run. We will try to help you."

The woman backed away. His worst fear confirmed, Liam left the cup on the tray. Could Janet run in her present state? Again, she eyed him curiously, as if she knew him but couldn't quite remember who he was. He wanted to rip the necklace away and shove it down Finvarra's throat.

"All right, Your Majesty," he said, "I'll tell you a story."

Like small children, the fairies oohed and aahed. They settled themselves around the banquet tables, filthy things covered with leaves so old and dry, they crackled. Cobwebs held the leaves together. Wooden bowls and platters on each table contained spoiled fruit and moldy nuts.

The legends said the fairies had fine taste in food and wine. Somehow, Liam doubted that better provisions awaited them in Galway, or that this was only their "road show," as Finvarra claimed. The Good Folk seemed to have hit an economic downturn.

A rough plank bench appeared behind the king. The witch claimed one end. Finvarra took hold of Janet's arm, and she sat beside him on the other. "You may start, *shanachie*," he said.

Struggling to hide his animosity, Liam eyed his peewee host and pint-sized audience. The perverse idea of telling them a story about giants appealed to him. He began with the standard "long, long ago" and eased into the tale of the giant Finn MacCool's encounter with his Scottish rival, Benandonner.

"Finn shouted across the sea to Scotland and challenged Benandonner to do battle. The two had never met. Now Finn being a thoughtful sort, he set a trail of mighty stones into the sea between Scotland and Ireland so Benandonner might keep his feet dry when he came."

Liam continued, stalling for time by embellishing details and adding new twists no one had ever heard. His words enthralled the fairies, and he was only warming up. Janet's vacant stare left him doubting that she understood a word he said. Would she know what to do when the time came? Even if she did, how was he going to get them both out of here?

Unless the women really could help them...

He paced as he spoke, making the fairies' heads turn, careful to avoid the chandelier. "The Scottish giant crossed the sea to fight with Finn, but when Finn saw Benandonner's monstrous size, he ran home and asked his wife to hide him."

"Oooooh," the amazed fairies said as one.

"She dressed him as a baby and placed him in a giant cradle. Benandonner entered their house, and when he saw what he thought was an infant, he screamed in fright. 'If this is the baby, why, the father must be huge indeed!'"

The fairies belly-laughed at Liam's theatrical imitation of the terrified giant's hasty retreat to Scotland. "He tore up the stepping stones as he went, so Finn couldn't follow."

Liam paused. Benandonner had given him an idea. He must rip up stones, so to speak, to keep the fairies from following him. He decided to give his story a brand-new ending.

Edging toward the wall, he improvised to shield his intentions. "Finn climbed out of the cradle and held his arms out to his wife." Liam slowly raised his arms. "She gave him a great...big..."

With his right hand, Liam yanked a torch from the wall and tossed it onto the nearest table. His left hand shook the chandelier. Candles flew over the rest of the tables. The dry leaves serving as tablecloths ignited with an enormous whoosh.

Fairy shrieks pealed through the hall like alarm bells. Finvarra leapt to his feet. Liam ran at the unsuspecting king, knocked him down, and grabbed Janet's hand.

"Come on!" he shouted.

She seemed to realize she must run. Thankful for that, he pulled her from the room to the passageway. Keeping a tight hold on her hand as they fled, he yanked torches from the wall and tossed them behind him. They continued to burn on the tunnel floor, stinking, smoking, and, Liam hoped, blocking the way.

Not bad, he thought, though he didn't slow down. Squeals of outrage twittered in his wake. Bellowed threats and taunts resounded through the passage. When the din began to fade, he dared to look at Janet.

Her growl made him jump. Her face was that of a snarling wolf.

What had that ballad said, what, what, what? He knew it well enough. What had the Scottish knight, Tam Lin, told his Janet when the fairies changed him to different beasts to frighten her away?

Hold me fast and fear me not...

Liam held fast to Janet's hand.

"Old tricks!" he shouted. "Can't you knackers come up with something more original?"

The wolf's fangs grew. The face turned to a snake's head with hypnotic black eyes and powerful jaws that snapped at him.

"Ah, Jayz!" he cried, leaping back, but he held fast to Janet's hand and ran. Her face morphed to a snarling lion and then to a growling black bear. He tried not to look at her. Maybe if he didn't look, if he focused on what was ahead, kept tossing the torches down…

They reached the end of the tunnel. The standing stone, solid and cold, blocked the exit. Liam punched it in frustration. Then he remembered: the witch had used some sort of password. "What did she say?" he shouted to no one. "Terra Nova!"

The stone remained unchanged. The twittering fairy squeals behind him, however, grew louder.

"Tantra Rula!"

The squeals changed to chirps and yipping squeaks. He knew the sound from a childhood spent playing in castles: rats. A pack of fairy rats was closing in on him and Janet.

She had a rat face now, beady eyes and a long gray snout filled with sharp yellow teeth that laughed at him.

They were coming. Clicking. Squeaking.

Coming.

Trembling now, Liam repeatedly punched the stone. "Toora-feckin'-loora!"

"*Tatther rura!*"

He whirled at the commanding shout. The serving woman who'd warned him not to drink the wine emerged from a nook in the stone. She pulled a plaid shawl over her head. "I'm leaving with you."

The stone hummed. Light spun in its center. When the glow grew big enough, she stepped through. Tugging Janet's hand, Liam followed. He glanced back once, in time to see a stampede of rats charging at him. He nearly gave up. What good would running do? The rats would only follow them through the stone.

But when he and Janet reached the other side, the woman repeated the words, "*Tatther rura!*"

The stone calmed. The woman ran into the orchard. "We must hurry. They'll need some time to open the stone again, but they'll follow if they can."

Janet had regained her human appearance. Whether she understood what was happening or not, she ran with Liam. He worried about the woman. How long could she run like this? She looked so old. Most women stayed with the fairies either a year and a day or for seven years. Could she have aged so much in seven years?

"Who are you?" he asked as they flew past the pond with the leaping salmon. "Where are you from?"

"I am Berneen Dolan. I was born in Connemara."

"How long have you been with *Them*?"

Berneen glanced back at Janet, who'd grown silent and docile again. "They took me when I was her age, in the year of our Lord 1585."

More than four centuries ago. Impossible, but Berneen was here, alive and well because of fairy enchantment. What would happen to her when they got outside? *If* they got outside.

They'd reached the souterrain that led to the hut. No one followed them, not yet. Liam stopped to catch his breath and check on Janet. "What made you decide to leave now, Berneen?"

"I always knew time had passed, that my family and everyone I loved were gone. My home beside the sea must be gone too. I loved the sea. I smelled its perfume when Becula brought the girl to Finvarra. I would return to the sea, sir. I'm an old woman now. The fairies themselves have aged, immortal though they perchance might be." A smile bloomed on her wrinkled face. "Besides, I had to help you. You're a brave young man, Prince Liam Boru. You have the red hair, but I feared you might not escape Finvarra unaided. Few have." She entered the passage.

"But if you leave this place—"

She paused and turned her head toward him. Her consoling smile glowed with the gentle reassurance of a resolute soul at peace. "I will return to the sea."

Her footsteps tapped the stairs. Liam hurried after her, clutching Janet's hand, daring to believe they'd escaped. A moment later, they stood inside the hut.

Berneen strode to the door and reached to open it. Her hand hovered over the latch. She turned unsmiling to Liam. "You violated the fairy realm without permission, young sir. He'll want his revenge. He'll come after you. Mind yourself." She closed her eyes. Her lips moved, and she crossed herself. "I'm ready. God bless you both."

They dashed into the salty breeze and rushed away from the

roundhouse, already disappearing. Berneen ran ahead. She stopped on a high spot and gazed at the Irish Sea. Slowed by Janet's robotic pace, Liam followed. He wanted to help Berneen, but by the time he reached her, he knew he could only wish her Godspeed.

Tears flowed down her timeworn cheeks. She raised her face to the sun and smiled. "I am home!" she cried, and she slowly crumbled away, first to a skeleton, then to fine white dust that blew over the cliffs to the sea.

Liam dabbed his sleeve at his eyes. Hating Finvarra more than ever, he mourned for Berneen and for all the women the fairies had stolen. At least he'd saved Janet. He turned her so she faced him. Her blank expression infuriated him.

"Give me that!" He wrenched the sapphire necklace from her throat. The chain caught her hair as he pulled it over her head, and she cried out in pain. Horrified that he'd hurt her, he kissed her gently, barely touching his lips to hers. "Wait here, darlin'. I'll be right back."

He ran to the end of the trail and skittered down a small slope overlooking the sea. The familiar lighthouse on the jutting arm of Howth Head to his right reassured him. So did Ireland's Eye, off to his left. The place was still deserted, and now he knew why: the fairies had claimed Howth Head for a feckin' Sunday morning dance.

Poising himself to fling the necklace into the water, he raised his arm and noticed Janet's locket tangled in the wicked thing. Carefully, he picked it out and slipped it into his pocket.

He hurled the necklace hard and far. "Here's a present for Manannan MacLir!" he shouted. "You feckin' fairy kings can sort it out between yez!"

The necklace sailed. It seemed to fly. He thought it might keep going, that the King of the Sea didn't want it, but at last it tumbled sparkling into the water.

"Good riddance." A sense of calm fell over Liam. His hammering heartbeat slowed as the adrenaline eased and he caught his breath. He spun on his heel to climb back up the path to Janet.

The sea roared behind him. He turned and stared in horror at churning white-capped waves rising impossibly high. A monstrous wind blew at him, buffeting him, capturing him. Arms flailing, he reached for something to save him from falling but found only angry air. He lost his footing and tumbled over the edge of the cliffs.

CHAPTER FIFTEEN

Two giant hands seemed to squeeze Janet hard, so hard she couldn't breathe. She felt she'd popped right out of herself, that she was floating, watching herself totter along the cliff path. Floating and cold. And stupid. What was she going to tell Gram?

In the distance, a boat left a sudsy trail in the sea. The water reflected the blue sky above it. No clouds. No rainbows. The rainbows were gone, like her locket. She wanted to lie down and sleep. The salt air must have exhausted her, or maybe all the walking. So much walking.

She couldn't believe what had happened. How could she have been so gullible? From that first bite of pizza at Manetto's, Liam had lied to her. Tricked her. He'd probably crashed into her on purpose in Temple Bar.

He'd said he wanted to show her the lighthouse, but he'd stolen her locket instead. Yanked it right over her head, catching her hair and hurting her before running off like a common thief. And he'd had the nerve to kiss her before he made his escape!

His mocking voice taunted her: *Not many girls wear such classic jewelry these days. It's a fine old thing. Is it gold?*

Is it gold is it gold is it gold?

Janet had lost her last link to her parents. Her eyes filled. She sobbed once and held her breath. Crying would do no good. She would call the police. Tell them he'd robbed her. From the way he and Kevin had avoided the policemen in Temple Bar, they knew him, even if he had lied about his name. Maybe they could get her locket back.

Brushing her useless tears away, she looked about to get her bearings.

She was somewhere on the path at the edge of the cliffs, the same path she and Liam had taken from the car park. Could she find her way back to the village? Yes. She pulled out her cell phone.

Matti answered on the first ring. "What's going on, Jan? You don't sound so good. Where are you?"

"Up on the hill. The cliffs. I don't know exactly where. Liam ran off and left me here." She couldn't tell Matti about the locket. Not yet.

"That's weird. Kevin got a call and took off like a rock from a slingshot. He didn't even say goodbye."

Because Liam called and said he'd finished the job. Matti was right. They're drug dealers or something. "Where are you, Matti?"

"In the parking lot."

Janet glanced left. The car park had to be that way. People were coming toward her. If she got lost, she could ask them the way, but how could anyone get lost here? Liam had told her the Nose of Howth only had one main path. He'd said the hill had lots of shortcuts, but she wasn't going to waste time trying to find them. She'd only lose her way, and what if he'd lied about that too?

If she stayed on the main path and hurried, she'd be back at the car park fast. Hustling along the narrow trail, she passed the spot where she and Liam had sheltered from the rain. Where he'd first kissed her.

"You scum-sucking jerk!" She despised him, but she despised herself even more for crying. Determined to pull herself together, she fished for her sunglasses and put them on so no one would see how upset she was.

Soon she approached the people she'd seen, two middle-aged couples dressed for a casual hike. The bits of conversation she heard sounded German. They smiled when she passed and said hello and *guten tag*. She nodded and hurried by them, not caring if she seemed rude.

When the car park came into view, she ran. Matti rushed toward her. They met where the heather gave way to the asphalt. Comforting whiffs of burning peat ushered Janet away from the cliffs to the safety of the parking lot, which contained about ten cars now. She saw no one but Matti. Thank goodness.

"Liam stole my locket, Matti. Ripped it right off my neck!"

Matti's glasses enlarged her gawking eyes, making them look absurdly big and round. "I knew it! I knew they were no good! We have to call the police. Did he hurt you, Jan?"

Janet shook her head. "We can't call the police. I thought I should, but Gram said we mustn't do anything to embarrass Gramp. I'll tell her I lost it. I'll say the chain must have broken and slipped off, and by the time I realized it was gone, it was too late." She was going to cry again. She pressed her lips together and held her breath, quashing her helplessness by assuming an air of strength. "It's only a locket. I can get another one."

The concern in Matti's gaze sharpened. "It's your *locket*, Jan. Your parents gave it to you. I know what it meant to you. The pictures—"

"My grandparents have lots of pictures of my parents, and I can get another locket." Janet raised her chin. "Or maybe I won't. Lockets are for little girls."

Matti flashed her "yeah, right" smirk. "If you're not going to call the police, you should at least tell your grandparents about the guys."

"No! They'd never let me out of their sight again. Promise you won't say anything."

"Don't you think—"

"Promise!"

Sighing loudly, Matti agreed.

"They think we went to the zoo today." Janet glanced at her watch. "Too bad it's so late. We might still have gone."

"What do you mean, so late?" Matti checked her own watch. "It's only a little past noon. We can grab lunch somewhere and take the bus to the zoo. The baby giraffe will help us forget those evil dudes. Of course, the monkeys behind bars will remind us of them."

Janet laughed. Laughing felt good. She shook her wrist. "My watch must be broken. It says four o'clock."

"You need a locket *and* a watch. Come on, let's catch that bus."

CHAPTER SIXTEEN

Liam twisted as he fell, instinctively raising his arms to shield his face. Punishing blows bashed him all over, pummeling him so fast he couldn't think. He skidded to a stop on an outcrop of grass-covered soil. His left arm took the brunt of the impact.

The tumble knocked the breath from him. Lightheaded and queasy, he sensed he lay much too close to the rim of the slanting ledge. One wrong move and he'd plunge into the sea. He curled himself up, gritted his teeth, and willed the throbbing in his head to ease.

He wasn't sure he'd been completely conscious since he'd slammed onto the blessed piece of earth that had saved him from certain death. From the ache in his head, he suspected the spill had knocked him out altogether. Yes, he thought, the whole fairy thing had been a bad dream, the hallucinatory result of an accident.

Moving slowly, he assessed his position. He wasn't as close to the edge as he'd feared, yet only a few feet separated him from the solid side of the cliff and thin air. He tried to move. Blood trickled down his face from a gash on his forehead. Pain shot through his left arm, though he doubted he'd broken anything. He'd felt worse after being tackled by a swarm of rabid rugby players.

At least his contact lenses were still in place. Wiping the blood from his face with his sleeve, he fumbled through his pockets for his cell phone. His probing fingers brushed a metal chain: Janet's locket.

No dream. It had happened. Not only had it happened, the disgruntled fairies had taken exception to his tossing the necklace into the sea and tried to send him after it.

Where was Janet? The horrid thought that Finvarra's filthy pack of rats had shanghaied her back to fairyland worried him, but only for a moment. Most likely she'd seen him fall and gone for help. Or perhaps she was still confused after her ordeal and needed help herself. Either way, he had to find her and take her home, wherever that was.

He studied the hillside above him. An easy climb for an able-bodied lad. With one arm banjaxed, Liam required assistance. Annoyed that his hands were shaking, he thumbed the speed dial for Kevin's phone.

Kevin answered right away. Briefly stating that he'd fallen and injured himself, Liam told his sputtering cousin where he was. The sound of Kevin's familiar, if panicked voice bolstered him. Confident that he'd soon be back on the trail, he inched closer to the cliff wall.

The phone slipped from his hand. As he watched it plummet into the sea, he thought that, all in all, he'd been lucky.

Kevin would be frantic, Liam, embarrassed. Nothing could be done for it now but to wait. The sun's glare had him looking for his baseball cap, but he failed to find it in his pockets. At least it wasn't raining, and the clouds and the sea breeze would keep the sun from baking him. A fella stuck on a ledge in Howth could be in worse straits. He was warm and alive, and he'd beaten the fairies twice in one day.

He glanced at his watch. Nearly half-four. Where the devil was Kevin?

Right above him, it seemed. "Li! Where are you?"

"Here," he called back as loud as he could. Squinting in the speckled sunlight, he spotted Kevin on the path, wild-eyed and out of breath from what must have been a record-breaking run.

Kevin's downward rush sent stones caroming over the cliff and left his jeans stained with grass and mud. He knelt beside Liam, hands jerking through the air as if he were afraid to touch him. "You're bleeding! You're hurt! How bad? I'm calling the Coast Guard chopper!"

Liam suspected he looked much worse than he felt. Touched by Kevin's concern, he sought to reassure him. "I don't need the Coast Guard chopper. I'm all right, Kev. Just cuts and bruises, but my arm is bollixed. Help me get back to the trail and we'll be off home."

Considerably relieved—and perhaps a tad annoyed—Kevin sat back on his heels. "I knew it! You told the girl one story too many, and she pushed you over the edge. Why did you feckin' hang up on me?"

"I didn't. I dropped the feckin' phone." Liam tilted his head toward the water.

Kevin's eyes widened in renewed horror. "Mary and Joseph, Li! You could have gone with it!"

"I could have, but I didn't. Now give us a hand, Kev." Liam held out his uninjured arm.

Kevin helped him to his feet. "Maybe we should wait for my father to get here."

Liam winced, and not because his arm hurt. "You called your father?"

"Of course I did! What do you think? I thought you were—never mind. Come on, let's get out of here."

"Where are the girls?"

"How the devil do I know? I left Matti in the car park, and I haven't seen Janet at all. I came over the top of the hill. She didn't come looking for you?"

If Liam told Kevin about the fairies, he had no doubt his sensible cousin would think he'd suffered a serious head injury. "I don't know. She probably went to find help. I can't call her. I lost the phone."

"They're probably waiting in the car park. What's her number? I'll call her."

"I don't know her number. It's in the feckin' phone! We have to get to the car park and find them." Liam turned to tackle the hillside. His traitorous knees buckled.

"Easy, Li." Kevin grabbed his good arm and steadied him. "The girls will be fine. You're hurt. You're coming back to Garrymuir with me right now"—Kevin's hold tightened—"unless you want me to call my father back and tell him to send the rescue chopper."

Defeated, Liam smiled at Kevin's atypical adamance. "You're a hard man, Kev."

"We'll ask him to send someone to the car park. I can't believe you disremember the girl's number after going to so much trouble to get it."

"I don't clutter my head with numbers."

"No, just useless stories. Maybe you'll think of it later."

With Kevin pulling, pushing, and generally supporting him, Liam climbed a little at a time. He was almost to the top when a mighty grip seized his underarms, lifting him up and onto the path. Wobbling and mortified, Liam stared into the bearded face of his unsmiling uncle.

An hour later, Peadar Boru still hadn't smiled. Liam rested on the bed in the room that was his when he visited Garrymuir. Forehead loosely bandaged, arm wrapped in ice, he absorbed the soothing rumble of his uncle's muted voice.

"The helicopter is on its way, Li. We'll get you to St. Brigid's and have them check you out. Tell me again about these two young ladies. My lads saw no sign of them in the car park or anywhere else in Howth."

Even without his contact lenses, Liam saw that concern had replaced the perpetual sparkle in Peadar's keen brown eyes. The big bear of a man sat beside the bed speaking gently, listening intently, and to Liam's increasing dismay, probing persistently.

For as long as he could remember, his uncle had doted on him and Talty. Peadar had been a kind second father to them, a good-humored soul who'd helped them grow up in the public eye. He'd indulged his brother's children as well as his own, providing guidance and discipline, reminding them who they were and what they stood for while grounding them so their privileged status didn't go to their heads.

But Peadar wasn't all sunshine and rainbows. Liam knew well that his affable uncle could be ruthless when necessary. In his role as Ard Laoch, the High Warrior who protected Ireland, he'd developed a nose for trouble—and he was sniffing at Liam now.

Liam longed to tell him about the fairies, to have his warrior uncle reassure him he needn't fear Finvarra and his kind. Instead, he recapped how he and Kevin had met the girls in town and invited them for a Sunday walk. "Janet went to see the lighthouse from the top of the hill. I went to take a look at the sea. She didn't know I fell. She probably thought I did a runner on her."

"So you called Kevin, and he left the other girl in the parking lot, and they both disappeared."

"That's about it."

"I see." Lost in thought, Peadar glanced at the window. The thunderous bat-bat-bat of an approaching helicopter swelled in the distance. "The chopper will be here soon." He returned his attention to Liam, studying him through narrowed eyes. "Do you want to tell me what really happened, Li?"

Yes, but you'll think I'm crazy. Liam turned his head to escape Peadar's scrutiny. "No, sir."

"Did the girl push you? Did she try to rob you?"

The idea that Janet might have pushed him had amused Liam when Kevin said it as a joke. Peadar's suspicion that she'd caused deliberate harm wasn't at all funny. If Peadar thought the girls were scam artists, he'd hunt them down, and not to invite them to tea. Assaulting a member of the royal family—Peadar's family—carried grave consequences.

"No, Uncle. They didn't know who we were. We had nothing they'd want to steal. The wind knocked me over. It picked up so fast, I had no time to get back from the edge."

Peadar rose from the chair. "All right, Liam, here it is. You have no way of contacting this Janet person. You don't even know her last name. Given your secret identity shenanigans and the potential for a family scandal, it might be best if you never see her again. I'm thinking your father will agree."

Liam thought he might find her cell phone number through his phone bill, but he had no idea where the bill was sent or who paid it. Perhaps he could find out. Maybe his uncle would help him. He raised himself on his good elbow. "I have something that belongs to her. I'd like to return it. Is there no way you can find her? Or if your lads can't find her, maybe Kieran's could. All I want to do is return her property."

The vertical lines between Peadar's eyebrows deepened ominously. "We can track her down very easily, Li. All you have to do is tell me the truth. If not, you'll have yourself a fine memento of the girl."

Kevin knocked and opened the door. "The paramedics are here, Dad."

"Bring them up, Kevin. As for you, Liam," Peadar said after Kevin closed the door, "we'll continue this discussion when you're feeling better. I'll learn the truth of the matter eventually, with or without your help, though I'd rather have the real story from you."

He left the room. Devastated by his uncle's glaring disappointment in him, and dreading an even more harrowing encounter with his father, Liam closed his eyes.

CHAPTER SEVENTEEN

The glimmer failed to subdue the chill in the troop's interim lodging. Finvarra paced back and forth on the damp stone floor to warm himself. He glared at Becula, seated before her basin of mystical water, and pulled his white cloak tighter around his shoulders.

When the troop first arrived at their rocky outpost beneath Howth Head, he'd claimed the puddly inner cavern for his private quarters and left the others to make do in the larger outer cave. Moisture dripped nonstop from the ceilings of both chambers, and some of the fairies were sneezing. They couldn't linger here too long.

But they wouldn't return to Knock Ma until Finvarra retrieved the girl and evened the score with the boy who'd stolen her from him. "We would have had him if not for that traitor Berneen!"

Becula wheezed as she cackled. "I wouldn't be so sure, sire. I told you that boy had the heart of a lion. A true son of his noble lineage."

Only Finvarra's distance from her kept him from striking her frightful head. Hands balled into fists, he increased the speed of his pacing. "I don't care whose son he is! How dare he sneak into our realm and spy upon our revelry! I'll personally slice off his eavesdropping ears and pluck out his prying eyes. He'll lose his hair one night, his finger and toenails the next, and his teeth the night after that! Once I flay his skin from him bit by bit and he's bleeding and writhing in agony, I'll send in the rats to gnaw on him." Finvarra paused. He thought that last bit a stroke of genius. "Did you know he hates rats?"

Becula glanced up from the basin of water and smiled. "Yes, sire. I did."

Of course she did. She was the one who'd divined it. But Finvarra couldn't let her become more full of herself than she already was.

He resumed his pacing. "After that, I'll twist every meddling bone in his miserable mortal body. Then I'll decide if I'll let him die."

"Whatever you do, tread softly, sire. The King of the Sea knows we're here."

Finvarra jerked at her grim pronouncement. "How could he know? We've been most discreet."

"The boy tossed my bridling necklace into the Irish Sea. Manannan MacLir didn't care for that. Considered it fouling his home, he did."

"The necklace is gone? One of our most valuable spell casters *gone*?" An even more distressing thought presented itself. "Can you find the girl without it?"

"No, but it won't be gone for long. The necklace is a special pet. It always comes back to me. Only I know its secrets."

"The princely pup will pay for the theft of the necklace!"

"He already has. Manannan MacLir's outrage has injured him."

"So will I, when I find him. He spoiled our dance!" Finvarra's longing to hold the girl in his arms lodged itself in his mind like a bee trapped in an empty wine jar. "I want to waltz with that girl, Becula. She left with my best dancing spell still upon her."

"You shall have your chance, sire, but perhaps we should not interfere with the son of the King of Ireland. After all—"

"I mean to teach the boy a lesson. The mortals will learn to respect me. So will MacLir. If they want a war, I'll give them one!" An idea occurred to Finvarra. "We have no way of finding the girl without the necklace, but you said she'll attend the mortal king's ball. The boy will be there too. When is it? And where?"

"I don't know exactly, sire. Soon, I expect, and in one of their castles, as always. But there's no need to attend. I expect to regain the necklace soon. We'll find the girl."

Her desperate tone annoyed him. Why was she being so troublesome? "The necklace won't find the boy. Look in your water, Becula. Determine the details. Before I'm done, King Brian will regret excluding us from his soirée."

Becula's eyes sharpened. "I beg you, sire, do not provoke the mortals. They have great power, much more than they did when they sent us to live beneath the earth."

"Enough, hag! My power is also great. I mean to wield it at the ball. The mortals will believe in us again, and it will be greater still!"

Pleased with his plan, Finvarra repaired to the outer cave in search of a cup of wine.

CHAPTER EIGHTEEN

Gram jostled Janet down a torchlit corridor. "I want you to see Kilkenny Castle, dear."

The passageway was cold and filled with putrid smoke that stung Janet's eyes. She stopped to tell Gram she didn't like this place. The light from the torches glittered on Nora's sapphire necklace. Why was Gram wearing it?

Little by little, Gram's face changed. She turned old and ugly, and as she described the castle, her voice grew higher and higher until she sounded like a wicked old witch. "I'll teach you to play with boys and lose your locket. It's the dungeon for you, little girl!"

A powerful shove sent Janet stumbling into a cold, damp room that smelled like a city sewer. The door banged shut and left her in pitch-black darkness. Shivering and afraid, she groped for the door but found no trace of it. "Let me out, Gram! Please let me out!"

A razor-sharp cackle cut through the walls. Successive bursts of the evil laughter dwindled away. Gram was deserting her, leaving her in this awful place.

She hugged herself. Why did her grandmother hate her so much?

Blinking dots of light appeared in the dark. The lights grew bigger and brighter until they flickered like candles and scented the air with a pleasant aroma that quickly overpowered the chamber's noxious smell. Strains of music grew louder. Both the perfume and the music seemed familiar somehow, but for some reason, they frightened her.

A handsome young man appeared in the room. His long blond hair brushed his shoulders; his golden suit shone in the twinkling light. She felt as if she knew him, yet she doubted she'd seen him before. Whoever he was, maybe he'd help her escape this horrible place.

He held out his hand. "Dance with me, Janet."

Her name floated in his hypnotic voice, echoing through the room, bouncing all around until the sound faded away. She tried to say she couldn't dance, but her mouth wouldn't work.

Something in his eyes compelled her to obey. She touched his hand, and her jeans and sweater sparkled into a golden gown.

Transfixed by his smile, she danced with him, whirling until the dungeon resembled a huge bright ballroom. Other dancers spun around them, dancers in golden suits and gowns.

Dancers with rat faces.

Confused and afraid, Janet glanced back at her partner. He, too, had a rat face. Long black whiskers twitched on either side of his furry snout. His smile revealed sharp yellow teeth covered in dripping slime.

Janet screamed. The rat squeezed her arms.

"Jan! Wake up, Jan!"

The rat face vanished. Matti appeared in its place, her worried expression dramatically lit by the moonlight shining through the bedroom windows. Gasping for air, Janet raised her hands to her eyes and shook her head. "Oh, Matti, what an awful nightmare!"

Matti switched on the lamp between their beds. "You're shaking worse than my mom's washing machine. Who were you dreaming about? Light-fingers Liam?"

"That loser! No. He wasn't there." Janet tried to describe the rapidly vanishing dream. "It was Gram. She said she wanted me to see Kilkenny Castle."

"She said that at dinner. That's where she and your grandfather went today, remember? Your grandfather said he wanted to take us both to see it before I go home."

"Yeah, but Gram locked me in the dungeon 'cause I lost my locket."

"It was a dream, Jan. You feel bad about the locket, and it merged in your head with what your grandparents said at dinner. Maybe you should tell them what happened today."

Matti's assessment made perfect sense. Janet puffed out a relieved breath. "I'll tell them tomorrow, but not how I really lost it." She hugged her arms around her knees. The sheets rustled reassuringly. "That dream really scared me. Gram turned into a witch, and she was wearing Nora's necklace."

"Who's Nora?"

"The woman I bumped into on Wicklow Street, remember? She works at Louise's dress shop. She let me try on a necklace to see how it looked with the dress. And I was dancing with some guy in the dream. He turned into a rat."

"Eew! That *had* to be Liam!"

Janet almost laughed. Matti's confident tone chased away the cloying remnants of the nightmare. "He wasn't. I don't know who he was, but I felt like I should."

"You probably dreamed you were dancing with that guy because you're afraid to dance at the ball. All your fears rolled up into one neat nightmare."

Janet glanced at the alarm clock on the night stand. Two o'clock in the morning. "It doesn't matter. It was just a dream. Sorry I woke you, Matt. I wish you didn't have to leave on Thursday."

"Me too. I'd love to see you at the ball dancing with Prince Geek."

Janet winced. "Great. Now I'll have more nightmares."

"No, you won't. Keep thinking you live in a great house most kids would kill to have, your grandparents get you almost everything you want, and you're going to be the world's greatest actress some day."

Comforted by Matti's logic and support, Janet relaxed. Her annoyance with herself gave way to a burst of confidence. "I guess I'm stupid. The dream just seemed so real, y'know?"

"Nightmares always do until you wake up and turn on the light. We can leave it on if you like." Matti spoke the last words in a prim maternal voice.

Janet pushed her off the bed. "What am I, two years old?"

She and Matti were laughing when Matti turned off the lamp. The dream seemed funny now, the frightening rats no more than harmless cartoon characters. Liam's betrayal bothered Janet more, but she ousted him from her thoughts and slept without dreaming for the rest of the night.

CHAPTER NINETEEN

Rain bucketed down on Dublin early Monday morning. Seated at the small round table between his bedroom window and the gently flickering fireplace, Liam shifted to keep the spandex sling from digging into his neck. His arm ached. So did his head. The stitches over his eyebrow stung, and the purple bruise on his forehead would linger for weeks. Peeved at the world, he frowned at the ruthless downpour through his gold-rimmed glasses.

The day before, the rain had blessed him, granting him a sweet romantic encounter—one that would haunt him forever if he failed to find Janet. Evil infected the weather now, a loathsome reminder that danger lurked in a part of the world he'd always considered safe.

He rested his uninjured arm on the Dublin Ledger, the newspaper that had caused him to gaze out the window in the first place. He scowled at the King's Garden two stories below. When his hostile glare failed to wither the roses, he returned it to the Ledger. His good hand slapped the filthy rag.

Citing an anonymous hospital source, a feckless female journalist with nothing better to do had reported his accident, and the Ledger had printed the story on the front page. The column was thankfully short on details. The author had been in such a rush, she hadn't taken the time to learn the location of the fall or the nature of Liam's injury. Still, her report that the king's son had suffered a mishap left Liam royally indignant at the invasion of his privacy.

His father's summons to a meeting at half-nine this morning had darkened his already dour mood. He'd received scant sympathy from his old Da at the hospital the night before. Once the doctors had assured Liam's parents that he'd live, that his worst injury was a sprained wrist and forearm, his mother had wept.

His father, however, had eyed him with the same suspicion Uncle Peadar had. "Your mother and I are glad you're all right, but we're late for an engagement because of this incident. Peadar will take you home. We'll discuss this further tomorrow."

That discussion, scheduled to take place in twenty-five minutes, hung over Liam like the newly sharpened blade of a guillotine. How could he tell anyone what had really happened? His parents would send him off to the head doctors faster than a fiddler's elbow.

But if he wanted to find Janet, he'd have to confess the whole story. And he wanted to find Janet.

"Will that be all, sir?"

Liam straightened the slump from his brooding form. He'd forgotten that Ross was still in the room. The stalwart aide had helped Liam before and after his morning shower, offering towels and easing him into his clothes. Old Ross had even unscrewed the cap on the toothpaste, but Liam resented the special care. No one had helped him dress since he'd escaped his nanny's clutches at the age of eight.

Yet Ross hadn't caused this predicament. Regretting his uncharacteristic ill will toward his devoted aide, Liam strove to be pleasant. "I'm grand, Ross. Don't need another thing, thanks. Above and beyond the call of duty for you today, eh?"

Ross smiled, crinkling a dark brown beard that nearly hid old acne scars. "Not at all, sir. I'm pleased to have been of assistance. Have a pleasant morning, sir."

The door opened and closed. Liam checked his watch. He now had twenty minutes before locking horns with his father. Uncle Peadar had reset the watch after he'd noticed it running four hours fast. He'd blamed the discrepancy on Liam's fall, and Liam hadn't corrected him. How could he tell his uncle that the time change reflected the hours he'd spent with *Them?*

Rapping sounded at the door. Ross had probably forgotten something. Tired of feeling helpless, Liam crossed the room and wrenched the door open.

"Howya, Li."

His sour mood burst like a soap bubble playfully popped by a gleeful child. "Talty! What are you doing here?"

His sister wore her dark red hair in an informal twist, a sign that she'd hurried. Her chestnut eyes, a prettier and much more incisive version of his, took in the sling and the narrow bandage on his forehead. Her lower lip wobbled, but she wouldn't cry. Not Talty.

"I wasn't supposed to come home until Thursday," she said, "but I got special leave. A chopper brought me here late last night. I'd have come straight to see you, but Mum said you were already asleep. What on earth happened, Li? I've been so worried!"

He took her right hand and kissed it, a gesture of respect so ingrained, neither of them noticed. "I'm fine, Tal. No harm. Come in."

She coasted into the room, her head turning as if to convince herself that all was the same as she remembered. Her casual outfit—perfectly tailored jeans and a silky teal jersey—accented the tension in her arrow-straight stance.

Her attention switched from the room to Liam. As she studied him, she relaxed. "You look a bit bocketty, but I think you'll do."

"I'm altogether grand, Tal." He pointed to the table, and they sat as they often had over the years. "I have to see Dad in a few minutes, or I'd call for tea."

"I know. He told me the two of you were going to have a serious talk. He seemed grumpy about it. Never mind him. What did the doctor say about your arm?"

"That it's only a bad sprain. Not even any swelling or bruising. I'm to keep it in the sling and do nothing with it for two weeks. The arm should be better by then."

"Two weeks! Sounds like you won't be dancing this Friday, but you'll come, of course. We'll have Ross get you a fine black sling to match your dinner jacket."

Was she teasing or serious? He couldn't tell. "I'm not going. I'll malinger a bit, say I don't want to jostle my arm or something."

"Not going?" Talty tilted her brilliant head. "What sort of codology is that? The whole clan will be there. They'll want to see you, to know you're all right. I can't wait to see everyone myself. It seems I've been away forever."

"It seems that way to me too. I've missed you, Tal. Mum and Dad are driving me out of what little mind I have left."

"That's nothing new. Why don't you want to go to the dance?"

Liam sighed and leaned back in his chair, settling his swaddled arm carefully over his stomach. "The rumor is, the new American ambassador has a teenaged granddaughter, a lonely orphan, from what her granny told Mum. Mum wants me to keep the girl company all night and present her with a gift from the family so she'll feel welcome."

"What's wrong with that? I think it's a fine idea. Imagine the poor girl come to a new country with only her old grandparents to look after her. She should be with people her own age."

Refusing to be drawn in, Liam wagged his head. "I'm not in the mood to babysit a spoiled prima donna who's probably still in braces and can talk of nothing but herself. Anyway, I won't be much good to her with only one arm."

"That's unlike you, Li. I'm guessing your abnormal lack of charity is the result of your accident. What happened, anyway?"

Could he confide in his sister, his closest ally in the world? No. Even she would think him loopers. "I'd tell you, but you'd never believe me. No one will. I wouldn't even tell Dad if not for Janet."

Talty's eyebrows shot up. "Janet is it? The plot thickens. All right, let's hear about this girl who's got you all soft-eyed. From the beginning. I promise I'll believe you." Talty checked her watch and folded her arms. "You have twelve minutes."

Liam's absolute trust in his sister won him over. He'd always thought her magical, the one born to be queen some day, the leader he could never be. She'd been training since the age of nine to be a warrior, an endeavor she took seriously. At first, their father had tried to discourage her interest in martial arts, saying such sport was a waste of time for a proper princess destined to rule the kingdom.

Uncle Peadar had intervened. He'd assured his brother that the discipline would not only keep Talty fit and round out her intense education, it would give her the advantage she'd need to rule one day in a world run by men. Brian had reluctantly agreed. Peadar had taken her under his wing, and she'd never disappointed him. Not like Liam had.

Talty had never made fun of Liam's storytelling. In fact, she'd encouraged him, assuring him he had a special gift. If anyone would believe him, Talty would.

Heartened by her promise, he told her how he'd met Janet. He described the pizza they'd shared and the outing to Howth, omitting the snug little nook that had sheltered them from the rain. Even Talty would hear none of that.

Not much time remained before he had to report to his father. Could he tell her about the fairies? "You have to promise you'll never repeat what I'm going to tell you, Tal."

"I can't promise that. I can only promise I'll say nothing as long as my silence does no harm. Come on, Liam. You've gotten this far. Tell me the rest. Remember, 'Truth stands when all else falls.'"

If he couldn't confide in Talty, he'd never tell anyone. Before he could change his mind, he poured out the tale of how Janet had run off to find the music only she could hear. He told his sister everything. "When I threw the necklace into the sea, the waves and the wind rose like living demons. I got blown right off the cliff walk."

Talty's eyes narrowed, making her appear suspicious of his story, a mistaken impression on Liam's part, as it turned out. "You challenged the King of the Fairies? I'm in awe of you, Li, not a word of a lie."

"You don't think I'm astray in the head?"

"Well, not for this anyway," she said, grinning. "If you said it happened, it happened. Dead sound. Where's the locket now?"

Liam drew the chain from his trouser pocket. "She probably thinks I stole it. I have to get it back to her. Do you think you can help me find her?"

"Maybe." Talty took the locket and turned it in her hands. She opened it, glanced at the picture, and snapped it shut. "Nice little trinket. Do you suppose the magic from the necklace rubbed off on it?"

A prickly chill shot up Liam's spine. "I hope not." He peered at the locket, silently daring it to harm him or his sister, yet he sensed no malice in the thing. "No, Tal. I'd feel any evil in it. So would you."

His sister eyed him thoughtfully and smiled. "I wasn't thinking evil. Maybe it has its own magic." She reached across the table and planted the locket in his hand. "If it stood up to the old hag's necklace, it must be a potent thing. Keep it with you for good luck, Li."

Janet had said the little gold heart was her good luck charm. He recalled seeing her touch it, and more than once. She must have repeated the gesture often since she'd received it some years ago. Could it really retain the power of all her hopes and dreams? More determined than ever to return her treasure to her, he slipped it into his pocket.

"I'll need more than a locket to deal with Dad. Will you come with me? Keep him from eating my head off?"

"Didn't I tell you? I'm to attend your meeting, too." Talty pushed back her chair and rose. "I'm sure we'll set things straight if you tell Dad exactly what you told me."

CHAPTER TWENTY

The morning downpour had stopped by the time the driver passed through the main gates of Hazelwood College, the private school Janet had vowed to hate. From the limo seat she shared with Matti, she warily eyed the enormous trees, sweeping lawns, and ivied stone buildings tucked away in the foothills eight miles south of Dublin. The clouds broke apart, and a rainbow burst over the sky. She couldn't help smiling.

"We want you to see the place, Ladybug," Gramp had said at breakfast. He'd surprised her by rescheduling his Monday morning meetings so he and Gram could bring her to visit the school.

Gram had altered her plans too. She'd changed her hair appointment to the next morning and sent her regrets to a charity luncheon. "Your grandfather and I didn't realize how frightened you were about attending a new school, dear," she said as Rosemary briskly cleared the breakfast dishes. "We've obtained recommendations for several secondary schools, and we've looked them over carefully. We think Hazelwood is the best choice for you."

Gramp reached over an empty juice glass and squeezed Janet's hand. "That's right, Ladybug. We think it will be perfect for you. I know you'll feel better once you see for yourself what a wonderful place it is. Would you like to come along, Matti?"

"You bet, Mr. Gleason. That way I can picture where Janet is when we talk on the phone and email."

A cheerful smile crinkled Gram's face. "Get your jackets, girls. We can't wait to tour the place ourselves. We want to see where our girl will be spending her time."

Sitting opposite Gram and Gramp in the back of the limo now, Janet soaked up their affection. The previous day's trauma in Howth had left her badly in need of what she'd once considered their smothering. How silly her nightmare seemed now! Gram was no witch. She only wanted what was best for her grandchild. Janet chided herself for thinking anything else.

"Thanks so much for changing your appointment, Gram."

"Not at all, dear. I think tomorrow will be better anyway. The hairdresser is on Dawson Street, not far from Grafton. Your final fitting with Louise is tomorrow morning. I can meet you and Matti after my trim and go with you. I can't wait to see the dress you'll wear to the ball."

As he often did when talk of hairdressers and wardrobes cropped up, Gramp tuned out. He seemed lost in thought, and finally said, "I wonder if Prince Liam will go to the ball. Such a shame about his accident. I must remember to have my office send flowers or fruit, something suitable for a young gentleman."

Gramp had seen the sketchy story in the morning paper and relayed the news. Janet cringed at hearing the name "Liam." Though sorry for whatever had befallen the prince with the same name as the slimy creep who'd conned her, she hoped Liam Boru wouldn't attend the ball. If he didn't, maybe she could sit in a corner by herself and not have to dance with anyone. She'd said so to Matti before they left the house, but she'd received little sympathy from her friend.

Gram glanced out the tinted window beside her and tsked. "I wonder what happened to the poor boy. Probably a sports injury. Your father had those all the time, dear. Well, if Prince Liam doesn't attend the ball, you'll still have plenty of young people to keep you company. Prince Liam and Princess Talty have several cousins their own age, and I hear they're all wonderful dancers. You and your grandfather should practice waltzing."

Matti smothered a snort and dug an elbow into Janet's side. Nearly laughing out loud, Janet dug back. The idea of dancing suddenly fell into a "not-so-bad" place. Dance partners didn't steal jewelry. She'd be safe at the ball with her grandparents nearby, and with Gramp's help, she felt sure she could master a few waltz steps by Friday.

Somehow, she felt she already had.

If Gram noticed the girls' horseplay, she ignored it. "You still need shoes and a necklace. We can pick those up after your fitting tomorrow.

Are you sure you don't want to wear your locket with the dress?" She glanced at Janet's neck and frowned. "Where is your locket, dear? I don't believe I've ever seen you without it."

Matti stiffened. So did Janet. She wanted to tell the truth, but she couldn't admit she'd been duped by a smooth-talking thief. Her grandparents were treating her like a grown-up. If they found out about Liam Murphy, they'd go back to treating her like a child.

But she wasn't a child. She was an almost-adult young lady, and she thought she should act—no, really behave—like one. Even if she fibbed a bit. Bracing herself for Gram's anger, she took a deep breath and told her cover story. "I lost it, Gram. It must have broken or something and fallen off my neck while Matti and I were in town yesterday. When I went to take it off before bed last night, it was gone."

Gram put her hand over her heart. "Oh my! I know how much you loved it, dear. We'll try to find you a new one tomorrow."

Heat surged over Janet's cheeks. She almost wished Gram would scold her instead of being so nice. "It's okay, Gram. I don't need another one. Lockets are for kids, and I have plenty of pictures of my parents."

The car stopped in front of an old mansion made of gray stone blocks. Weeping willows and several other trees that Janet didn't recognize surrounded the building, making it look like someone had dropped it into the woods. A black and white sign on the lawn said "Admissions."

The driver opened the door, and everyone got out. Squinting in the sunlight, Janet inspected the campus, quiet except for a medley of birdsong. Newer buildings nestled among the old, linked by inviting paths lined with beds of colorful flowers. Salt air scented a gentle breeze already sweet with the fragrance of fresh-cut grass. She looked for the sea and found it: a sliver of Dublin Bay twinkled in the distance. The neatly landscaped grounds seemed to welcome her, and she let herself feel at home.

"Wow," Matti said, "what a beautiful place."

Both elated and nervous, Janet nodded and followed her grandparents up three granite steps. The mellow peal of church bells rang half-past the hour. She glanced at her watch. How odd, she thought. Yesterday she'd been sure it was broken, but it seemed fine now.

Nine-thirty on the dot.

CHAPTER TWENTY-ONE

The grandfather clock struck half-nine as Liam and Talty turned down the hallway to their father's study. As they passed the gallery of family portraits, Liam's dread increased.

By the time they reached the curio case displaying their father's collection of antique naval instruments, he felt downright squeamish. Easy for Talty to be so nonchalant, he thought as she raised her hand to knock on the double oak doors. She wasn't about to receive a sentence of death.

Kevin breezed around a corner at the opposite end of the hall. Bundled under his arm was a large green book, an old one from the looks of it. "Hey, Tal. I didn't expect to see you before the dance Friday night."

As Liam had done earlier, Kevin kissed her hand. When she hugged him and kissed his cheek, the book he held slipped. He shifted to reposition it under his arm.

Liam greedily eyed the faded cover. "What've you got there, Kev?"

"A history book my father asked me to bring from his library. For the meeting."

Liam and Talty exchanged surprised glances. Talty pointed toward the door. "Your father is in there?"

"Yeah. He stayed the night after he brought Li home from the hospital. Kieran is here too."

"Ah, the Blessed Trinity," Liam said. "I must really be in trouble."

Talty patted his arm. "We'll do our best to keep them from eating you alive. Come on, we're late."

Holding his breath, Liam knocked. At his father's gruff "Come in," he opened the door and stepped aside so Talty could enter first. He and Kevin followed her into the sumptuous, dark-paneled study. Liam exhaled and breathed in the familiar aromas of old books, leather, and Prince Brian's Dance, the apricot-salmon hybrid rose named for his father when he was born.

Brian stood at his usual spot near the fireplace, and so Liam looked to the tea cart first. The pastry-laden barrow stood between his father's massive desk and the built-in bookcases. Dressed in a gray blazer and dark slacks, Kieran rummaged about the cart fixing himself a cup of tea. No doubt the jacket concealed his gun. He peered at Liam and nodded curtly.

Peadar sat grim-faced before the fireplace. His black pullover sweater and khaki trousers, a tad too tight for his robust frame, were clearly borrowed from Brian's wardrobe. He rose when the young folk came in, a mark of deference to Liam's status as the king's son and Talty's as Crown Princess.

Attired in casual cashmere and tweed, Brian stood with his back to the hearth. Despite his garb, his mood was far from casual. The savage snarl that had terrified Liam when he was a child twisted the old fella's face, deepening the furrows in his forehead. The cheeks above his silver-streaked beard blazed as if sunburned, and he appeared prepared to pounce on any hapless wretch who got in his way.

All in all, Liam thought he'd rather be back with the fairy rats. Beside him, Kevin gulped.

Talty, however, breezed over the thick blue carpet in elegant princess mode. "Good morning, Dad." She held and pecked the hand he raised to her. "We're here. How can we help?"

Brian's face softened the slightest bit. "Get yourself a cup of something and sit down." He pointed to the half-dozen black leather chairs grouped before the hearth. "You too," he added, glaring at Liam and Kevin.

Talty declined the tea and selected a seat by the fire. Teacup in hand, Kieran sat beside her, greeting her warmly. Kieran was Talty's godfather.

Peadar was Liam's, but other than a brief hand-kissing greeting for Talty, Liam sensed little warmth in his burly uncle's demeanor. He began to resent their annoyance with him. What had he really done wrong? Nothing.

Forehead throbbing, arm aching, he sat opposite his sister knowing her supportive glances would sustain him through the coming ordeal. Kevin claimed the chair next to him, placing the old book, which under different circumstances Liam would have stolen away and devoured, on the coffee table.

Brian remained standing. Scowling. Ferocious. "How are you feeling, Li?" he growled.

Did he really care? Liam bristled with a ferocity of his own. "A bit sore, but I'll do."

"I'm glad to hear it. Let's get started. Tell us the family motto."

Caught off-guard, Liam stared unblinking at nothing until the old slogan popped into his head. "'The Strong Hand Rules'," he replied.

"And what do we always add to that motto? Kevin?"

Kevin seemed just as surprised. "'But There is No Strength Without Unity.'"

"'No Strength Without Unity.' Don't any of you ever forget it." Brian's piercing gaze took them all in. "Tell us what happened yesterday, Liam. The truth this time, if you please. For all we know, you were away with the fairies."

Liam's head jerked. His mouth fell open, but he couldn't make it work. Too stunned to even draw a breath, he gawked at his unflinching father.

The color drained from Brian's face. "Heaven help us, you *were* with them, weren't you? Stop gloating!" he shouted at Peadar. "I hate it when those warrior instincts of yours are right!"

"I'm not gloating, Bri. I honestly wish I were wrong. All right, Li, let's hear it."

How could they know? But they did, and Liam resigned himself to getting the whole affair done and dusted. Still, he sputtered and bobbled about until Talty's smile and barely perceptible nod reassured him.

He repeated the tale as he'd told it to her, speaking timidly at first, growing braver and louder when he realized he had engrossed his listeners. He might have been telling the story of a nameless young man's rescue of a damsel in distress until he reached the part about Berneen's warning. The thought of her and the certainty that he and Janet would still be down there if not for the poor woman's help reminded him that his recitation was no fanciful adventure.

He described how he and Janet had fled the pack of fairy rats. His voice grew soft as he described Berneen's fate but sharpened when he told how the necklace had still controlled Janet even after they'd escaped. Each word fueled his anger anew. He pictured himself flinging the necklace over the cliff and relived the horror of the wind and waves summoned by magic to crush him.

"Janet's locket got tangled in the necklace, but I kept it. She was gone by the time Kevin helped me back to the path. I want to find her, to give her back her locket."

Peadar rubbed his beard the way he did when worry beset him. "We'll talk about that later, Li. Let's deal with Finvarra first. Did this Berneen, rest her soul, give you any advice? Any warning?"

Liam had been so focused on Janet, he'd forgotten Berneen's ominous prediction. "She said I violated the fairy realm without permission. That Finvarra would want revenge. That he'd come after me."

Brian punched the wall. Everyone but Peadar jumped in their seats. "That feckin' son of a Connaught banshee! How dare he harm my son! I'll wrap his cheating chess board around his thieving throat and shove the pieces down his feckin' fairy gullet until he chokes on them! I'll flatten every feckin' fairy fort on this fairy-infested island if he starts twisting hay with us again!"

His fists swung in time to his bellowing rant. Liam cringed even as he realized his father wasn't angry with him at all.

Talty moved to the edge of her seat, clearly eager to hear more. "You sound as if you've met Finvarra, Dad. Have you?"

Brian plopped into the last vacant chair. "No, Tal, I haven't. We've all heard the stories, though."

"Fairytales!" Kevin sat white-faced, gasping for breath. "They're not real!"

"They were real enough for Liam," Peadar said gently. "The Good People exist, Kevin. They call Ireland home, just as we do."

"The Good People," Brian said. "The Gentle Folk. The Other Crowd. I haven't thought about them for years. Contact between us diminished over time. I thought they were gone." His chest heaved as he sighed. "Apparently I was wrong."

Kieran returned to the cart and brought Kevin a glass of water. "Our grandfather, King Declan, was the last Boru to have dealings with them, at least that we know of. He told us the story when we were boys. A farmer in County Roscommon had a fairy fort on his land. He went to his barn early one morning to milk his cows and found someone had already done so. When it happened again the next day, he hid in the hay loft. Kept watch all night. Just as the moon rose, a gang of fairy women came in with pails and milked the cows. He was too terrified to confront them—he said they were glowing and taller than most men—but he followed them and their milk buckets back to the fairy fort. They went in through a door he'd never seen before. He didn't know what to do, so he told the authorities."

Peadar took over the telling. "Old Declan heard about it. A great respecter of the fairies, he was. He went to Roscommon and paid the farmer for his best milking cow. That night, Declan brought the animal to the fort and left it grazing there. The next day, they found no sign of the cow, and no more of the farmer's milk went missing."

"Declan figured the fairies had hungry babies," said Brian. "He told the farmer to leave them something every night."

Talty seemed miffed. "Why have we never heard such a grand tale?"

Brian smiled sadly. "'The man long absent is forgotten.' I suppose that goes for fairies too. As I said, I haven't given them much thought in years."

"None of us have," said Peadar, "but they're out there."

"I can vouch for that," said Liam. "How did you know I was with them, Uncle?"

"I grew suspicious when you wouldn't tell me what happened. Then, at the hospital, when I saw your watch set four hours ahead, I remembered the legend about the thin spot on Howth, near where you fell. Your refusal to tell me what happened made sense." Peadar chuckled. "You thought I'd be wondering what meds the doctors had given you."

Talty glanced from Peadar to Liam and back. "What on earth is a thin spot, Uncle?"

"Thin spots are all over Ireland. They're places where our world and that of the fairies intersect." Peadar lifted the green-covered book from the table. "I asked Kevin to bring this down today. *The Annals of Binn Éadair.* A very old chronicle of the history of Howth. When Peggy and I first moved into Garrymuir, I went through the library. I wanted to know all about the place. Some of what I read matched the history we all know, such as Finn MacCool and his Fian warriors setting up a lookout camp on Howth Hill centuries ago to watch for Viking invaders. But, like Kevin, I put down most of what I read to legends and folklore. At least until yesterday."

Peadar flipped the pages until he found what he wanted. "According to these annals, there's a thin spot on the Ben of Howth. The book doesn't call it a thin spot, yet there's no mistaking the writer's meaning. The Good

People built a fort beneath the ben, but they abandoned it after some sort of fairy battle ages ago. No mention of the outcome or who the victors were. Ah, here it is."

He read aloud:

Fierce are the fairy hosts upon the Ben of Edar. Stormy strong kings atop noble steeds, they take refuge in the ghostly air beneath the fragrant heather. Many a shield they cleave in bloodless battle as dire as any slaughter by sword. They of the blue-starred eyes and yellow-gold manes do rouse the spirit of the sea. There is no strand which the wave does not pound. The hair of the wife of Manannan MacLir blows wild. The King of the Sea himself flies over the waves in a chariot of gold drawn by seahorses swift and bold. Fires burn atop every fairy fort. Phantoms plague the people, and the seas around Erin groan.

Silence fell over the room until Kieran spoke. "Sounds like the land fairies had a big donnybrook with the sea fairies."

"Lots of myths have a basis in fact," said Talty. "I wonder what happened?"

Peadar shrugged. "We'll never know for sure, but whatever it was, it appears the fairies were battling each other, and those on land took refuge somewhere beneath Howth Head. We know there are caves around the cliffs, but this sounds like something different."

"A thin spot." Liam said the words slowly. "One where their magic can surface. I wondered how that hut got there, and why no one was around when Janet and I started our walk."

"At certain times," said Peadar, "certain places belong to *Them*. When you're feeling up to it, Li, you'll show me the spot. I'll decide what to do with it, though I doubt the people of Howth or the hill walkers are in any danger. Your friend Janet was under their power because of that necklace. Somehow it lured her to them."

Kevin was gaping at Liam. "And you saved her, Li," he whispered in awe.

Liam still had trouble believing it himself. "I did, Kev, at least for the moment, and if you ever tell me again that my stories are useless, I'll, why I'll—"

"He'll tell you a story," said Talty.

The brief bit of laughter died away in a flurry of questions: *What are we going to do? What made Finvarra decide to steal a young woman now, after all these years? Hasn't he learned he can't get away with it? How can we stop him?*

"We can't threaten him," Brian said. "We can only try to reason with him. Remind him of the agreement he and his kind made with our ancestors to remain underground and out of trouble. But the fairies, especially Finvarra, can be notoriously disagreeable when they want something."

Peadar was rubbing his beard again. "So what does he want? What the devil is he doing in Howth? He belongs in Galway."

Talty's darting eyes and faraway expression reflected her spinning thoughts. "Is there any way to ask him?"

"Not to my knowledge," Brian replied.

Kieran riveted his piercing gaze on Liam. "That woman said he'd come after you, Li. We must take defensive measures. The fairies don't die from natural causes, but they can be and have been killed. Even with all their magic, we're stronger than they are, and they know it. It's one of the reasons the little pains in the pants agreed to the truce in the first place."

Brian shook his head. "We don't want to kill them, Kieran."

Kieran half-smiled. "A minute ago you wanted to bulldoze every fairy fort in Ireland. Not that you'd get anyone to do it. The country people, the old-timers, anyway, would never touch the things. Hell, I don't think I would. Even the army would balk at the job."

Liam recalled the creatures he'd seen, their ragged clothing and meager food. He thought of the milk cow his great-grandfather had given them. "The fairies need help. The ones I saw were old. Their clothes were tattered, and they had little to eat. Maybe they need some sort of support."

"Maybe," Brian said. "We'll support them if we can, but first we must find the girl. It's not just getting her locket back to her. We have to be sure Finvarra isn't still after her. The legends are full of the kind of *support* he likes."

"The necklace has something to do with it," said Liam. "I doubt he can influence her without it."

"Still and all," Peadar said, "we'd best find her and her friend. You said they're visiting from America. We'll check with customs. They must have a record of their entry into the kingdom. If so, they'll have an address for them. And we'll have airport security keep an eye out in case they leave. Janet Smith, you said?"

"And Matti Jones," said Kevin.

Kieran rolled his eyes. "What did you two geniuses do, tell them your name was Kelly?"

Recalling the conversation in the pizza shop, Liam smiled. "No, Murphy."

One of Kieran's malevolent chuckles broke the tension. "Lying to the women does a man no good, young fella-me-lad."

"Too bad you lost your cell phone," said Peadar. "We could've found her fast enough with that."

Brian leapt from his chair. "You lost your cell phone? That droid thing that cost more than a small Caribbean island?"

Despite his earsplitting outburst, humor sparkled in the old fella's eyes. Glad to be back in the family's good graces, and relieved that his ordeal in Howth was out in the open at last, Liam grinned at his playacting father. "Sorry, Dad."

The big hand that tousled his head seemed to bless him. "No harm, Li. We'll get you another."

Chuckling away, Peadar said he'd track down Liam's phone bills. "Whatever the girl's real name is, her number should be there somewhere. As for you, Li, I want someone with you at all times until we resolve this matter."

Liam groaned. "Can't I just wear an enchanted mushroom or something? I've read the stories. Things like a blackthorn stick and holy water will keep *Them* away."

"What you need is a four-leaf clover," Talty said.

A ruthless chill hardened Kieran's eyes. "No. What you need is steel."

That idea held no appeal for Liam. "I'm not about to tailor my clothes to conceal a handgun, Kieran."

The chill spread over Kieran's face. Both his mouth and the scar on his jaw curved diabolically. "A pistol would work. So would a sword, but I had in mind the more classical fairy defense of a dagger."

Talty agreed. "Good idea. We have plenty of throwing knives in the training room."

Liam stared openmouthed at his sister. "I will not carry a weapon. Period!"

"You don't need a knife or a sword to protect you," said Peadar. "You can carry a nail or two in your pocket."

Brian shook his head. "Not very practical. Men nowadays wear all sorts of stainless steel jewelry. Chains, rings, even bracelets. I'll call Adam DeWitt this afternoon, and we'll get you geared up."

"The jewelry will work," Kieran said, "but a knife is better. Stick it in the doorframe of whatever room you're in, especially when you're sleeping. The fairies won't pass by it. And in a pinch, it will give you the means to defend yourself."

Sighing in frustration, Kevin shook his head. "Listen to the lot of yez, discussing charms against hobgoblins! This is the twenty-first century, for feck sake!"

Eyeing Kevin with apparent amusement, Brian smiled. "Still unconvinced that the fairies exist, Kev?"

"No, Uncle Brian, I believe they exist, even if it does sound like a bunch of codology. But if they're real, there must be some way we can contact this fairy king fella and talk sense to him."

Talty agreed. "I'd love to speak to him!"

Liam started to say, "Don't even think about it."

His frowning father cut him short. "Don't worry about contacting Finvarra. I have a feeling he'll be contacting us soon enough."

CHAPTER TWENTY-TWO

Janet reminded herself that she didn't want to attend a boarding school. Annoyed by Matti's perky exuberance, she followed her grandparents through the door to the Admissions Office. Easy for Matti to like the place. She wouldn't be stuck here like a guppy in a fish tank full of goldfish.

A tall, slim gentleman in an olive sports jacket and brown slacks greeted them in a paneled reception area filled with leather chairs and artwork. "I'm Martin Tobin," he said with a handshake that left Janet's fingers tingling. His delightful Irish accent shattered her already weakened resolve to detest everyone and everything about Hazelwood.

Engaging his guests in polite conversation and witty remarks, Mr. Tobin strolled down a flower-lined walkway. The silver flecks in his sandy sideburns hadn't yet reached the clump of hair that tumbled over his forehead, no matter how often his fingers combed it back. Suntanned and debonair, he conducted himself like a confident young actor playing an older man in a play, though no actor's ego hampered his flawless manners.

"For nearly three centuries," he said, "Hazelwood has occupied two hundred acres here in the Dublin Mountains. As you can see, we have a good mix of building styles. The newest are the Library and the Blackthorn and Alderwood dorms. The school has extensive sports fields. Our rugby lads are already in residence, getting a jump on their practice."

Gram linked arms with Gramp. "You look as if you once played sports yourself, Mr. Tobin."

"I did, Mrs. Gleason, for most of my life. Played rugby and hurling at Cork University. I haven't played regularly since I taught social studies at

Trinity. I'm altogether busy here at Hazelwood, but I still like to kick a ball about when I can spare the time. The girls' teams here are first-rate, and for those who don't care for the rough stuff, we've recently added an archery range, all-weather tennis courts, and a nine-hole golf course."

Gramp stopped on the path. "A golf course? I may be visiting you often, Janet."

Everyone laughed, and the tour continued. Mr. Tobin showed them the academic buildings, the main dining hall, the non-denominational chapel, and the gymnasium, which reeked of chlorine thanks to its massive swimming pool.

Every building Janet saw amazed her in a different way. As far as she knew, no such schools existed in Boston. Her grandparents weren't exactly paupers, but two years of tuition and boarding fees would set them back considerably. She could never repay them, not with money. Overcome by love and gratitude, she resolved to make them proud of her.

Mr. Tobin walked backwards down the path that led away from the gym. "We'll have a gander at Blackthorn, the dorm where you'll be staying, Janet. Then we'll see the theater." He spun around and brought them to the center of the campus.

They ambled beneath blue skies stippled with fair weather clouds. Only occasional puddles remained to attest to the day's rainy start. They reminded Janet of the puddles she and Liam had dodged on the cliff path.

From somewhere up ahead, the high-spirited voices of teenage boys ricocheted merrily through the air. Their good-natured shouts evoked Liam's sly smirk. Annoyed with herself for thinking of him, Janet focused on the voices. She waggled her eyebrows at Matti, who responded with a knowing wink and a double thumbs up.

Mr. Tobin and his charges turned right at a monstrous evergreen he said was a yew tree. Its branches seemed to grow right out of the ground instead of the tree trunk. On the other side of the tree, a pack of rowdy boys in royal blue shirts with white collars approached. They looked scruffy and fit and wonderful.

Their banter stopped when they saw Mr. Tobin. He greeted them warmly and introduced them collectively as Hazelwood's rugby team. Then he kept right on going.

So did the boys, furtively appraising Janet and Matti as they passed. The tallest one, the one with jet-black hair and ivory Irish skin, winked at Janet.

Her cheeks blazed, and she turned her head away, but she was smiling.

Glancing at the grownups ahead, Matti put her hand to her mouth and whispered, "Those guys make Ricky Gagnon look like a fish-lipped cybergeek."

Janet held her breath to keep from giggling.

Gram asked Mr. Tobin who was in charge of each dorm. "Back home they have resident advisors called R.A.s," she said. "Older students who help the younger ones."

"We call them House Tutors here," said Mr. Tobin. "They act as assistants to each Housemaster or Housemistress. Ah, here we are."

Though still apprehensive about the school, Janet couldn't wait to see where she'd be living during the week. She followed Mr. Tobin and her grandparents through the revolving front door. Matti whistled at the dorm's sleek interior.

Mr. Tobin continued the scripted part of the tour. "Blackthorn is the newest building on campus. Its common area includes a big screen television and gas fireplace. It's centrally located, has its own dining hall, a small kitchen, and wifi throughout. Each room has a private bath, a small refrigerator, and individual environmental controls. You'll be quite comfortable here, Janet."

He escorted them to an elevator, and they rode to the second floor, which to American Janet was the third floor. It was also the top floor of the streamlined dorm. Each window they passed presented a perfect view of either the landscaped grounds or the vintage campus buildings and the sparkling sea beyond them.

At the end of the hall, Mr. Tobin entered the room reserved for Janet. The bare mattresses and empty closets did nothing to detract from the first-class look of the spacious double room.

Gram inspected the closet and bath. Her head twisted back and forth so much, she looked like a wound up doll. "Oh my, this is nothing like the dorm I lived in at Smith. Just picture your things here, dear."

Janet already had. And she'd have a roommate! Maybe not Matti, but at least someone her own age. Someone to talk to. Someone who'd know other kids and introduce her around. She'd have friends.

Gram and Gramp were clearly pleased when they left the dorm. Matti's unflappable good cheer matched Janet's growing excitement. How could she ever have thought her grandparents were being mean by sending her to this wonderful school?

"Our last stop is the Carriage House," Mr. Tobin said. "I understand you have a special interest in drama, Janet."

His words might have been chocolate, or honey, or a magical rainbow popping up to paint the sky. "Yes. It's one of the reasons my grandparents chose Hazelwood for me." Janet's affection for them swelled.

Mr. Tobin explained that the Carriage House had once contained extensive horse stalls and watering troughs. Staff and visitors had kept their wagons and coaches inside. With the arrival of automobiles, the building fell into disuse until its recent refurbishment as a theater.

"Areas that once stored hay and riding gear are now prop and dressing rooms," he said, opening the main door to the old building. "Sorley Griffin is in charge of our Music and Performing Arts School. He's inside preparing for the new school year. I'll let him describe the program."

They passed through a simple lobby with a tiny caged box office at one end. Symphonic classical music trickled from behind double doors that Janet assumed led to the theater. She didn't know the name of the piece she was hearing, but she recognized it as a Strauss waltz. Her stomach lurched. She reached for her locket, but it wasn't there.

Beaming as if he knew a secret, Mr. Tobin opened the nearest door. The music blared. Gram went in, then Janet and Matti. Gramp and the headmaster followed, and the door closed behind them.

The auditorium's main lights were off, but the stage glowed brightly. In its center, a red-haired man in a sweatshirt and jeans waltzed with an upside down mop whose yellow loops wobbled in three-four time. The man's eyes were closed, the music so loud he didn't seem to realize anyone had entered his domain.

Mr. Tobin chuckled. "Come on, I'll introduce you." He marched down the center aisle, up the side stage steps, and over to the CD player, where he bent and lowered the volume.

The man kept dancing, though he opened his eyes. "Is it yourself, Toby? How's she cuttin'?"

"We have guests, Griff." Mr. Tobin waved an arm at Matti and the Gleasons, who had followed him onto the stage. "This young lady is Janet Gleason, all the way from Boston in America. She'll be a third year transfer student this semester, and she's interested in our drama program."

Sorley Griffin froze and pinned Janet with a demented gaze she wasn't sure he was faking. He suddenly bounded toward her with the mop still in his hands. Just as he reached her, he tossed it aside. "We'll know all about you after one dance, Miss Janet from Boston in America."

Before Janet realized what was happening, he'd grasped her wrists and pulled her to the middle of the stage. She nearly shrieked when he took her hand and placed an arm around her waist. But a sudden calm fell over her, and as he started waltzing, she followed his steps in perfect time, in perfect form, in perfect unison.

Faster and faster the music flew. Janet grew dizzy whirling around the stage, but she loved the speed, the increasing momentum, the laugh-out-loud fun of it.

Dance with me, Janet...

The grand finale smothered the eerie whisper like a brisk wave washing over the sand and retreating into the sea. Had she heard it at all?

The music stopped, ending the waltz. Mr. Griffin released her and bowed gallantly. "You're a far better partner than a mop, Miss American Janet."

He wasn't even winded. Janet, however, was struggling to catch her breath. Struggling and smiling. "Thank you," she said. "That was fun." She pivoted toward the others.

Matti and Gramp stared curiously at her, but Gram was gushing. "All that practicing with your grandfather has done wonders for you, dear. You're a lovely dancer!"

Mr. Griffin agreed. "I'm Sorley Griffin," he said. "Everyone calls me Griff. Why don't you two young people bring a few chairs from the side there?" He pointed to a dimly lit offstage spot that Janet yearned to explore.

As Mr. Tobin made introductions, she and Matti found a row of folding metal chairs.

"I thought you couldn't dance!" Matti whispered

"I can't!" Janet whispered back. "At least I couldn't. I can't tell you how many times I stepped on my grandfather's feet. Maybe it's Mr. Griffin. He's a good leader."

Matti grunted as she lugged out a pair of chairs. "Yeah, if you're a mop." Holding a chair in each hand, she walked a few steps and then rested the chair legs on the floor. She released the chair on her right side, letting it lean against her thigh so she could straighten her glasses. "Janet Gleason, you are going to have the most wonderful time here. If you weren't my best friend, I'd hate you!"

Janet wrestled her own pair of chairs from the heap. Like Matti, she rested the legs on the floor. "We'll always be best friends, Matti. Promise?"

Matti raised her hand and made an "X" over her chest. "Promise. Cross my heart and hope to die, stick a needle in my eye."

"Ouch! What happened to 'Kiss the boys and make them cry?'"

"That too!" Matti hefted the chairs to the stage. "The whole rugby team will be crying before you're done with them."

She and Janet set up enough chairs for everyone to sit in a semicircle. The sense that Sorley Griffin didn't sit still often had Janet taking advantage of the break to study the wonderfully eccentric man she hoped would be her drama teacher.

As he described Hazelwood's theater curriculum, Janet's attention shifted from his carrot-red eyebrows and freckled face to his detailed remarks. Each new tidbit fascinated her. The scope of the program dazzled her.

"All grades are welcome to participate in our annual production," he said, eyeing everyone in turn, even Mr. Tobin, "from major and minor roles to costumes, props, and scenery. Those in the upper grades produce smaller shows throughout the year, work with video critiques and attend performance technique workshops."

"Your drama program sounds like more than an extracurricular activity," said Gramp.

"It's much more, Mr. Gleason. Drama training helps build self-confidence. It also encourages team work and accustoms the students to speaking in front of large groups, a skill a gentleman in your esteemed position can surely appreciate."

Gramp grinned and shook his head. "Indeed I can. I still freeze up when I have to make a speech. Speaking of which, we must be on our way. As much as I've enjoyed our tour, I have to check in with my staff at the embassy. Right after I take these lovely ladies to lunch, of course."

He stood as he spoke. So did Gram. Mr. Tobin and Mr. Griffin rose for a final round of handshakes. Mr. Griffin told Janet to make an appointment to see him the minute she arrived on campus. She thanked him, and Mr. Tobin led the way back to the Admissions Office.

Lively conversation about all the wonderful things Hazelwood offered filled the limousine on the ride back to Dublin. Gramp treated everyone to lunch at Roddy's Bistro, his favorite restaurant in the embassy district, before the driver dropped him at his office.

"I have to catch up on a few things," he said. "Tonight we're having dinner at Malachy's to celebrate Janet's new school, and I have tickets for that play we've been wanting to see at the Abbey Theater. You might be performing there yourself some day, Ladybug!"

Janet had never been to the Abbey Theater, but she knew how old and famous it was. When had Gramp gotten the tickets? He and Gram had gone to a lot of trouble to make her happy—and they'd succeeded.

Later that afternoon, while Matti was in the shower, Janet raided her closet for something grown-up to wear to dinner and the show. As she considered and rejected several tops and skirts, she relived every minute of the memorable day: the rainbow arcing across the sky, Mr. Tobin bringing her to her dorm room, and Mr. Griffin—Griff, he'd insisted she call him—spinning her around the stage and making her feel like the greatest dancer on earth.

Treasuring that wonderful moment, she continued hunting through her clothes. She came across the shirt she'd worn to Howth the day before. Her fingers curled like claws. She tugged at the cloth and tore the collar. How could she have been so naive about Liam Murphy?

She glanced at the bathroom door. The shower was still running. Hurrying to her bureau, she thumbed her cell phone until she found his "Unverified Sender" text messages. She'd replied to them before. She could try again. What would she say if he answered her? She thought of a few choice phrases. Holding her breath, she hit "Options" and chose "Reply," just as she had when she'd texted him about where to meet him in Howth. A message that his phone was no longer in service popped up, deciding the matter for her.

Of course it was no longer in service. He probably got a new phone every other day so the police couldn't find him. Well, to hell with him!

The world had plenty of other boys. Boys who weren't lying thieves. Boys like the dark-haired rugby player in the blue and white shirt who'd winked at her today.

She touched the spot on the front of her neck where her locket once hung. The prettiest necklace in the world could never take its place.

The shower stopped. Janet set her cell phone on the bureau and hurried back to the closet before Matti came out and caught her crying.

CHAPTER TWENTY-THREE

In her guise as the elderly woman called Nora, Becula found a specialty shop in the heart of Dublin and filched a half-dozen bottles of wine. So many newfangled labels, she told Finvarra when she returned to the cave. Unsure which ones to appropriate, she'd nicked an assortment of burgundies produced in a place called California.

As she took her seat in the dreary underground den and set up her basin of water, Finvarra sampled a substandard Pinot Noir. The wine tasted nothing like the French vintages he relished. How low the mortals' taste had sunk!

"It's Tuesday morning Out There, Becula. Two mortal days since the boy tossed the necklace into the sea. Where is it? I assumed you'd have it back by now."

Becula annoyed him by focusing on her basin. The water in it shimmered and hummed. "A family of seal people owes me a favor," she said, her grating voice a lifeless drone. "They're scouring the seabed below the cliffs now."

"What have you learned about King Brian's ball? When is it? And where?"

"This Friday night at Clontarf Castle, sire."

Finvarra knew the castle well. He'd often danced in the stronghold back in the days when the mortals invited him and Oona to their parties. The first King Brian had built the castle right on the spot where Finvarra had saved his life after the Battle of Clontarf. Said he'd chosen the spot to commemorate his friendship with the *Daoine Sídhe*. So much for friendship!

The modern mortals needed a lesson in keeping in touch.

Mechanically sipping his tawdry wine, Finvarra plotted his vengeance against Prince Liam. "A most worthy domain, Clontarf. I assume the girl will be there."

"She's having a dress made for the occasion, sire."

"Will Prince Liam attend?"

"I can't say, sire. He might not. He's injured, you might recall."

Finvarra recalled. He was still annoyed that Manannan MacLir had punished the boy before Finvarra could get his hands on him. "Prince Liam's family will surely be there. His sister is the Crown Princess. She'd make a fine hostage. I'm considering taking her and negotiating an exchange."

Becula's head snapped up, her hag's eyes round as Celtic brooches. "I beg you, sire. Do nothing to incur King Brian's wrath. The mortals have more than enough power to destroy the *Daoine Sídhe*. They always have, and the weapons they now wield are far superior to the spears and swords that secured their ancient victory over us."

"They don't believe we exist, Becula. They won't fight an enemy in which they don't believe."

"But we are not enemies, sire! Please—"

Finvarra shot her a warning look. "I wonder what sort of food they'll have at their ball?" He eyed his goblet with distaste. "Hopefully they'll have a decent burgundy. Yes, I fully expect we'll eat and drink our fill. For such a fine event, we must have our Oona and the rest of the troop. Where is she?"

Becula lowered her head. Fingers fluttering, she waved her hands over the basin. Light glowed from her fingertips, glazing her grotesque face with shimmering shadows. "The queen has returned to the palace beneath Knock Ma. Shall I summon her to the marble stone, sire?"

"Please do." The prospect of seeing Oona, of conversing and sporting with her, kindled a warmth in Finvarra that spread from the core of his being and chased the damp chill from the rocky chamber, at least temporarily. He summoned his glimmer to make himself presentable.

Becula surrendered her seat to him. He allowed her messaging magic to encase him, knowing he must hurry. The old crone couldn't sustain the connection for more than a few minutes.

Dust-like particles bubbled deep within the basin. The sprinkles glittered and shot through the water like tiny fish, coalescing into Oona's glimmer-clad face. Affection for her drew Finvarra closer to the basin. "Greetings, pet."

"Fin? Where are you? I thought you'd be back from your dancing by now."

"It's complicated. I'll explain when I see you. We're near Dublin, beneath the Ben of Howth. Would you like to attend a party? I'm thinking of crashing King Brian's ball."

He expected her to scold him for such foolishness, but her feline eyes sparked like Roman candles, shuffling through the rainbow of colors he never tired of seeing. "Ooh, Fin, I'd love to go! It's been ages since we danced at a mortal ball. When is it? Will they know we're there? What will I wear?"

Finvarra smiled. No matter how many outfits Oona tried on before a party, she always chose her gossamer gown of silver and gold. "The dance is in a few mortal days," he said, "and they'll most definitely know we're there."

"Where is the party?"

"Clontarf Castle will be the venue. Do you remember it? We camped beside it ages ago, when we helped the mortals defeat the Vikings at the Battle of Clontarf. If I recall correctly, we can gain access through the basement. I've sent out scouts to see if our old camp is still habitable. If so, we'll settle in, and I'll send for you. Do try to keep from flitting off on another of your adventures in the meantime."

Oona's enticing pout appeared. "All right, I'll wait to hear from you. Don't take too long. I miss you, sweet." She blew him a kiss, and her image dissolved in the rippling water.

He wanted nothing more than to be with her. Why did he bother with mortal women? They were so much trouble.

Still, he shuddered with pleasure recalling how softly solid the mortal called Janet had felt in his arms when they'd danced.

Yes, the mortal women were trouble, but ah, they were worth it!

CHAPTER TWENTY-FOUR

Shivering from cold and fright, Janet hugged herself. She wore jeans and a T-shirt instead of a golden gown this time, and Gram wasn't with her. Nothing was in the murky cave but frigid darkness, until the yellow loops of a mop began to glow in the gloom. The handle took human form, though the mophead remained faceless. It stalked toward her, its extended hand holding Nora's sapphire necklace.

"Look what I have for you, Janet," the creature said in Liam Murphy's Irish lilt.

The familiar inflection enraged her. She wanted to beat him senseless, but was this monster really Liam? Somehow she knew that it wasn't, that the necklace would harm her, that the mop-headed thing was evil. Unable to respond, she backed away from it.

Laughing with Liam's voice, the fiend closed in on her, trapping her against a cold, damp wall with jagged bumps that dug into her back. As the outstretched hand closed in on her, the necklace turned into her locket.

Janet woke gasping for breath. Why was she having these horrible dreams? She didn't think she'd screamed this time: Matti still slept in the bed beside her. Relief washed over her. She closed her eyes and scolded herself for letting a dream frighten her. Forcing herself to think of more pleasant things—her new school, the blue dress, shopping with Gram, and doing something special with Matti before she flew home on Thursday, Janet fell back to sleep.

By ten o'clock the next morning, she and Matti were leaving Bewley's on Grafton Street, where they'd polished off a pair of enormous chocolate muffins and a pot of good strong tea. They'd already picked up the shoes Janet would wear with her dress. Beneath a typical Irish mix of lively clouds and peekaboo sun, the girls maneuvered through the crowds to Wicklow Street and dashed up the stairs to Kincora Designs.

Gram was already there, relaxing in the sitting area. Steam wafted from a silver tea service on the coffee table before her. Fingers lacing a delicate china teacup, she chatted with Louise, who stood behind her glass reception desk. The pink and white chunks of Louise's former 'do had given way to short black tresses daubed with yellow, as if someone had spilled ink on her hair and sprinkled it with dandelions.

Janet thought it looked fabulous. "Your hair looks great," she said, addressing her classically coiffed grandmother first. "Yours too, Louise."

Both women thanked her. Despite the disparity in their age and hairstyles, they were getting on like long lost friends. Their identical smiles were way too big, and Janet had the oddest sense they were in cahoots over something.

"Except for the hem," said Louise, "the dress is done. Try it on with your new shoes and we'll finish it up."

Trembling with excitement, Janet left her jacket on a chair and picked up the bag that held the shoebox. "Is Nora here today? I'd like to say hello."

The question seemed to befuddle Louise. "We don't have anyone named Nora here."

Befuddled in turn, Janet nervously crumpled the bag. "Are you sure? She was here the first time I came. An older lady. She let me try on a necklace."

Louise frowned and shook her head. "I'm sorry, Janet. No one by that name has ever worked for me."

"Oh. I must be confused with another shop." Leaving Matti sitting beside Gram, Janet hurried into the back room.

She wasn't confused. Nora had come to this very dressing room and handed her the necklace. What was going on?

They say this necklace is magic...

A slide show streamed through Janet's thoughts: Nora bumping into her on the street. Nora parting the curtain and offering Janet the sapphire necklace. Nora in the pizza shop. Nora on the cliffs of Howth.

Howth? Janet's skin crawled. Was she losing her mind? How could Nora have been on Howth?

But she had been. Janet remembered now, saw the little hut where Nora had waved and asked her in for tea. What had happened after that?

Janet couldn't remember. Maybe Nora had drugged her tea. That had to be it. And maybe the drug was still in her system, giving her nightmares. She'd heard of that happening.

A terrible thought occurred to her. Were Nora and Liam Murphy partners in crime? Things were starting to look that way, but why go to so much trouble to steal a measly locket?

Whatever the reason, Janet's blood boiled. She should tell Gramp what happened. He'd know what to do. Yes, she'd speak to him soon.

Her decision made, she slipped into the dress. She felt like Cinderella when she stepped into the low-heeled shoes.

Louise knocked, came in, and helped with the zipper. She then directed Janet to a wooden block in the center of the work area. "Stand up here and we'll pin the hem."

Janet obeyed. Measuring tape and pincushion in hand, Louise knelt. She finished the job in minutes, and Janet dashed back to the dressing room to study her mirror image. The beaded strip fit her waist perfectly. The tiers of mesh on the skirt gave her a dreamy look. And Gram was going to buy her a beautiful necklace, something to hang just so in the square, open neck.

Elated, she glanced at Louise's reflection. "Can I show my grandmother?"

"Of course. I want you to step about a bit. We have to be sure the length is right."

Janet had no difficulty retracing her steps to the waiting room. Graceful and confident, she spun and posed for Matti and Gram. They applauded, and Matti whistled.

Louise laughed. "I think we're all set. We'll finish the hem, and I'll have the dress delivered to Deerfield House by late tomorrow morning."

"All we have to do is get you a necklace, dear," said Gram. She and Louise smiled their "too big" smiles again. Why would they be so excited about a necklace?

"You'll find several suitable jewelry stores nearby." Louise named a few. "Adam DeWitt, the royal jeweler himself, is right at the end of Wicklow Street. You'll see the sign for DeWitt & Sons. His shop is upstairs, like this one."

"The royal jeweler? We should be able to find something suitable for you there, dear." A look of rapture glowed on Gram's face.

Janet coughed and covered her mouth to hide a smile. Profusely thanking Louise, she and Gram left the dress shop with Matti, who gushed nonstop about the dress. They reached the street and headed toward DeWitt & Sons.

"Here it is," Matti said, reading the sign aloud.

But a second sign on the door said the shop was closed.

Gram looked like she was going to cry. She rallied quickly, however. "Oh well. As Louise said, there are other shops. We'll try one of them, and then we'll have lunch somewhere."

"That sounds fine, Gram. All these stores have necklaces."

"Yes, dear, they do, but what a shame the royal jeweler isn't in." Gram turned toward the opposite end of Wicklow Street. "I wonder why?"

CHAPTER TWENTY-FIVE

Liam didn't see why the royal jeweler had to come to the King's Residence to meet with him. He'd have been happy to pop up to Wicklow Street, but his father refused, saying the trip "would tax your injured arm."

The old fella wasn't fooling anyone. He was worried about *Them*.

Adam DeWitt's visit served a double purpose. He'd come to deliver the necklace Liam's mother had selected, the one he was to present to the American Ambassador's granddaughter at the dance Friday night. The idea still nettled him, though not as much as the second reason for Adam's visit. Liam's father had called the jeweler and asked him to bring a selection of stainless steel jewelry.

Uncomfortable receiving people in the formal front reception room, especially for such personal business, Liam met Adam in the den. Dressed in a dark suit and tweed tie, the jeweler rose from a leather sofa awash in morning sunshine. A stack of thin black cases sat on the coffee table, an old oak thing that fit in well with the room's casual decor.

Adam's forebears had been the royal jewelers for generations. A recognized authority in metallurgy and gemology in his own right, Adam had worked with his late father, the former royal jeweler, all his life. He'd already produced a son who would likely continue the family's venerable commission one day.

Though only in his early thirties, Adam's once dark hair had turned completely white. The contrast with his boyish face and black falcon eyes was startling. Those eyes darted up and down now, undoubtedly noting Liam's sling and bruised forehead.

A flicker of concern wrinkled the jeweler's brow. Then he smiled and said, "Good morning, sir," in the soft-spoken voice of a confident craftsman.

Liam had received deferential treatment all his life, but sometimes he felt silly being only seventeen and having a grown man, especially a fine gentleman like Adam, address him as "sir." He'd known Adam forever, knew his shop well, and would prefer a more easygoing relationship with the man who would be his "surprise gift" co-conspirator over the coming years.

Striving to set a less formal tone, he held out his good arm and shook Adam's hand. "How's things, Adam? Bringing the show on the road again, eh? Nothing 'guaranteed worn by rock stars and celebrities,' I hope."

"Only my finest wares, sir. I have plenty to show you, of varying quality. Shall we start?"

They sat side by side on the couch. Liam noted that only a plain gold wedding band adorned the long, slender fingers that opened the first black case. Inside, an assortment of men's watches sat in tidy rows.

Just what I need. Another watch.

Most of the pieces were silvery steel; a few were light brown and coppery. Knowing that Adam would educate him, Liam asked about the darker watches.

"Chocolate stainless steel, sir. It's all the rage. It's formed when a protective coating of ion plating coats the metal to form a seal that's not only attractive, but protective."

Liam wondered if that coating would seal in whatever power the steel might have over the fairies. He decided he'd stick with the uncoated steel.

He selected two watches, both with the Roman numerals he preferred. The first featured a stainless steel bracelet and a large black dial with luminescent hands he could read without his glasses. The second, a sleek classic model with gold woven into the bracelet and an opalescent dial, would do for more formal events.

He liked the solid Celtic knot bracelets and chose one with a barely noticeable gold weave for everyday wear. For dress up, he chose a cable link bracelet inlaid with braided gold. The dance Friday night was a state affair: white tie, no wristwatches, no bracelets. Liam eyed the sling and sighed. Without it, he might have gotten the bracelet past Ross, but with only one hand, he'd need help with the fold-over clasp. Hell, he'd need help with everything. He thought he'd ask Kevin to help him dress and slip on a piece of steel or two.

"I like this bracelet, Adam, but it's a tad loose. Can you adjust it by the dance this Friday night? It's white tie. Can't have it slipping from under the sleeve."

The question that flashed in Adam's eyes lingered no more than an instant. He knew very well that accessories such as bracelets weren't worn to white tie events. "I'll have it for you by tomorrow," he said dutifully. "We can easily adjust the size by removing a link or two." As he scribbled a note, he said he had no stainless steel shirt studs, cuff links, or pocket watches in stock for white tie attire, though he offered to order some. "But I don't know that they'll arrive by Friday, sir."

Liam declined. His gold pocket watch would do, should he decide to wear it, and he'd inherited several vintage pairs of mother-of-pearl cuff links with matching shirt studs that served him well for both white and black tie events. A steel bracelet and wristwatch ought to provide enough protection for the dance, and Adam still had more to show.

Rings, bracelets, chains, tie pins, and cuff links for business casual attire occupied the remaining trays. The pieces intrigued Liam. Most of his casual cuff links, all gold or silver and dotted with jewels, had been gifts. He had none in stainless steel. The square links with round diamonds in their centers caught his eye right away. Perhaps he could wear those Friday as well, if he kept his sleeves tucked up.

"Well done, Adam. At this rate, I'll have enough stainless steel to form an arsenal. How about a ring or two?"

Worry, or perhaps fear, swept over Adam's face. "Most are wedding bands, but we have a few etched with Celtic and other designs. What about earrings, sir?"

"I don't do earrings, but I suppose I could wear a chain under my shirt."

Adam fidgeted for a moment, glancing about the room as he did. "Is it *Them*, sir?"

The DeWitts weren't the royal jewelers for nothing. Liam patted his sling and sighed. "My family feels I may be under some sort of threat, yes."

"I wondered about it when the king asked me to bring so much steel. My father taught me that the Good Folk do pop up from time to time, and not always with kind intentions. Our family records contain descriptions of the various protective pieces we'd provided to the members of your family over the centuries. Armbands, wristlets, brooches, all in different grades of steel. The notes mentioned a fine jeweled dagger in particular. Perhaps some of these items are still in your family's keeping."

Liam doubted it. His father and Uncle Peadar would have mentioned any such pieces—unless they didn't know about them. "A dagger, jeweled or otherwise, wouldn't go well with my dinner jacket. Anyway, I wouldn't know what to do with such a thing, unlike my dauntless sister. As for the other items you mentioned, I'm sure they're around somewhere, but I don't have time to go searching now. We'd best stick with the modern steel for the moment. Do you really think it will work?"

"Yes. I can't say how, exactly, but steel, stainless or otherwise, affects unseen energy forces in some manner. I suppose things haven't changed much over the years. Many New Age health practitioners provide pendants and amulets of crystals and other materials to help people who are sensitive to electrical waves. Microwaves, cell phones, computers, that sort of thing. Why would fairy magic be any different?"

"So it's not really magic, just a type of energy we don't understand?"

Adam shrugged. "Not my area of expertise, sir. I can, however, obtain additional steel items for your everyday use. Bookmarks, key rings, even money clips."

"Thank you, Adam, but this is plenty for now. I do have a favor to ask, however." Knowing he could rely on Adam's discretion, he drew Janet's locket from his trouser pocket. "Can you find me something similar to this? Age and quality-wise, I mean. Not necessarily a locket, but an old-fashioned necklace a young lady might consider a keepsake. And not stainless steel. Something fine and tasteful. The best you can get."

Adam took the locket. As Talty had, he turned it in his hands. Would he wonder, as she had, if it contained magic? "This goldwork is quite old. I'm sure I can come up with comparable pieces for your consideration, sir." He set the locket on the table. "Would you prefer something with a gemstone that might provide...protective properties?"

"Gemstone?" Liam grinned. "I see how it works. The ladies get the gemstones, and I get stainless steel. Still, it's not a bad idea. I'll leave the details to your good judgment."

Adam gently shut each case, emptying and setting one aside to hold the pieces Liam had chosen. "Ordinarily I'd take the items you selected back to the shop for proper preparation and wrapping, but you should have these pieces now. Only the cable link bracelet will require adjustment. I'll take care of it right away and deliver it myself tomorrow morning. I'll also bring appropriate containers for your other selections."

"Bring them to Clontarf Castle, please. We don't usually move in until the day before a clan gathering, but my father wants us up there early. And Adam, if it's not too much trouble, could you bring a copy of those descriptions from your family records? My curiosity is getting the best of me."

"I'll see what I can do, sir. One last item and I'll be on my way." Adam plucked a small velvet box from his inside pocket. "The necklace the queen chose to match the young American lady's dress. A star sapphire. The chain is white gold."

Liam opened the box and stared transfixed, not at the finely detailed chain, nor at the pendant's circle of tiny, matching diamonds, but at the deep blue oval sapphire they enclosed. He wished he were giving it to Janet instead of the ambassador's granddaughter.

Yet as he studied the sapphire's glittering facets, a disturbing image of the necklace he'd thrown into the sea appeared in his mind's eye. Confused, he snapped the case shut and set it on the table beside the locket. "What do you know about sapphires, Adam? Not their actual makeup, but the legends about them."

"Sapphires have a wealth of lore attached to them. As you may know, they come in different colors. The ancients believed the gods painted the sky with blue sapphires. They considered it a holy stone, one that ensures good luck and prosperity. Legend has it that the Ten Commandments were carved on tablets of sapphire."

"The original blue laws, eh?"

Adam grinned and continued. "Talismans of blue sapphire were thought to ward off evil spells and return the evil to the sender. At the same time, magicians and witches reportedly wore them to boost their occult powers. Nowadays, the blue sapphire is considered a meditative stone that promotes the ability to tap into the subconscious mind."

A startling idea compelled Liam to pick up the locket. "Does gold do anything to sapphires?"

"Folklore holds that gold intensifies the power of most gems. Gold contains the warming power of the sun. It evokes strength, builds confidence, and helps its wearer conquer the paralysis caused by fear. I suspect that the gold in that locket has served its various owners in this way."

The locket seemed to twitch in Liam's hand. More determined than ever to find Janet, he returned it to his pocket and stood. "It's almost as if these things have a life of their own."

Adam rose too. "It's only legend, sir, but I'm not prepared to discount it as nonsense. Not when we're outfitting you with a hoard of protective steel."

They shook hands. "Thank you for that," Liam said, "and for your incomparable tutoring."

"I'll be up to Clontarf by early afternoon tomorrow. The best potatoes to you, sir."

Liam laughed at the old country farewell. "Good man yourself, Adam. Take care."

Adam saw himself out. Bombarded by troubling thoughts, Liam brought his new steel jewelry upstairs and prepared for the move to Clontarf Castle.

CHAPTER TWENTY-SIX

For the umpteenth time since Janet returned to her room that afternoon, she drew the long black jewelry box from her bureau drawer and admired her brand-new necklace. The azure topaz didn't quite match the gown's rich blue, but Gram and the jeweler had both pointed out that the gem's lighter shade would suit the dress better. Janet had agreed, and she loved the twist in the fine gold chain and the way the stone glowed in the trinity knot setting.

Matti had come away with a present too. Gram bought her a sterling silver Claddagh ring as a souvenir of her visit to Dublin. Stunned into uncharacteristic silence by the generous gift, Matti had promptly placed the ring on her right hand, worn as instructed by the jeweler with the heart facing outward "so the world will know your heart hasn't yet been won."

Janet snapped the jewelry box shut and glanced at Matti, sprawled on the sofa before the fireplace, engrossed in a book of Irish fairytales. She'd bought so many books, they'd never fit in her suitcase. Gramp had suggested she mail them home.

Matti planned to so do tomorrow. She'd be packing all her things tomorrow, and she'd be leaving Thursday. Janet would miss her terribly, but she no longer felt so afraid of being abandoned. Anyway, tonight was only Tuesday, and she meant to enjoy Matti's company while she was still here.

"It's almost seven, Matti. Let's see my grandparents off."

"Huh?" Matti glanced up from her book. "Gimme two minutes. I have to find out how the kidnapped piper gets away from the fairies."

Dance with me, Janet...

Fragments of a desperate flight through a murky tunnel burst from Janet's memory like strobe lights. Someone was holding her hand, and she was afraid.

Matti snapped the book shut and pushed up her glasses. "Cool! They took him to play his pipes for their dance, but he learned the secret password and got out of the fairy fort."

Tatther rura...

Whose voice was that? The eerie whisper lingered in Janet's ears and slithered away. She repeated the cryptic words: *"Tatther rura."*

"Hey, that's right! When did you read this story?"

Confused and disturbed, Janet shook her head. "I didn't. I don't know how I knew it. I must have read it somewhere." She stared at her friend. "That stuff doesn't really happen. Fairies are make-believe. They can't kidnap people."

"They kidnap lots of people." Matti nodded toward the anthology she'd just set down. "In that book, a fairy king called Finvarra is always bringing human girls to his fairy fort, but someone usually saves them."

The necklace allowed me to hear your wish...

Janet hugged herself. What was happening to her? "Fairies aren't real!"

"Who knows? This is Ireland, after all. I've been reading tons of stories about fairies. They steal women to take care of their kids, but mostly they want to party."

Dance with me, Janet...

Blue eyes blazed from the shadows of Janet's thoughts.

"What's wrong, Jan?" Matti tilted her head and frowned. "You look awfully white."

The image vanished as quickly as it appeared. Could fairies be real? Had they kidnapped her somehow? Or was it a dream? Janet squeezed her eyes shut.

I've come to reclaim the young woman you've stolen...

Her eyes opened wide. Her fists tightened. Real or not, she wasn't buying it. Bad enough a thief had stolen her locket. No one was going to steal *her*! If she met any fairy kings, she'd defend herself the way her father had taught her.

But she wouldn't meet any. Fairies weren't real. She'd been having weird dreams lately, that's all. Too much stress over moving to Ireland and worrying about the Ambassadors' Ball. Now she had a new dress and a beautiful necklace, she could dance—a little—and soon she'd attend a great new school and make lots of friends. Everything would be fine.

"Nothing's the matter. Come on, let's get downstairs."

They found Gram and Gramp in the open reception room off the foyer, not one of Janet's favorite places. All that yellow and gold in the rug, the curtains, and the couches, overwhelmed her. Tonight, however, light from the crystal chandelier brightened the gilded tones, creating a perfect backdrop for Gram's sequined gown. She looked gorgeous in green.

Ever handsome in his black tuxedo, Gramp wore a black bow tie and vest. Gram was straightening his tie when the girls came in. Matti whistled.

Janet would miss those whistles. "You guys look absolutely stunning. Spanish embassy tonight, right?"

Gramp beamed at her. "Yes, Ladybug. I sure do wish we could eat dinner here before we go. Spanish food gives me heartburn. Say, how about a brush-up dance for your old Gramp?" Holding his arms out to her, he hummed something off-tune but in waltz time.

Janet giggled and indulged him. He spun her over the carpet in little circles, and she didn't step on his feet, not once. Her spirits skyrocketed— but she was in her comfy jeans and sneakers. "We'll have to try this again on Friday when I'm all dressed up," she said.

He released her and bowed. "Don't you worry, Ladybug. You'll be the star of the show."

Rosemary came in and announced that the limousine had arrived. "I left plenty of food in the refrigerator for you, girls," she said in her thick Irish brogue. "You only have to heat it in the microwave."

Gram plucked her evening bag and lacy black shawl from the sofa. "Thank you, Rosemary. Enjoy your evening off."

The housekeeper nodded and left the room. Gram smiled her wooden smile at Janet. "Are you sure you'll be all right home alone tonight, dear?"

That particular smile, Janet now knew, was simply part of Gram's formal ensemble. She smiled back warmly. "Of course we will, Gram. We won't starve. Have a great time, and don't worry about us."

"We'll be fine, Mrs. Gleason," said Matti. "We're going to watch movies upstairs."

Gramp helped Gram with her shawl. "The alarm is set, Henrietta. There's a guard at the gatehouse. They'll be perfectly safe." He held out his arm, his elbow bent in gentlemanly invitation. "Shall we, Sugar?"

After they left, the girls turned off the big lights and retreated to the upstairs den. An hour into a corny tale of a high school prom queen who'd returned to her hometown after being in jail for years for a crime she didn't commit, Matti paused the DVD.

"I'm starving, Jan. Let's raid the kitchen."

Janet's stomach grumbled. Food sounded good. "Let's see what Rosemary left for us. And let's watch something else when we come back."

The den was right beside the grand staircase. Janet opted to go that way. The dimly lit hall didn't seem so scary with Matti around. Treasuring Matti's company this second-last night before she left, Janet spouted a scathing critique of the movie.

Matti added her two cents about the scenery. "They should shoot a movie in this house," she said. "A horror movie. I'm glad you'll be away at school, Jan. I hate thinking of you all alone here when your grandfolks go out at night."

"I'm glad too." Janet wondered what she would do after Matti left. School wouldn't start for almost two weeks.

Still chatting about the movie, the girls crossed the foyer. The corridor to the kitchen suddenly started to glow. The shadows deepened. Janet held her breath. Was she seeing things again?

Matti stopped beside her. "What the heck is that? Are there timers on the lights?"

"I don't think so."

The shadows moved. Someone was in the hall.

"Don't be afraid, Janet…"

A man's voice. A man who knew her name. Terrified, Janet twisted her head toward Matti. "Did you hear that?"

Matti stepped back. The glasses on her chalk-white face slipped down her nose. Instinctively, she pushed them up. "Yeah. Maybe we should go back upstairs and call the police." Her voice sounded hoarse. "Or maybe they're on their way. Is the alarm silent?"

"I don't know." Janet gulped and stared transfixed at the growing light. "Who's there?"

"I want to dance with you, Janet. Your friend can come too…"

In a flash, Janet knew that whoever had spoken was somehow involved with the strange things happening to her. Rage overpowered her terror. "Who are you? How did you get in here?"

A flickering man appeared in the center of the foyer. The girls shrieked and hugged each other. Young and handsome, the invader wore jeans and a pullover shirt. His longish blond hair and startling blue eyes seemed familiar.

Janet knew him. But how? Who was he?

He finally grew solid. "Hello, Janet," he said with the saintly smile of an innocent child. "I've been looking for you. You left my party too soon." His spooky words had turned solid too. He spoke in a cultured voice with a deep silky rumble.

Janet nudged Matti away and folded her arms. "I don't know how you did that, but whoever you are, you'd better disappear again. Get out of here. Now!"

Matti tried to speak but only managed a pitiful croak. She tried again. "He's a...are you a...one of those fairy guys?"

"No, he's not!" The self-defense lessons that Janet's father had drilled into her streamed through her turbulent thoughts, as if he were right there coaching her.

You're a girl but you're not helpless. Push your thumbs in his eyes, knee his groin, scream in his ear, bite him if it comes to that...

If she had to, she could do it. She braced herself to attack the intruder.

He peered down his long thin nose at her. "You don't believe in me? I am Finvarra, the King of the Fairies. I want to dance with you, Janet."

For the briefest instant, he wore a jeweled crown of gold and a long white cape pinned with a round gold brooch. Then he was back in jeans.

No doubt about it: he was a fairy. The one Matti said stole women. Charged with red-hot anger, Janet spread her feet and glared at him. "I'm not dancing with you, you weirdo! This house is the property of the United States of America. As long as you're in it, you're on American soil. You have no business here. And no power! Now get out, or I'm calling the police!"

Finvarra's face twisted with rage. "You cannot defy me! I am Finvarra!" He raised his hands. White light shot from the tips of his fingers.

Matti screamed.

Janet flew toward the stand of antique walking sticks and seized a shillelagh. She lunged at Finvarra, swinging the stick at him, striking his arms, his shoulders and back, whacking him repeatedly, releasing all the fury that had simmered inside her for weeks.

His raised arms did little to thwart her attack. Grunting and shouting, he backed away. "Stop! That hurts! Stop, evil hellcat!"

Matti joined her, flogging him hard with a stick of her own. Like brush strokes of phosphorescent paint, red streaks seemed to burn through his clothes wherever their blows made contact. With each blow, he seemed to shrink and grow older. Soon he looked like a middle-aged man with a week's growth of bristly white beard.

"Enough!" he cried. "I'll go! Whatever made me want to cavort with such violent creatures? Becula, get me out of here!"

As he flickered, he gaped at the girls with the pitiful look of a sad little boy. "I only wanted to dance," he said, and then he vanished.

Huffing between breaths, Janet leaned on her knobby shillelagh and stared at the spot where Finvarra had stood. "Did we just beat up a fairy?"

Equally winded, Matti tapped her stick on the marble tiles. "Unless we're both astray in the head, as they say over here, yeah. These walking sticks must be made of blackthorn. I read about how blackthorn wood keeps fairies away."

"And apparently it hurts them." Janet banged her shillelagh hard. "What else keeps them away? I doubt we'll see that jerk again, but maybe we should find out, just in case."

"He seemed to know you, Jan. Have you met him before?"

"I'm not sure. I think I've been having nightmares about him."

"I wonder who or what Becula is? Backup fairies? We should call the police."

"Yeah, right. Hello, Officer O'Toole. This is Janet Gleason, the American Ambassador's granddaughter. I'd like to report a fairy break-in at Deerfield House. No need to come over. We kicked his fairy butt with a couple of magic canes we keep in the front hall."

Matti sighed. "I see what you mean, but you should at least tell your grandfather. What did that guy mean when he said you left his party too soon? Were you there, Jan? Is that how you learned that secret password?"

Janet wasn't sure. Hazy memories teased her and then scattered away like windblown tendrils of smoke. "I don't know. I promise I'll talk to Gramp. Tomorrow. Right now, I'm really hungry." She smiled and banged the stick on the floor again. "I'm always hungry after a great performance. Let's eat. Then you can tell me what you've read about fairy charms."

"Good idea. The movie stank anyway."

Blackthorn sticks firmly in hand, they thumped victoriously into the kitchen. The shillelaghs vanished before they reached the refrigerator. The girls didn't notice, didn't recall that they'd used the sticks to defend themselves only moments before.

They forgot all about Finvarra.

CHAPTER TWENTY-SEVEN

The outpost below Clontarf Castle was warm and dry, a topnotch encampment compared to the hovel the *Daoine Sídhe* had left behind in Howth. Though hardly the opulent fairy palace beneath Knock Ma, the subterranean chambers would house the entire troop, and they'd require less glimmer to maintain. The airtight conditions had preserved the furnishings well.

Finvarra hadn't visited Clontarf in ages, but the moment he entered the underground camp, he fully recalled lodging here in the days when the mortal kings had welcomed him and Oona to their splendid soirées. More important, he remembered how to get into the castle. The thin spot, as the mortals called it, reposed conveniently near the storerooms.

And the wine cellar.

Not only bottles, but dozens of kegs of wine were on hand for King Brian's ball. The mortals would never miss one or two. When he'd first seen the cellar, Finvarra thought he might play a trick and replace the kegs he nicked with barrels of rancid buttermilk.

Yet his visit to Deerfield House had left him feeling far from playful. He sat at an oak trestle table whose narrow plank top rested on a pair of thick legs carved from tree trunks. Twirling a goblet of exquisite red burgundy, he watched as Becula worked a spell on the gold-labeled bottle whose contents he'd nearly drained.

A simple sniff of the cork from the Grand Cru Chambertin had set his wounds to heal. The burgundy's ruby red color, glorious bouquet, and spicy-smooth aftertaste had expunged all signs of the mortal girls' vicious attack. Becula's incantations boosted the wine's effects, and Finvarra's spirits soared.

"This domicile is more suitable, Becula. More appropriate to my kingly status."

Becula glanced up from the candlelit corner where she sat mumbling magic. "Aye, sire. The queen will be comfortable here."

"She does love camping out."

He couldn't wait to see Oona. He'd already summoned her and the rest of the troop. Those who'd accompanied him to Howth and Clontarf were in the outer chamber preparing a feast for those en route, a proper feast procured by strategically pillaging the stores the mortal servants were bringing in for the ball. Finvarra himself had led a covert raid on the castle's pantries.

And the wine cellar.

The storerooms had served as dungeons the last time he'd seen them. The conversion left him wondering what else had changed, and he'd made a game of exploring the rest of the basement. Much was the same, but the updated kitchen impressed him. The hearth remained, though the cooks didn't use it. They had fancy ovens and things they called microwaves, and all sorts of gadgets that spun and whirred.

Of all the additions, his favorite was the lift. He'd made himself invisible and had a hoot of fun riding up and down with the workers, who had unwittingly shown him how the mysterious buttons worked. He thought he might install one in his palace. Oona would love it.

Preparations for her arrival were nearly complete. No glimmer was needed to fashion a feast in her honor. The storerooms contained good meat and fowl, potatoes and brown bread, butter and cake and honey, all of which would wash down well with ample servings of fine French wine. The troop would only require their glimmer to spruce up the banquet hall. Finvarra had ordered them to create hundreds of sweet-scented candles and golden tableware. Happy to take their turn at serving, a dozen fairies had already donned the troop's hunter green livery. Even now, music filled the air. The *Daoine Sídhe* would dance tonight.

Finvarra would gladly dance with his loyal Oona instead of the fiend who had burned him with the blackthorn stick. Thanks to the wine, he'd nearly forgotten the attack. Still, he wished he'd won the girl over instead of dismissing her as a failed endeavor.

He drained his cup and peered at the hag. Halfway between the bottle and her basin of water, the sapphire necklace sparkled. The seal people had returned it to her at sundown, and Finvarra had quickly employed it to find and approach the girl. A failed endeavor indeed.

"Ready for another glass, sire?"

"Why not?" He held out his goblet. "Top it off for me, if you please."

The bottle floated through the air, tipping and filling Finvarra's glass with a most delightful chug. Empty at last, it floated back to the stool.

"Feeling better, sire?"

Finvarra resented the reference to his humiliation at the hands of the savage mortal girl and her equally savage companion. He snapped a gruff "Yes!" back at her.

Becula seemed unfazed by his snipe. Her attention was on the water. "I did remind you of the mortals' violent natures, sire. Luckily I was able to expunge all memory of your visit and return those wicked blackthorns to their case. Did you manage to reclaim your dancing spell?"

He glared at her, though again, she ignored him. "The hellcat gave me no chance," he said, "yet it's of little consequence. The spell might vaguely affect her dreams, but it will wear itself out in a century or so. She may keep it, for all I care. I'm done with the vile creature—but I'm not done with the boy."

As he drained his glass, Finvarra envisioned the red-haired prince, the thief who'd stolen Janet and led Berneen to her death. In her youth, Berneen had been an agile dancer, one of his favorites. "I've a score to settle with him," he said, essentially to himself. "He's in the castle now. I can feel him."

Becula glanced up sharply. "Sire, please—"

"Silence! For the next few nights, we'll dance and laugh and partake of King Brian's honey and wine. But before we leave for Galway, I intend to have a word with Prince Liam Conor Boru."

Finvarra rose and thumped his wineglass on the table. He closed his eyes and pictured the men at work in the larders, studying their attire. When his eyes reopened, he wore leather sneakers, drab modern trousers, and a dark red jersey with large white letters that read "Galway Gaelic Football." A leather thong secured his hair at the nape of his neck, and he'd applied enough glimmer to appear as young as he always pictured himself.

"If anyone needs me, I'll be in the wine cellar."

CHAPTER TWENTY-EIGHT

After the Battle of Clontarf in 1014 A.D., High King Brian Boru ordered his men to build a castle to memorialize his victory over the Vikings. For centuries, the old stone fortress stood guard over the northwest coast of Dublin Bay and its rolling, gray-green waters. Secure, spacious, and set in a picturesque park of mature trees and gardens, Clontarf Castle had always been the Boru clan's favorite gathering place. Most members of the present-day clan drove to the stronghold, though some flew in by helicopter, landing on the helipad behind the enormous garage. Others arrived by sea, mooring their boats at the nearby yacht club.

The primary members of the royal family liked to stay at the castle when it served as a party venue. A few days before they arrived, their household staff descended upon the place to freshen the private apartments, the great hall and kitchen, and the public rooms. They'd been cooking, cleaning, and decorating for more than a week to produce the Ambassadors' Ball.

By late Wednesday morning, Liam had settled into his top-floor suite. He had little to do, thanks to his efficient aide. Ross had overstocked the closet with several suits of formal attire and enough casual outfits to last a few days. His brow had briefly puckered when the stainless steel trinkets caught his eye, but he'd said nothing.

Liam wore several bits of steel now. His black polo shirt concealed a neck chain. A casual bracelet dangled from his right forearm. His thumb kept rubbing the thick new ring on his right hand, while his watch-clad wrist still idled in the demonic sling that imprisoned his left arm.

Shortly after he'd come to the castle, Adam DeWitt delivered the last of the bracelets along with a neatly typed list of the steel charms his forebears had obtained for the royal family over the centuries. Liam thanked him and hurried upstairs.

Sipping his favorite Kenyan tea, he sat on a sofa reading descriptions of wristlets, buckles, and bodice chains. Though he wondered what had become of all the stuff, he wondered more why his ancestors had needed it. Were the fairies really that threatening?

"Yourself chased by a pack of rats, and you're askin' that?" he said aloud. At Kevin's special knock, he set the papers down. "Come in, Kev," he called.

The door opened. Kevin was there, all right, but Talty barged past him. "Howya, Liam!" Eyes gleaming, mouth turned up in her matchless smile, she pulsed with front-page news.

He rose and kissed her outstretched hand. "Have they found Janet?"

"Not yet. Don't worry. They'll find her."

"So what's up? I doubt you're grinning like a tipsy chimpanzee because you're happy to see me, Lady Sister."

"I'm always happy to see you, Li." Ponytail whipping, her head swung toward Kevin. "Aren't we, Kev?"

Kevin seemed more worried than happy, not an unusual state of affairs. Yet that unmistakable Boru mettle gleamed in the un-Boru blue of his eyes. "Right. We've been digging in the archives at Tara Hall. Reading King Declan's diaries."

Indignant, Liam eyed the dust-streaked jeans and shirts his sister and cousin wore. "You went through the archives without me?"

"And you with one arm and a bocketty head," Talty said in her older sister tone. "We also found a list of pieces the royal jewelers made or obtained to protect the family from fairies. Are you and your one arm up to a jaunt?"

They'd found the old steel jewelry! "Adam DeWitt gave me a similar list, but it didn't say where the pieces were."

Kevin pointed to the floor. "Declan says they're right downstairs."

"His diaries referred to a vault in the basement of Clontarf Castle," said Talty. "A chamber hidden below the drawbridge room."

Liam pictured the castle layout. "There's nothing below the drawbridge room. The builders indented the walls like that to allow for the moat that used to be there."

"Apparently there's a room there too," said Kevin. "Your father gave us two keys from a set he inherited when he became king. He said they were the only ones he knew nothing about. He told us to try them. We're going to have a look." Kevin unclipped a flashlight from his belt and shone it in Liam's face. "He also said we'd be altogether safe poking about in the basement. The rats are gone."

Liam flinched as the light hit his eyes. "Put that thing away, you eejit! You're lucky I only have one arm!"

Kevin laughed and returned the flashlight to his belt. Talty gave Liam's sling a playful tug. "The room should be easy cakes to find. Come on, let's find it!"

The staff had the lift tied up, so the trio took the stairs. During the castle's construction, the builders deliberately laid the stone steps at random intervals to trip attacking swordsmen. Such an attack had never occurred, but the stairs remained unchanged. Every Boru child knew their irregular pattern by heart. With Talty in the lead, Liam and Kevin hurried down to the great hall.

Ladders and cleaning supplies cluttered the gargantuan room. Aproned men and women arranged piles of logs in the massive hearth, dusted the chandeliers and sconces, and vacuumed the tapestries and stags' heads adorning the granite walls. Sneakers squeaking on the ancient limestone tiles, Liam and Talty exchanged greetings with the workers. Kevin remained silent.

The trio turned down the corridor that led to the lift, the public rest rooms, and a seldom-used conference room. At the end of the hallway, they stopped at the main stairway to the basement. Kevin switched on the overhead light, and they scuttled down the stairs.

The dry cellar air was cool, though not uncomfortably so. From the far side of the basement, hand trucks and rolling barrels rumbled like thunder as workers brought in party goods. Liam enjoyed the familiar sound.

Just as familiar were the cloth-covered statues and tables huddling in corners and alcoves. The wall hangings remained uncovered, however. They marked the way through the cellar maze, if one knew which ones were which. Liam and Talty and Kevin knew.

Talty pointed confidently to her left. "This way."

They strode through the bare-bones corridor whose long woolen runner muted their footsteps. Liam watched for the holy water font that preceded the French hunting tapestry. The colorful wall hanging not only marked the intersection of two passageways, it also concealed a door that led to a tiny chapel.

When he spotted the pewter font, filled to the brim as always, he quickly calculated the location of the drawbridge room. "Take a right at the tapestry," he said, and they turned. "Give us a few of the finer points you found in Declan's diaries."

"The biggest thing I noticed," Kevin said as if he were telling a secret, "was how often he repeated that since the first Celt set foot on Ireland, the fairies have been among us."

Talty chuckled. "Why are you whispering, Kev? They're not down here. Didn't you say the rats were gone?"

Kevin stopped, his eyes as round as saucers and darting about as if they were trying to flee the scene. "Don't be talking like that, Tal!" His voice grew softer. "They're all around us, and they don't like it when you make fun of them."

If Liam hadn't encountered Finvarra himself, he might have laughed at the ludicrous sight of his usually confident cousin bug-eyed with fright. "You're the one who called them hobgoblins, Kev."

"Maybe I put no pass on them before, but I'm not so sure after reading those journals."

Talty hadn't stopped. She was halfway down the corridor. "All right, you two," she called over her shoulder. "No bickering. We're here to find the steel."

For an instant, Liam wondered why she was so enthusiastic, but Talty was like that when things caught her fancy. He and Kevin overtook her easily enough.

"I have to admit," she said, "when I first started reading, I thought poor old Declan was gone for his tea. Altogether loopers, like Mad Sweeney in the old tales. But Declan's hand was steady, his thoughts coherent. Almost scientific."

"They were," Kevin agreed. "He wrote down the story the old fellas told us about the cow and the fairy fort. We found others too, but mostly he bemoaned the loss of contact between the *Daoine Sídhe* and us."

A faraway look came over Talty's face. "They used to visit us often. I wonder what happened to make them stop coming and hide in the long grass all these years?"

Curiosity seethed through Liam like a burning electrical current. "I want to read those diaries."

"You may have to get in line," said Talty, her head turning as she scanned the walls. "Dad came by while we were going through them. He said he felt lost about all of it. Said he thinks his own father must have known something about the *sidhe*, but he died before he could tell him. We left him in the archives reading away." She stopped at a spot where the wall curved out. Carved oak panels covered the stone. "Ah, here it is. The drawbridge room is right above this wall, I think. We've always thought these panels were decorative, but I'll bet one of them is a door."

Picturing the drawbridge room, Liam glanced up.

* * * * *

The three young mortals stood frozen by Finvarra's quickly conjured spell. It was the best he could do for now. The evil aura of baneful steel would catapult him to hell if he drew any closer. Not only did the deadly force emanate from Prince Liam, it pulsed and thrummed from behind the wall. Angry that they'd thwarted him—for the moment—Finvarra edged as near as he dared to the mortals.

Prince Liam's swathed arm and bruised forehead provided a pleasing spectacle. On his way to the wine cellar, Finvarra had recognized Liam's voice and couldn't believe his luck. From the bits of chitchat he'd overheard, the other boy was a kinsman, the girl, King Brian's daughter. Elated, Finvarra had pursued them, intending to wreak his vengeance on Liam and kidnap his highborn sister.

He'd tracked them to a passageway with stone walls on one side and wood on the other, an area his magic could easily encage.

He had them.

Or so he'd thought until the unseen but definite presence of steel stopped him cold. Even without it, the sight and sound of the girl had confounded him. It still did. Confused and curious, he'd cast his spell to view her unmoving form from beyond the sting of the sorcerous steel.

Could it be? Her melodious voice was the same. So were her chestnut eyes, her thick auburn hair, and her gently curving chin. And her lips might have been those rosebud lips he'd dared to kiss so long ago.

Impossible images leapt from the depths of his unretentive *sidhe* mind, recollections of a girl who greatly resembled the princess standing before him. A mortal girl of royal Celtic blood who'd danced and laughed and made him…yes, he'd loved her, as much as his kind could love any mortal woman. As much as he loved even Oona.

Treasa Boru had declined his offer of a long and carefree life in his fairy realm. She loved another, she said. He told himself he didn't care, that there were other mortal women, but he never stopped watching for her. Each time he met her, he forgot all else, even after she married a worthy chieftain. He danced with her at her wedding, and at several subsequent celebrations. Each dance filled him with joy, for when he danced with Treasa Boru, she smiled for him.

She died bringing forth her first child. He closed his eyes to banish her haunting smile. What unkind gods had brought back her memory to one for whom only the bliss of the here and now mattered?

Unaccustomed to sorrow, he shook it away. He wouldn't allow it. He must concentrate on the present, spy on these mortals to learn where they'd be for the next few days. At an opportune moment, he'd trap Prince Liam and settle the score between them.

His plans for the girl, however, had changed. He could never harm her now.

Finvarra released his spell and withdrew to the shadows, watching.

* * * * *

Kevin ran his hands over the frames that held the panels in place. "I don't see any door, but I'm guessing it's here somewhere. I don't get it. Why would they hide the stuff if they thought they'd need it?"

Feeling useless, Liam studied the Celtic patterns carved into the wood. Talty and Kevin had forbidden him to prod at the wall and risk further injury to his arm. "I doubt it was a secret at first," he said. "The family must have forgotten about it after a while. Maybe they made peace with *Them* and had no further need for it."

"Not according to Declan's diaries." Talty pressed and poked the wood as she spoke. "Declan said that every so often, the fairies would stir the pot, and trouble would start again. The steel would come out, though it hasn't for ages now. Maybe the simple fact that we have the steel precludes the need to use it. Like magical weapons of mass destruction. No one really wants to launch them."

Liam agreed. "I wonder what caused the falling out in the first place?"

"Who knows?" Kevin switched on his flashlight and shone it over the paneling. "Declan mentioned nothing about that. The situation between us and *Them* was strained long before his time, it seems."

Talty knelt. Her fingers skimmed the wood as if she were reading Braille. "I'd love to meet Finvarra and ask him what happened. Tell him we'd like to be friends again. Invite him to some of our parties."

"Send him a feckin' email, why don't you?" said Liam. "Finnie the Worm at Knock Ma dot com."

"I wish it were that easy. I'm not finding anything here, fellas."

Liam noticed a glint in the wood, the same sort of spark that gleamed in the door hidden next to the hearth in the great hall. "Tal," he said, "there's something just over your left shoulder. Shine the light there, Kev."

With a triumphant "Hah!" Talty tickled what looked like a metal clasp. The wood strained and popped, and the outline of a tall slim opening appeared. She teased the edges, tugging until the door came loose.

*****

Malevolence lurked in the hidden room. Finvarra sensed its deadly presence the moment the door opened. The danger to him was great, but he stood there shuddering, hunching his shoulders, watching until the mortals entered the evil chamber before he returned to the wine cellar. Inexplicably sad, he bethought what the girl who resembled Treasa—her accursed brother had called her Talty—had said:

I'd love to meet Finvarra and ask him what happened. Tell him we'd like to be friends again. Invite him to some of our parties...

He thought he'd like to dance with her. Perhaps he could ask for a waltz at the ball. From what she'd said, she wouldn't refuse him. Suddenly cheerful, he jig-stepped into the wine cellar. Already he saw himself up in the great hall hopping a hornpipe with Talty Boru—and her miscreant brother would surely be there.

Finvarra had no idea what email was, but the boy had clearly called him a worm.

*****

As Liam expected, the room lacked electric lights, though black iron sconces with fat yellow candles clung to the walls. Logical Kevin had thought to bring matches. Talty shone the flashlight as he lit the candles, infusing the circular room with the honeyed scent of burning beeswax.

Eager to see what the light revealed, Liam scanned the hoard of steel that covered the rounded walls. Most of the pieces hung on wall pegs. Some dangled from ceiling hooks. Hints of rust dulled their once shiny surfaces, yet colored stones gleamed in the candlelight. Graceful swags of bodice chains accented by semiprecious jewels drooped beside chokers and necklaces, tiaras and chaplets, and chains with long thick pendants that looked like dog tags. More than a few of the pendants were miniature swords cast with sharp downward points.

A handful of steel medallions bore religious symbols, though most flaunted the royal lion of the Boru clan. The opposite side of the room showcased an array of bracelets, armbands, and boot spurs. A suit of armor stood before the only portion of the wall on which nothing hung.

"The real reason why knights wore armor," said Liam. "To protect them from the fairies. This place is like an armory of jewelry."

"I see no real weapons here. Only things you can wear." Talty sighed dramatically. "But alas, none of it matches the dress I'm wearing Friday night."

The disappointment in her voice had Liam wondering what she was after. "That's the idea, isn't it? You wear the stuff to protect yourself."

"You'd be a lightning rod if you wore this stuff," Kevin said. Metal jingled as he handled one of a half-dozen canteen-like flagons attached to long, finely wrought chains. "Look at these beauties! You can still smell traces of liquor in them. I'll bet they didn't mind schlepping these over their shoulders."

A puzzled look crinkled Talty's face. "So where are the smaller pieces? The brooches and rings and earrings? The records we saw listed dozens of them."

"So did Adam DeWitt's list," said Liam. "The armory off the drawbridge room houses antique swords and other grisly things. Maybe there's a similar room off this one."

"Li, you're a genius!" Talty spun, searching.

"Amn't I though." His arm ached. His head hurt. He wanted to lie down, but curiosity kept him going.

Kevin pointed toward the vacant wall behind the suit of armor. "Maybe there's a door there."

They converged on the wall. Balancing care with impatience, Talty and Kevin moved the armor. As candlelight invaded the space, a slim wooden door appeared.

Kevin jiggled the latch. "It's locked."

"Let's try the keys Dad gave us." Talty drew them from her pocket. One was large. Both were ancient.

Tired of feeling useless, Liam snatched the bigger key. "Allow me. I should at least be able to open a lock."

He inserted and turned the perfectly fitting key. The lock clicked; the latch yielded.

Armed with his flashlight, Kevin entered the chamber first and lit more candles. The room was so small, he barely fit. "There's a cabinet in here," he said. "It's locked. I'm thinking the other key might open it."

He backed out to let Talty in. As he and Liam watched from the doorway, she knelt before the carved wooden cupboard. Soon the double doors opened, exposing a dozen narrow drawers.

Starting at the top, she rapidly opened and closed each drawer, indifferent to their contents until she reached the sixth drawer. She drew out what looked like a piece of oilskin cloth. "Give us more light, Kev," she said, unfolding the cloth.

The flashlight spotlit the bejeweled hilt of an ornate dagger. Talty eased the double-edged blade from its matching sheath, also adorned with precious gems. "There you are, you gorgeous thing."

"What have you got there, Tal?" asked Kevin.

"A lady's dagger." Talty stood hefting the knife in her hand. "Made for Queen Evlin in 1585."

The same year the fairies had taken Berneen Dolan. A time of trouble with *Them*? Liam recalled what Adam had said: *The notes mentioned a fine jeweled dagger...*

"Not only beautiful," Talty continued, "but practical. A fine grip and well balanced."

She moved so fast, Liam cringed and shut his eyes. When he dared to look, the quivering dagger was lodged in the doorframe above his head.

"You might have hit us!" Kevin cried, his voice an octave higher than usual.

Talty only smiled. "We're to lock everything up and report back to Dad. He said if I found Evlin's dagger, I might borrow it for the ball." She pulled the knife from the doorframe and slid it into its fancy case. "Now this will match my dress!"

CHAPTER TWENTY-NINE

Janet sat cross-legged on her bed enjoying Matti's comical attempts to fit a small library of books into one little box. Matti had reshuffled the contents of the shipping carton several times trying to decide which book to pack in her carry-on bag. Her latest round of possibilities littered both her bed and the night stand.

She clasped a thick paperback in both hands and frowned. "Should I bring a novel? A novel would last the whole flight." But the book landed on the rejection pile. After digging some more, she plucked a small hardcover from the box. "Maybe poems would be better. That way I can read in spurts and do other things, like eat lunch and watch the movie, if it's good."

Janet winced at the thought of eating airline food. "You'd better have a good breakfast before you leave tomorrow. I've already asked Rosemary to make all your favorites. Why don't you download a bunch of different books onto your e-book reader?"

Matti set the poems aside and resumed her rummaging. "Because that would cost, and I'm already in trouble for going way over my vacation allowance. Besides, I want to read something I bought in Ireland. Ambiance, Janikins, ambiance." Adjusting her glasses, she studied a sizable softcover volume. "Hey, I never did finish this book of fairytales." Another frown. "Nah, I'd finish it too fast. I only had a few more stories to go."

The book seemed to fly in slow motion from Matti's hand. When it landed, something compelled Janet to reach across the space between the beds and pick it up. The colorful cartoon cover depicted mermaids and leprechauns, clear-winged pixies perched on the petals of pink morning glories, and a beautiful lady with tumbles of long blond hair.

The lady winked. The fairies waved. Gasping at their tinkling teehees, Janet reached for the ghost of her locket.

"What's wrong, Jan?"

Janet glanced up. When her gaze returned to the cover, the images had settled. "Nothing. My eyes are playing tricks on me. I thought the pictures moved. Just my actress imagination dreaming up friendly fairies." She continued to stare at the cover.

"After reading some of those stories, I'm surprised I'm not seeing the little rascals all over the place. Speaking of dreaming, what's up with these nightmares you've been having? Last night makes three in a row. I don't know if I should leave you here." Matti rubbed her chin. "Hmm. Think you can fit in the box?"

Janet giggled and tossed the fairytales onto Matti's bed. "I'd love to, but I'm not sure all the characters in your books would leave any room for me. Don't worry, Matt. I'll be okay. It doesn't feel so scary here anymore, and Hazelwood will be great. I'm sure the nightmares will stop after I start school. I just wish you could stay a little longer. I'd love it if you could come to the ball with me tomorrow night. Then I wouldn't be such a nervous wreck."

"Think of it as a role, Jan. A dress rehearsal. Opening night. You're a debutante, or maybe the Queen of the May. You can do it. And I want pictures!"

Matti's pep talk helped, but their fast-approaching separation had Janet close to tears. "I'm going to miss you so much, Matti." No amount of acting could keep the wobble from her voice.

Matti didn't seem to notice. "Oh, I'll be back. I may have to babysit every night for months to save up the airfare, but I'm coming again. I love it here. In Ireland, that is, not in this creepy house, but I guess I'd stay here if I absolutely had to."

Janet's burst of laughter dispelled her gloomy mood. She jumped up and grabbed a few books. "Here, I'll help. We have to get that box out before the post office closes." She picked up the fairytales again. "I'd really like to read these."

"Hold on to it. You can mail it to me when you finish."

"Okay. Thanks." Janet set the book on the night stand.

Working together, she and Matti filled and sealed the carton. While

Matti addressed it, Janet picked up the house phone and called Rosemary, who in turn called a courier to take the box to the post office.

Matti had spent the morning packing most of her clothes. With extra time on their hands, the girls hopped a bus into town and spent a few hours laughing and planning, teasing and comforting. They stopped at Bewley's for chocolate muffins and tea and returned to Deerfield House to change for Matti's farewell dinner. Afterward, Gram and Gramp took them to see a fabulous Irish dance show at a theater near Grafton Street.

That night, Janet dreamed a red-haired man was trying to tell her something important. Sorley Griffin's face came into focus. He was calling to her from the stage at the Hazelwood College theater, warning her that Liam was in danger and only she could save him. She woke up feeling afraid for Liam, though she sensed no danger herself. Wishing the eerie dreams would stop, she closed her eyes and slept until the alarm went off at six.

Rosemary set out a full Irish breakfast of scrambled eggs, bacon and sausage, toast, brown bread, scones, baked beans, porridge, juice, tea, hash brown potatoes, and fried tomatoes and mushrooms. Matti sampled all of it, and she thanked the housekeeper several times "for the awesome feast."

Janet, however, barely picked at her eggs.

Gram dabbed a napkin at her lips and poured herself more tea. "Aren't you hungry, dear?"

"If I eat all this," she said, "I'll never fit into my gown tomorrow night." Her response seemed to satisfy everyone.

Before Gramp left for the embassy, he gave Matti a hug that made her squeal. "Come anytime, Miss Matti. We loved having you, and you made our Ladybug happy."

The limousine driver placed Matti's bags in the trunk and drove to Dublin Airport. Janet sat with Matti on the back seat; Gram sat opposite them. She and Janet were getting their nails done after Matti left.

They stayed with her until she checked her bag and went through security. "Send lots of pictures, Jan," she called from the long line of passengers. "I want to show everyone how gorgeous you look in your dress!"

"I will!" Janet answered, waving and sniffling and waving some more. "Email me when you get home! Email me every day! Call me too!"

She didn't cry until she returned to the limousine, and Gram didn't chide her a bit.

CHAPTER THIRTY

Liam's parents arrived at Clontarf Castle late Thursday afternoon. His father went straight to the basement with Talty to see the "Steel Room." On his way, he brought Liam a pair of leather bound journals.

Declan Patrick Boru's initials were tooled into the diaries' soft but durable leather covers. Settling into his reading chair, Liam unbound the straps, checked the dates on the title pages, and delved into the earlier chronicle. As he always did when he handled timeworn books and manuscripts, he drifted into the past, entranced by the hand-stitched binding, the handwriting's old-time flourish, the fusty smell of the pages. After a break for a casual supper with his sister and parents, he returned to his task and finished a third of the volume by midnight.

He removed his glasses and rubbed his bleary eyes. Pondering Declan's apparent good will toward the fairies, he set the sewn-in bookmark and went to bed. One perplexing passage ran through his thoughts, repeating itself to lull him to sleep:

> *They are my subjects too, these noble, mysterious creatures of magic and myth. I am honor bound to look after them and would gladly do so, but they elude us. Why?*

By late Friday afternoon, Liam had finished both diaries. His reading confirmed his suspicion that the *Daoine Sídhe* had fallen on hard luck. Although Declan did what he could to help and managed to live in peace with *Them*, he never learned what had caused the rift with the mortals. The latest truce had lasted for generations, until Liam challenged Finvarra and rocked the boat.

Though unrepentant—he still thought the fairy king had his glue to be stealing mortal women—Liam regretted his inadvertent involvement in the disruption of a detente he'd never known existed. His rancor toward the fairy folk softened as he recalled their rags-and-tags clothing and wretched food. He rubbed the steel ring on his finger, resenting the clumsy feel of it, of the bracelet and chain that chafed both his skin and his conscience. Could the present-day Borus make peace with the *sídhe* and restore *Them* to their former well-being?

I have ordered the steel locked away in an effort to gain their trust.

Old Declan was either a shrewd visionary or a naive fool. A little of both, perhaps. Liam brooded about fairies and steel until Ross arrived to help him prepare for the dance.

Liam had attended gala affairs since he'd been a toddler. As comfortable in a dinner jacket as in jeans and a T-shirt, he enjoyed dressing up in his finely tailored evening wear. Socially savvy Ross always ensured that he looked his royal best, but tonight he'd need Kevin's collusion to slip a piece of steel or two past his diligent aide.

Poker-faced Kevin arrived at seven o'clock looking dapper in his evening wear. Perched on his lapel, his signature rose, the Apricot Derry, added a whiff of cinnamon to his guileless presence. Ross took his jacket and hung it over a chair. Together they helped Liam dress. Mindful of his stiff left arm, they eased him into his white shirt, black trousers, silk socks, and the black calfskin shoes that would have doubled as dancing shoes if he were going to dance.

"Why am I bothering?" He raised his injured arm as high as the sprain allowed. "I'm useless like this. The only redeeming factor is, I won't have to dance with Miss America."

A kindhearted half-smile appeared on Ross's face. He selected a perfect cream-colored rose from a vase on the table. "Time to prepare your jacket, sir," he said, and he disappeared into the closet.

Kevin straightened the front of Liam's stiff white shirt, lining up the stud holes. "I'll dance with her if I have to. So will Neil and Aidan."

"Aidan's coming? That's grand. I wasn't sure we'd see him tonight."

Liam and Kevin considered Aidan Dacey, Kieran's only son, more of an older brother than a second cousin. He and Neil had been away at the Military College, but one of Aidan's classes was scheduled to run an extra week.

"He got out early. Or they threw him out. Hold still." Kevin fastened the mother-of-pearl shirt studs, a gift from the boys' grandmother that included matching cuff links, to Liam's shirt. Kevin wore a similar set. "Adam didn't have any steel studs, eh?"

Liam glanced at the closet door. He doubted Ross could hear them. "No. It doesn't matter. The rest of it should be enough. Undo the top stud, will you, Kev? I can't wear this chain. The shirt's too stiff, and it's feckin' annoying me already."

Kevin obliged. "What other things do you have to wear?"

One-handed, Liam removed the chain and tossed it onto the bed. "Cuff links, a bracelet, a ring, and a watch. That should be plenty, though I doubt I'll need any of it. *They* wouldn't dare come here. With so many VIPs attending, security will be skintight."

"*They* don't know that." Kevin refastened the top stud. "I'll get your suspenders. You get the cuff links. We'll put them in fast so Ross won't notice."

Ross returned from the closet as Kevin finished buttoning the white suspenders to Liam's trousers. When Kevin reached for the cuff links Liam had set on the table, Ross rushed over, clearly appalled. "Oh sir, not those! They don't match the shirt studs. They aren't even chained. They're swivel posts!"

"No one will see them," said Liam.

"It's white tie, sir!"

"Even so, I believe I'm allowed a smidgen of individuality."

"But not impropriety." Ross pointed to the cuff of Kevin's sleeve and its proper, stud-matching cuff link. "Your dinner jackets are precisely tailored to show the shirt cuff. I'm begging you, sir, please wear the matching links."

Kevin's eyes narrowed, but he smiled. "Yer man's a right tyrant," he said, reaching for the mother-of-pearl cuff links.

"An old dog for the hard road," Liam agreed. He should have known better. "All right, Ross, matching links, but I will wear the ring. Any objection to the bracelet and watch?"

"Not as long as they absolutely do not show, sir." Ross licked his lips. "Forgive me for asking, but is there some reason for these...stainless steel accoutrements?"

"Just a fad," said Kevin. "You know how we teenagers are."

Liam had started to think the whole steel thing ludicrous. Declan had ordered the entire trove locked away to gain the Good People's trust, and he'd managed to peacefully coexist with them. This was all Kieran's fault. As usual, he'd taken his duty to protect the family far too seriously. What was he thinking, raising everyone's fears with his talk of knives and steel? Talty and Kevin had the right idea: find Finvarra and talk some sense into him. Talty had only wanted that fine lady's dagger for a souvenir, and who could blame her? Historically fascinating as Declan's steel relics might be, they belonged in a museum.

But what if by some slim chance Kieran was right? The few odd pieces of modern steel that Tyrannosaurus Ross had approved should protect Liam well enough, but what about Janet? Would Finvarra listen to reason where she was concerned? Probably not, and if steel could keep her safe from him, Liam would have her wearing the stuff head to toe.

He hoped she was already back in America. Finvarra couldn't harm her there.

"Help me into the waistcoat, lads. The guests will arrive soon."

CHAPTER THIRTY-ONE

Though nearly eight o'clock, the summer twilight lingered over Dublin City. Night would fall quickly when it did. Flames already thrashed in torches set around Clontarf Castle's ivy-covered walls. Something about the firelight unsettled Janet, but only for a moment. Clutching her new black evening purse, she rose from the limousine and gazed in awe at the thousand-year-old stonework.

Square walls with equally square gaps between them topped the main tower. Battlements, she recalled from a history class. The castle's defenders used them for shelter during a siege. In Janet's mind, swords clashed, horses whinnied, and archers up on the ramparts shot arrows at frenzied attackers.

Gramp took hold of her arm. Stately in his tuxedo, he looked every inch the dignitary he was, a calm and reassuring presence. Janet quashed her lingering jitters and slipped chameleon-like into the role of a princess attending a royal function. How easy it was! After all her worry and fussing about attending the ball, she stood calm, confident, and ready to walk on stage for the performance of her life.

Gramp hooked his other arm around Gram's yellow chiffon-clad elbow. "I'll bet I'm the only man here escorting *two* lovely ladies," he said, and Gram and Janet smiled.

They stepped under the canopy and joined the guests parading up the red-carpeted steps to the massive arched entrance. Two bronze lions with thickly maned heads as high as Janet's waist flanked the doorway. Mouths open in silent roars, they each held a paw up to greet a friend—or pounce upon an enemy.

The curtain was going up. Janet looked forward to meeting the young Boru royals, and she no longer feared waltzing with them. She and Gramp had practiced that morning, and again after she'd dressed for the ball. Gramp had declared her a master. She knew she could do it.

At breakfast and lunch, her grandparents coached her on protocol. "A reception party will greet us," Gramp said. "A line of top cat royals. After everyone arrives, the king and queen will make their grand entrance with a bagpiper leading them."

"It sounds wonderful," Janet said, and she meant it, but she still dreaded making mistakes. "How will I ever remember all those names and titles?"

"Few people can," said Gram. "Ma'am and sir will do very nicely. It's one of my favorite tricks. Don't offer to shake hands unless they initiate it, and for heaven's sake, don't worry about slip-ups. The Irish are delightfully friendly. Much less stuffy than the people in some of the other places we've lived."

"That's right, Ladybug. Just be yourself. Once they meet you, they'll love you. I guarantee."

Gram's hairstylist had come to Deerfield House and pinned Janet's hair up, allowing a few blond ringlets to fall to the back of her neck. Rosemary helped too, zipping up the dazzling blue gown and fastening the clasp of the topaz necklace. The housekeeper stared at the finished product, her assessing frown melting at last into a smile of approval. Janet grinned back at her, ready to rock.

"Remember to smile, dear," Gram had said as the limo turned into the castle drive. "Smile no matter how nervous you feel, and you'll be fine. If you see me touch my chin, I'm reminding you to smile."

Admiring the castle's lobby now, Janet doubted she'd ever stop smiling. How fabulous it all looked! The foyer of Deerfield House seemed like a closet compared to this. She and Matti had toured Malahide Castle, but Clontarf had to be at least twice as big, so much brighter and filled with amazing colors.

Tapestries, paintings, and gilded mirrors shared the soaring stone walls with antique maps and black iron sconces aglow with electric light. More bronze lions in various poses shared nooks with suits of armor and velvet-covered chairs so old, they looked like they'd come with the place. Dazzling displays of roses perfumed the air. A huge chandelier lit it all from above, creating a spectacle surpassing any theater backdrop Janet had ever seen—

and this was only the lobby!

Silently practicing her lines—*Hello, ma'am, hello, sir, I'm honored to meet you*—she followed her grandparents through another large doorway, where a small line moved toward two men. Silver flecked their dark-red hair, but they didn't look old. They towered over everyone, and from the light-blue sashes they wore under their jackets, Janet thought they must be royal. Beside the roses in their lapels, they each wore a round gold brooch with a tiny sword across it. Janet had seen similar pins in the museum in Dublin. She wondered why these men wore them and what they meant.

"The Duke and Duchess of Munster are first," whispered Gramp. "That's Prince Peadar and Princess Peggy beside them."

A real prince and princess! She couldn't see the princess yet, but the prince had a beard, and though he was built like a football player, he was handsome and friendly. So was the duke. They looked alike, familiar somehow, but then, a lot of Irish people looked alike.

Their dark-haired wives came into view, stunning in their respective plum and turquoise gowns. And the jewels! Diamonds and pearls dangled from their ears and hung in rows at their necks and wrists. Janet felt so out of place with her little topaz necklace.

She glanced at Gram, who touched her chin.

"Ambassador Gleason," the duke said, holding out his hand to Gramp. "It's fine to see you and Mrs. Gleason again. Say hello to my lovely wife, Breege."

Gram and Gramp exchanged introductions with the duke and his blue-eyed duchess. Then Gramp waved his arm toward Janet. "Our granddaughter, Janet, Your Grace."

As secure as she'd ever be in her role, Janet smiled and said hello. She only had seconds to wonder about the zigzag scar on the duke's chiseled face.

He took hold of her hand and squeezed it. "Kieran Dacey, Janet. I can't begin to tell you how much I've looked forward to meeting you. Peadar, look who's here!"

The prince slapped the shoulder of the man to whom he'd been speaking and swiveled toward the duke. "Ah, Ambassador Gleason. Mrs. Gleason, good evening."

"And this," said the duke, releasing Janet's hand at last, "is their granddaughter, Janet."

Amazingly, the smile on the prince's face grew bigger. "Janet," he repeated, grinning as if she were a long lost friend. "What a lovely young lady." He took her hand too, but instead of squeezing it, he brought it to his mouth and kissed it. His beard tickled her fingers, and she almost laughed. "We've heard so much about you," he said. "We're delighted you came to our party."

Why were they making such a fuss over her? They seemed a little weird. Even their wives were looking at them in a funny way, but their red-lipstick smiles quickly reappeared. They shook hands with Gram and Gramp and welcomed Janet.

The line behind the Gleasons had lengthened. They moved quickly into the great hall, where a fragrant wood fire welcomed them. Rows of linen-covered tables sparkled with china and crystal, though no one was seated yet. Men and women in glittering gowns and posh tuxedos milled in groups beneath the chandeliers. A handful of men wore turbans or kilts. Waiters in black jackets with gold trim flowed through the crowd with trays of drinks.

Two men greeted Gram and Gramp. They sounded French, and after saying hello to Janet, they started talking business. Already bored by their cryptic exchange and dying to see the castle, she told Gram she was going to find the ladies' room.

She cut across the banquet hall and found a quiet spot near a marble column. Wishing Matti was with her, she surveyed the cavernous room. She'd never seen such a monstrous hearth. The crackle and pop of burning logs seemed to keep time for all the melodic small talk.

Strains of music joined the mix. On the far side of the room, a man sat at a grand piano accompanying a harpist. Janet felt dizzy. The unsettling feeling returned. What was wrong with her?

Nothing. Just opening night jitters. She would find the ladies' room and rest for a minute or two. Behind her were several brightly lit corridors. Reasoning that they wouldn't be lit if guests couldn't go there, she chose the closest and strode toward it.

The noise of the party diminished once she entered the hallway. Feeling much better, she resumed her self-guided tour. She passed an elevator. Signs for the rest rooms were just ahead. At least she knew where they were now. She passed them and turned a corner. To her left was a doorway with a glass insert. A conference room, perhaps. Thinking to peek inside, she started for the door. After only one step, she stopped cold.

Dressed in sleek tuxedos and white ties, Liam Murphy and his cousin Kevin were coming toward her.

What were they doing here? But as they drew nearer, she realized they weren't Liam and Kevin at all, though they could have been their twins. Did all Irish people look so much alike?

"Can we help you?" said the one who resembled Kevin. "You seem a little lost."

"I…I was trying to find the ladies'…"

"You passed it," said the Liam clone. "It's back that way, just before the lift. That's 'elevator' to you, I'm thinking. This way goes to the cellar. Nothing down there for such a fine young American lady as your splendiferous self to see."

The Kevin twin rolled his eyes. "I'm Neil Boru. This eloquent fella here is my cousin, Aidan Dacey." Neil smiled and took her hand. "I know we haven't met. I'd remember if we had."

His handshake was perfectly polite, as was he. So why had her cheeks suddenly caught fire? Thinking herself silly, she smiled back at him and his cousin, glad that their Irish accents were easy to understand. "I'm Janet Gleason. The American ambassador is my grandfather."

The boys' eyebrows jumped. They exchanged glances.

Aidan spoke first. "So this is Janet. We've long awaited the coming of such an enchantress as your beauteous self." With a dramatic flourish, he snared her hand, bowed low, and kissed it. He stood tall then, gazing at her through reddish-brown eyes that twinkled with mischief.

Or was it something else? Janet had learned in history class that insanity ran in some royal families. Remembering Prince Peadar and the duke, she thought that maybe the Boru clan was one of them. She eased her hand from Aidan's grasp. "I believe I met your fathers when we came in."

"You did," said Neil. "Prince Peadar is my father. Aidan's old fella is Kieran Dacey, the Duke of Munster. We're on our way to the lobby to give them a break."

"You certainly look like your father, Aidan. You even favor Prince Peadar a little, but Neil, you look more like your mother."

"Lucky for him," said Aidan. "And you, Miss Janet, are an incomparable vision of pulchritudinous perfection."

Janet couldn't help giggling. "Does he always talk like that?"

"Only around pretty girls," said Neil. "Pay him and his blarney no mind."

More relaxed now, she noted that they wore roses in their lapels. Neil's was ruby red, Aidan's bright yellow. Their fathers had worn roses too. She wanted to stay and talk to these gallant young men, ask them if the roses had any significance, find out how it felt to live in a castle, but they'd already started walking toward the great hall. She walked with them.

"Here you are," Neil said when they reached the rest rooms. "We'll catch up with you later, all right?"

A mocking expression made Aidan look stern. "All right? She's more than all right, Neil. She's a golden-haired gossamer goddess who's even lovelier than we were led to believe."

...*even more comely than the marble stone depicted her...*

Janet shivered. Who had said that? Why did she have such peculiar thoughts? Maybe the Gleasons were the ones with the insanity. She pushed against the swinging door. "Thanks, guys. See you later."

She might have been in someone's living room. A wealthy someone's living room. This place had an oriental carpet, museum quality couches and mirrors, and marble counters with baskets of perfumes, lotions, and bottles of French mineral water.

A young woman sat on a chair fussing with something. She stopped and looked up when Janet came in. Startling chestnut eyes glowed from her creamy, fine-boned face. Her dark-red hair, loosely braided in a thick chignon at the nape of her neck, was entwined with bits of gold and ribbon that matched her rich teal dress. She needed no tiara to ooze royalty.

"Hello," she said in a cordial tone clearly intended to let Janet know she wouldn't bite. "I'm Talty Boru."

Janet's knees nearly gave way. She could play all the princess roles she liked, but this stunningly beautiful girl was the real thing.

Talty untangled the gold chain laced between her fingers and set it on the counter. When she stood, the gathered skirt of her gown rustled, unfolding into a slender feminine outline that conveyed exceptional strength. She wore a pink rose on a thick shoulder strap and a chain around her waist. What looked like a knife in a scabbard hung from the chain, covered with so many jewels, it had to be a prop.

She seemed to be waiting for Janet to speak.

"I, um, am, Gleason. Janet. Janet Gleason."

The chestnut eyes widened. The smile grew. "Janet, is it? You must be

Ambassador Gleason's granddaughter. I'm so glad to meet you."

Why was everyone so glad to meet her? Yes, the Irish were friendly, but her reception tonight seemed over the top. Still, she *was* being welcomed.

Her initial surprise at stumbling across the princess gave way to an image of Gram tapping her chin. Janet affected a smile, though she only had to pretend for a moment. Something about Princess Talty put her instantly at ease.

Talty extended fingers with clear polished nails and a gold ring whose opal reflected the blue-green tones in her dress. As they shook hands, her head slanted to one side, and she frowned. "Are you all right, Janet?"

"Oh, yes. I've been exploring and popped in to check the place out. I didn't expect to find anyone in here."

"Exploring, are you? I'll give you a proper tour sometime."

Excitement rippled through Janet. A tour from a princess who lived in a castle! Lots of castles, from what Matti had said. "I'd love that. Having so many different homes must be fabulous. Do you have a favorite?"

Talty's eyes glazed in thought. "Not really. They all have different moods, y'see. The King's Residence is the main place, old but up-to-date. Glensheelin is an old manor house in the country, a grand place for riding horses and hill walking. We have several such places to visit, but Clontarf is special. Being here makes me feel like I'm living back in time. That's why I thought I'd wear this dagger." She patted the knife at her waist. "Do you like it?"

Janet wasn't sure, but she thought it polite to say yes. "Oh, yes. Is it real?"

"It is indeed." Talty slid the knife from the sheath and held it up. "The steel protects you from the fairies. You stick it in the door frame"—she vigorously mimed doing so—"and they can't get in."

"That's…great." *This family is absolutely nuts.*

"What have you seen of the castle?"

"Not much. I got lost and was headed toward the cellar. I met Neil and Aidan."

"Ah, good lads. They went down to see the steel."

Janet was afraid to ask. "Steel?"

Talty picked up the chain she'd set on the counter. "Yes. We're only after finding it. A hoard of it put away by our great-grandfather. That's where I found the dagger. It belonged to an ancestor, a queen called Evlin."

Who used it to keep the fairies away. Right. But Janet had read some of Matti's fairytales at bedtime the night before. She could see how a person, especially a lifelong resident of Ireland, might think the creatures were real. Most likely, Talty was simply being playful. She seemed too intelligent to believe in fairies.

Janet changed the subject. "Why do you all wear roses...what should I call you? Princess? You're too young to be a ma'am, and 'miss' just seems wrong."

Silvery laughter pealed through the lounge. "Good woman yourself, Janet. Formally, I'm Your Highness, but the 'jacks' is hardly formal. My friends call me Talty, and I'm thinkin' we'll be great friends."

"I'd like that—Talty."

"There, wasn't that easy? I came in here on my way up front to help the old fellas greet the guests." She tossed the chain in her hand. "My necklace came loose. The clasp is bollixed. It'll hold through dinner, but it won't make it past the first dance. Come upstairs with me till I get another, and we'll have a lovely chat."

Janet doubted her grandparents would miss her. "All right."

The paneled confines of the elevator intensified the spicy fragrance from the rose on Talty's shoulder strap. Again, Janet wondered about the roses the boys and their fathers wore.

"That flower really smells great," she said.

"Ah, the roses. You did ask about them. They're selected for each member of the royal family at birth. In fact, when my brother and cousins and I were growing up, our parents called us a band of roses. They still do. A horticulturist bred mine specially." Talty touched the pink rose. "He called it the 'Princess Taillte.' Original, eh? Neil's is the Ace of Hearts, Aidan's the Yellow Rascal. Spot on names for both lads. My brother's is the Alba, an off-white hybrid tea." She gazed thoughtfully at Janet. "Have you met Liam yet?"

"No. I heard he had an accident. My grandfather wasn't sure he'd be here tonight."

"He's here, poor fella. He fell and hurt his arm. He's a little slow, our Liam, but he's a good boy. We do our best to be kind to him. You'll try to put up with him for one night, eh?"

A total geek, Matti had said. Maybe he was one of those idiot savants or something. Janet started to dread the rest of the evening. If only Matti could be here!

She had emailed that afternoon and said everything was okay. Maybe when she came back to visit, Janet would be friendly enough with Talty to ask her to show Matti the castle too.

The elevator doors opened. Janet followed Talty down a wide hall straight out of a Robin Hood movie. Modern touches like lighting and fire doors melded beautifully with the medieval decor.

Talty explained that she and her brother and parents had rooms in this wing of the castle. "My parents' suite is at the end of the hall. They'll be down later, after everyone arrives." She chuckled. "My father takes forever to get his sash on straight."

They stopped at a door of vertical planks with wide black hinges patterned like rambling roses. Talty tapped an electronic keypad on the doorframe. Something clicked, and she twisted the doorknob and turned on the lights.

Janet followed her into a short entrance hall thick with the perfume of flowers. To her left, a vase of Talty's pink roses sat on a pedestal in a small arched alcove.

The princess hurried into the bedroom. Janet lingered shyly in the hall, breathing in the roses, loving the way her feet sank into the carpet. To her right, her blue-gowned reflection shimmered in a floor-to-ceiling mirror with an elaborate gold frame. Beside the mirror sat a green velvet armchair and a potted floor plant with thick broad leaves.

"Come in, Janet. Have you seen much of Dublin?"

"A little." Describing her bus tours with Matti and the sightseeing drives with her grandparents, Janet drifted dreamlike toward a four-poster bed with a lacy white canopy. A folded green blanket lay across the white bedspread. An assortment of accent pillows matched not only the blanket, but also a pair of identical antique chairs set between two recessed windows. Just above the green and pink-flowered drapes, the wall bent sharply toward the ceiling. Talty really did seem to be living back in time.

Then Janet noticed more modern touches. A contemporary sofa and chairs in the sitting area faced a flat-screen television nestled above the fireplace. An electric kettle and tea things sat on a wet bar just like the one in Gramp's study. Shelves beneath the bar held a mini fridge and a microwave. A glance into the bathroom revealed a modern shower and what Janet guessed was a sauna. Across the bedroom, a vintage desk displayed a laptop and telephone.

"You've been busy," Talty called from her walk-in closet. "What about schools? Where will you go?"

Janet wondered briefly why the princess had no maid to help her. "Hazelwood College. We went to see it earlier this week. I'm going to study drama there. Do you know it?"

Talty emerged from the closet fastening a single strand of pearls around her neck. "Yes, I do. Several of my cousins and friends have attended Hazelwood. It's a grand school, and there's no better place on earth than Ireland if you're doing theater arts. You'll love it. Have you been up to Howth?"

She'd snuck in the question so fast, Janet blinked. Why would she ask that? Janet hated the place. She never wanted to see it again. "Yes. It's pretty."

"Now that's one of my favorite places. My uncle lives there in a fine old house called Garrymuir. Right at the top of the cliffs. Almost as big as Clontarf Castle. Plenty of room for dancing." She checked herself in the mirror over her bureau. "My aide has gone to supper, but I think she'd approve of the pearls. My parents will be going down soon, or I'd make you a cup of tea. I'd love one myself. We won't be eating for hours."

Janet's head spun from the lively discourse. She eyed the electric kettle. "Sorry, but wouldn't a princess send for tea?"

That silvery laugh again. "Not this one. It takes too long to get here, especially when the kitchen staff is up to their eyes preparing a banquet. I wouldn't dream of bothering them now. Well, we're ready to go, but I think you should meet my brother first. It will make it so much easier when they introduce you downstairs."

He must really be an embarrassment. Janet forced her tightened lips into a smile. "I'd like that, Talty."

"Grand. He's just next door. I'll have him come straight over." She picked up the telephone.

CHAPTER THIRTY-TWO

Contacts in, jacket on, Liam braced himself for the odious black sling. Ross had cleverly fashioned the thing from specially ordered material that matched Liam's suit. Yet no matter how Ross and Kevin positioned the vile encumbrance, the cloth drove Liam's new steel watch into his injured wrist.

The watch had to go. So did the bracelet, which kept slipping onto the heel of his hand from beneath the cuff of his shirt. Confident that the stainless steel ring was enough to protect him, and doubting he required any protection at all in Clontarf Castle, he returned the watch and bracelet to his jewelry drawer.

The necklace he was to present to Ambassador Gleason's granddaughter was there too, beside Janet's locket. He'd placed the locket in the drawer when he changed for the dance.

If it stood up to the old hag's necklace, it's a potent thing on its own. Keep it with you for good luck, Li.

Heeding Talty's advice, he slipped the gold chain into his jacket pocket and stood before his mirror. "I look like a feckin' eejit! Between the sling and my forehead, I'll frighten every dog and devil in the castle. I'm within an aim's ace of staying up here for the night."

Aided by Ross, Kevin slipped back into his dinner jacket. "And miss all the fun? You'll have the ladies fussing all over you, Li. Thank you, Ross."

"My pleasure, sir." Ross brushed something from Kevin's shoulder and whirled toward Liam for a final inspection. "You look roguishly mysterious, sir. I expect the ladies will lavish you with attention. The sympathy factor and all."

Liam scowled at Ross. "The grannies will lavish. The pretty young ones will abandon me for the likes of Kevin."

The telephone on the desk jingled quietly, as if reluctant to further upset its owner. Liam reached for the handset. "And don't think I don't see the two of yez smirking at each other like a pair of constipated hyenas!" Regretting his outburst, he thanked Ross for his help, told him to go have his supper, and picked up the phone. "Hello?"

"Hi, it's me. Are you ready to head downstairs?"

Liam envied the self-assured snap in Talty's voice. He wished he felt so confident. "I'm as ready as I'll ever be, sling and all," he said, watching Ross leave the room.

"Come next door. I want to see you before we go down. Bye."

A muted pop signaled the end of the call. Liam set the phone down. Talty's summons wasn't unusual. They often compared notes before a public dance, exchanging gossip and warnings. And he wanted to see what she'd think of the sling. Maybe she'd feel sorry for him and encourage him to skip the whole affair. "Talty wants me. I'll meet you downstairs."

"I'm not going down by myself," Kevin said. "I'll wait for you here." Fastidious in his finery, he sat on the edge of the sofa and poked through a medley of magazines.

Liam had hardly knocked when Talty opened her door. As always, she glowed in her party trappings. The jeweled hilt at her waist caught his eye right off. "You look savage wearing that thing, Lady Sister. The fellas will be afraid to dance with you."

"Then I'll dance with you," she said, eyeing him up and down. "We'll make a fine pair. You look like a pirate in that sling. Come in, Li. The American ambassador's granddaughter is here. I want you to meet her before we go downstairs."

He nearly turned and left. Why would Talty do this to him? Suppressing a groan before it escaped, he followed her into the suite's main room.

"Liam, I'd like you to meet Janet Gleason. Janet, my brother, Liam Boru."

The gown and hairdo confused him at first. She seemed just as confused. Neither spoke, and the charged silence gave him a moment to study the face of the girl he'd known as Janet Smith. His heart leapt so high, he might have been airborne.

She in turn gawked at him. Her shocked expression quickly turned to a vicious, lip-curling sneer. "You! You sleazy crud! Crawled out from under your rock, huh?"

Somehow, Liam kept from laughing. "Hello, Janet."

She raised her shaking fists. "Don't 'Hello Janet' me, you scumbag!"

Talty tensed, prepared to defend him if necessary. At least he hoped so. But she seemed more amused than worried. "You've an interesting way with the women, Li. Don't stand there grinning like a gobsmacked eejit. Speak to the girl before she has you wearing two slings."

"I don't want him to speak to me!" Janet's voice wavered with seething fury. Her glare threatened to incinerate him. "*You're* a prince? Prince Pickpocket! Do you have a klepto problem, Mr. Prince? Why did you steal my locket?"

A ripple of sadness for what she thought failed to dampen his joy at seeing her. He would set things right between them, and all would be well. "I didn't steal it. I've been trying to find you to give it back. The whole thing was a mistake. A misunderstanding."

"It was a mistake, all right!" Her right arm flew back as if she planned to launch a roundhouse swing at him.

Hands raised, Talty rushed between them. "No, Janet! He's telling the truth! He fell off the cliff the day he was with you. That's how he hurt himself. He didn't run off. He was hurt and couldn't climb back up to you."

Bewilderment softened Janet's rage. "He fell off the cliff?" Her eyelids fluttered as she took in Liam's appearance. "Oh. Oh, Liam. You fell off the cliff?"

Talty relaxed. "I told you he was slow," she said, smiling. Then the smile disappeared. "Please, Janet. Sit. We want to tell you what really happened, though I don't know as you'll believe us."

Pale and trembling, Janet collapsed onto the leather sofa before the hearth. Liam sat beside her, close but not too close.

Talty drew a bottle of water from the mini fridge and poured it into a glass. She sat on the couch opposite them and handed the glass to Janet. "Here, Janet, have a sip of this. Do you remember a sapphire necklace?"

Janet took a hefty swallow and held the glass in her lap, staring at the water as if she were reading a crystal ball. "Yes. A woman named Nora let me try it on with my dress at Louise's shop. When I went back for the final fitting, Louise said she didn't know her."

A quick lift of Talty's head hinted at her less than approving opinion of

Nora. "I'm thinking you met this Nora before you went to the dress shop. Where did you first see her?"

"Out on the street. I bumped into her accidentally." She glanced at Liam and blushed.

She had to be thinking about their collision in Temple Bar. "You bumped into *me* accidentally," he said, not quite restraining the smile that twitched at his lips. "Nora crashed into you altogether on purpose."

"But why?" A sob choked off Janet's question. Her eyes glistened.

"Oh, you mustn't cry!" said Talty. "Not only will there be photographers downstairs, but everyone will give Liam a good larrupin' if they think he upset you."

Janet almost smiled. She set the glass on the coffee table. "Matti and I were going to the dress shop. I said I didn't want to go to the ball because I couldn't dance. Matti said you got what you wished for in Ireland, so I wished I could dance."

"And right after that, the old woman crashed into you." Liam pictured the loathsome creature stalking this innocent girl.

"Yes. She said 'No harm' and went on her way, and we found the dress shop. Louise said she'd have someone bring me some costume jewelry. When Nora came in, I was surprised that she worked there, but I didn't think anything of it."

"Why should you?" Talty sounded calm, but an angry flush had crept over her face. "So she gave you this necklace to try on. Did she say anything about it?"

"Yes. That it was a wishing necklace. She said it was only a legend, but if you made a wish while wearing it close to your heart, your wish would come true."

"And again," Liam said, "you wished you could dance."

"Yes." Janet cast pleading glances at Talty and Liam in turn. "Did I do something wrong?"

Talty reached across the table and patted Janet's hand. "Absolutely not. Did you ever see the necklace again?"

Forehead furrowed, Janet thought hard. She finally shook her head.

"I saw it on Howth Hill," said Liam. "Nora was there with it. She fastened it around your neck, Jan. Do you remember?"

"I...I think I do, but I'm not sure."

Liam envisioned his hands around Finvarra's throat. "Do you remember hearing music?"

"Yes. I wanted to find out where it came from, but you pulled my hair and stole my locket." Her lips quivered alarmingly. "At least that's what I thought. What really happened?"

"Nora's real name is Becula. She's a…" Liam couldn't finish what he was going to say. He looked to Talty for support.

She didn't disappoint him. "This Nora…Becula…she's a…a fairy."

The color drained from Janet's cheeks. Her eyes grew round and glassy. "I think I should go. You people are—"

"A little nutty?" Talty said, her tone soft with kind understanding. "Maybe, but not about this. I tried a few times to see if you remembered anything, but it seems the Good Folk have taken measures to ensure that you don't. I'm sorry for it, but I'm afraid it's all true. They wanted you to dance with their king. Liam went after you and brought you back."

Janet eyed the door, undoubtedly thinking of making a break for it. Liam would have. Doubting he'd see her again after tonight, he reached into his pocket. "At least let me give this back to you, Janet. I really have been trying to find you to do just that."

The locket swung in his grasp. Wide-eyed with disbelief, she reached for it. He put it in the palm of her hand, closed her fingers around it, and kissed them. "I am sorry for all of it, Jan."

She opened the locket. Wistfully, reverently, she stared at its contents and closed it again.

"Your parents?" asked Talty.

Janet didn't respond. She seemed in shock, gasping for breath, clasping the chain with both hands, blinking and whimpering miserably.

Talty looked as worried as Liam felt. What was happening? What should they do? What *could* they do?

"It *did* happen!" Janet cried, focused on something only she could see. "I remember it all now. Nora and those strange people. And *him!*" She raised her head, viewing Liam through rapidly moistening eyes. "You were there, Liam. In the tunnels. You got me away from them. You saved me!"

"So the magic from the necklace did rub off on the locket," Talty murmured.

Liam shook his head. "That locket has its own magic, Tal."

"The fairies are real." Janet's hand suddenly shot to her mouth. "That woman. The one who turned to dust. She said he'd come after you, Liam.

What will we do?"

Smiling slyly at Liam, Talty mouthed the word *we*. "Don't worry about Liam." She slapped the knife at her waist. "Remember my dagger? Steel stops the fairies, and Liam has tons of steel, don't you, Li?"

"I do." Liam affected his finest expression of saintly innocence. "Why, I put on a neck chain, a watch, and a bracelet only a little while ago. And I have this ring." He turned his hand to display his new diamond and onyx steel ring. "As for you, Janet Gleason, I doubt the fairies have any sway over you without that sapphire necklace."

"Where is it?"

Reviewing the high points, Liam recapped the whole tale, from his struggle to climb the hill to the consequences of casting Becula's necklace into the sea.

Janet touched the black sling. "You nearly got killed. Oh, Liam."

They stared at each other as if an invisible string connected their eyes. Liam bent his head to kiss her.

Before he could, Talty jumped to her feet and clapped her hands together. "So! We should be getting downstairs, I think."

Rapping sounded from the hall. "Come in," she called, and the door opened. "Howya, Kev."

"You're lookin' lovely, as usual, Tal." Kevin strode into the room with a lopsided grin on his face. "My father called. Your parents are ready to make their grand entrance. We're all to come down. Hey there, Janet. You're lookin' lovely too. How's it goin'?"

Liam jumped to his feet, outraged that Janet's presence was no surprise to his cousin. "You knew she was here?"

"Sure. We all did. The old fellas thought it would be gas to have the two of you meet in front of everyone. Talty thought you'd rather get reacquainted more privately first. I was to keep you busy while she found Janet."

"But Janet found me first," said Talty.

Despite the shock she'd just endured, a soft smile glowed on Janet's face. She shook her head in admiration. "And I thought I was a good actress."

Talty chuckled. "All right, you two. Kevin and I will wait by the lift. You have two minutes. Do be watchful of his arm there, Janet," she said in her teasing tone, and she turned toward the door.

Liam intercepted her. He'd have hugged her if he could. Instead, he caught her hand and kissed it. "Thanks, Tal."

She bussed his cheek. "Two minutes, Li."

The door shut, leaving Liam and Janet alone. From the look in her eyes, he guessed that if not for the sling, she'd have jumped on him.

"Oh, Liam. I'm so sorry."

"For what? None of it was your fault."

"But I thought such awful things about you! And I'm afraid."

Damn the feckin' sling! "There's no reason to be afraid now, Jan."

"I'm remembering more. He came to the house."

Liam's head jerked. "To Deerfield House? Finvarra?"

She slowly repeated the name. "Yes. The King of the Fairies. Matti saw him too. We hit him with blackthorn canes, and he left. I forgot all about it till now. He called me an evil hellcat and said he only wanted to dance."

How had he found her? Either he'd retrieved the necklace, or the witch had devised some other means of tracking Janet down. Struggling to hide his concern, Liam touched her cheek. "I expect he'll think twice before tangling with you again, hellcat. Still and all, I don't think it would hurt to keep this in your purse." He slipped the ring from his finger and pressed it into her hand.

She tried to give it back. "No. You need it more."

"I have other things. Besides, we're safe here. Take it."

Lifting her purse from the sofa, she slid both the ring and her locket inside. She snapped the purse shut and slung the thin velvet strap over her shoulder. "I know I'm safe with you, Liam." She beamed at him adoringly.

He didn't deserve such devotion, but his father hadn't raised a complete eejit. Thinking the fairies had nothing on the spell a mortal girl could cast, he caught her in a one-armed hug and smoothly pulled her closer. She cupped his cheeks in her hands.

The minty taste of whatever was on her lips melted him. He kissed her again and again, tenderly sealing their reconciliation, losing himself in the process.

At last, she nudged him away. "We should go," she whispered.

He couldn't speak, couldn't move, the room was reeling so. And then the spinning quickly calmed, a carnival ride come to an end.

For now.

Fingers entwined, they strolled down the hall to the lift.

CHAPTER THIRTY-THREE

The elevator seemed to descend on a lazy cloud. Content in the glow of Liam's kisses, Janet held tight to his hand. So many things suddenly made sense: her nightmares, her befuddling reaction to Clontarf Castle's torches and music, even the odd feelings she'd experienced reading Matti's fairytales. The pieces had fit into place at last, thanks to her newfound friends. Gazing fondly at them now, she supposed she'd always envision Talty Boru as a formally clad princess. Liam and Kevin, however, would forever live in Janet's heart as two scruffy boys in hooded sweatshirts and jeans.

"You guys look so different in tuxedos," she said dreamily.

Kevin glanced up, torn from whatever he'd been pondering. "In our what?"

Liam squeezed her hand. "We call them dinner jackets on this side of the Atlantic. Tuxedo is an Americanism. Comes from *tucseto*, a Native American word used to describe a lake in New York. It means 'clear flowing water.' In the late nineteenth century, a wealthy bunch of fellas built a private country club in the area. They named it Tuxedo Park to keep the local flavor. The dinner jackets the members wore became known as tuxedos."

Kevin's face scrunched in disbelief. "Where do you pick up this feckin' stuff?"

Liam shrugged. "Ross told me."

Talty laughed. "You look quite stunning yourself, Janet. I've been admiring your necklace. Is it topaz?"

"Yes. A gift from my grandmother for attending my first royal ball."

"And not your last, we hope," said the serene Lady Princess as the elevator bobbed to a stop. The doors whooshed open; the occupants stepped out. "Isn't her necklace lovely, Liam?" Talty spoke distinctly and deliberately, arching her eyebrows as if willing him to understand her. Did she really think her brother was slow?

Oddly flustered, Liam released Janet's hand. "Yes. It's great. I, um, I forgot something. Wait here with Janet while I run up and get it, will you? I'll be right back."

He returned to the elevator. The doors closed, and the lighted red arrows above them pointed up.

* * * * *

Liam yanked open his jewelry drawer. What a dunce he'd been to forget the necklace! And he'd been a right dolt altogether for grousing over his mother's request to present it to the "spoiled American girl." Now he couldn't wait.

With the velvet box secure in his pocket, he jogged back to the lift and pushed the ground floor button. The doors whispered shut; the lift started down.

Liam leaned against the brass hand rail watching the numbers on the display board change: four, three, two, one. As each floor passed, he grew giddier. Soon he'd hold Janet's hand again.

The "G" for the ground floor appeared. He straightened to exit the lift.

But the lift didn't stop at the ground floor.

It went all the way to the basement.

* * * * *

The elevator's arrow lights pointed down. Between them, bright red numbers plotted its descent. Remembering that the second floor was the first floor in Ireland, Janet held her breath until the "G" for the ground floor appeared.

Kevin gazed at the display and frowned. "Why is he going to the cellar?"

Talty smiled. "The one-armed wonder probably hit the wrong button. He'll be back in a sec."

They waited. The elevator didn't move. Kevin pushed the call button. Nothing happened.

Kevin and Talty appeared unconcerned, but icy hands of fear squeezed

Janet, one cold finger at a time.

Liam is in danger...

"It's Finvarra! He's after Liam!"

"Not likely," Talty said. "Probably a malfunction in the lift. He'll be coming up the stairs any minute." She glanced toward the back of the corridor, from where her cousins, Neil and Aidan, had emerged and greeted Janet not so long ago.

No one came down the corridor. Talty's forced smile failed to mask her concern. "Don't worry, Janet. Even if it is Finvarra, Liam has his steel, the chain and the watch and the bracelet."

"No, he doesn't," Kevin said. "He did, but he took them off because they were uncomfortable."

"What? I'll beat the lard out of him! At least he has his ring. He showed it to us."

"He gave it to me." Janet patted the evening bag slung over her shoulder. "It's here in my purse." Her voice sounded like someone else's voice, high-pitched and trembling. "We have to help him!"

Skirts whirling, fists clenched, Talty paced in tiny circles. "I'm sure he's fine. Some botheration with the lift is all." Her businesslike tone held no trace of her former friendliness. Abruptly, the pacing stopped. She stood face to face with Kevin. "Just in case, go find your father and Kieran and get them back here doing ninety!"

Mouth crimped tight, Kevin nodded and sprinted away.

"We can't wait for them!" Janet started for the cellar door.

Talty grabbed her arm. "We have to wait. We don't know what we're up against, and they have weapons. They'll come flying, don't worry."

Only you can save him...

"Let me go!" Janet shoved Talty hard.

The princess grunted and stumbled against the wall. Before she could recover, Janet ripped the dagger from the hilt at her waist and bolted toward the cellar stairs.

* * * * *

Why the devil had the lift gone to the cellar? The staff wouldn't need it now. The wretched thing was probably banjaxed again. It couldn't have acted up at a worse time, with the castle full of guests.

Liam stabbed at the silver keypad. The mechanical hooligan failed to respond. Thoroughly vexed, he mashed his thumb against the "Door

Open" button. He'd have to take the stairs and report the breakdown to the service staff.

The doors parted. He stomped into the dimly lit hall. The cool cellar air felt downright chilly against his angry cheeks, no doubt because he was all dressed up and more than a tad annoyed.

A whiff of something akin to acrid air before a storm made him wrinkle his nose. Assuming the odor came from the kitchen, he turned toward the staircase, hurrying to make up the time he'd lost.

The stairs should have been on the other side of the Garden of Eden tapestry. They weren't, nor did Liam see the red exit light. Had someone moved the tapestry?

A few steps on, the Unicorn tapestry told him he'd nearly reached the wine cellar. He'd gone too far. He turned back, but the stairs weren't where they ought to be. Had he taken a wrong turn? Peeved that he had no cell phone with him, he returned to the lift in hopes it might be working now.

A solid wall had replaced the door to the lift. Before he could think what it meant, a rat ran across his path, pausing as if to say hello before skittering off and dissolving clean into the opposite wall.

Goosebumps broke out on Liam's arms and neck. He glanced around, stunned to see that the corridor stretched before him impossibly long with not a door in sight.

"Oh no," he muttered, trying to gulp down the lump of dread that threatened to burst in his throat.

Illusion, it's all an illusion. The doors are still here…

He ran his suddenly clammy hand along the wall to find the lift. The stone was cold and solid—but he'd just come through it, hadn't he?

They'd miss him upstairs and start looking for him, wouldn't they?

…at certain times, certain places belong to Them…

He had to get to the steel, and fast. Where was the drawbridge room from here? He ran, recalling that he and Talty and Kevin had taken a right at the French hunting tapestry.

Liam already knew that the "Other Crowd's" magic lacked power these days. That seemed to be the case here. Whatever spell had bewitched the place, the wall hangings seemed impervious. They were still on the walls, marking the way. Reassured by the sight of them, he vowed to grab a fistful of steel and pound his way through one of the fairy-enchanted doors.

As his footsteps thumped on the woolen runner, another idea occurred to him. If he reached the hunting tapestry, he could get to the chapel behind it. The stairway hidden beside the altar would get him upstairs in jig time.

But the faster he ran, the longer the passageway grew. Or so it appeared. Still, he kept an eye on the wall to his left. Moments later, the holy water font appeared, a tiny bump that gradually grew in size. Relieved, he slowed as he neared it, breathless as much from fear as from running. The tapestry hung beside the font, but the corridor that should be across from them wasn't there.

What if the doorway behind the rug was gone as well? Liam prayed that the fairies hadn't known about the door, that they'd missed it when they'd cast their spell. He hurried toward the tapestry.

"You called me a worm..."

Liam froze. He had felt more than heard the low-pitched voice purring with smug satisfaction. Apparently Finnie the Worm had witnessed the search for the steel in the hidden chamber. Liam suspected he'd never reach the chapel in time to escape. He pivoted to confront the fairy king. "Spying on us? That sounds like your style. Afraid of honest dialogue."

No one was there.

"I'm not playing this game!" he shouted, and grabbed the edge of the tapestry.

A potent shock flew up his arm to his shoulder. He cried out in pain. Unable to use his sling-bound hand to rub his burning fingers, he tucked them under his arm. As the stinging subsided, he studied the hallway, peering into the gloom, first right, then left.

Standing nearby in the subdued light, a transparent man peered back at him through glowing, electric-blue eyes. Liam stared transfixed as the white-cloaked figure grew solid.

"So here we are, Prince Liam Conor Boru." Finvarra took his time oozing out the words. His golden hair flowed in waves to his shoulders. He looked tall and youthful, not much older than Liam, and might even have passed for handsome if not for the malice pervading the air around him.

A cold sweat broke out on Liam's forehead. He was trapped, and the self-defense moves he'd learned would be useless here. Furious that he'd landed in this predicament, he boldly squared his shoulders. "I'd give you a nasty look, but you already have one. What do you want?"

"You, dear prince. I intend to put your eyes out for seeing what you had no right to see, but I'm in no hurry. Let's play a little first, shall we?" The fairy king raised his sparking fingers.

Liam ducked, but not in time. A bolt of pain shot through his chest. Teeth clenched, he dropped to his knees, unable to speak and gasping for breath.

Grinning like a cunning shark, Finvarra closed in on him.

* * * * *

Ignoring Talty's shouted commands to stop, Janet picked up her skirt and ran. Knife in hand, she hurtled down the stairs straight into a transparent wall. She tried to push her way through, but the rubbery membrane barred her way.

Liam had said a similar barrier or force field prevented him from climbing the hill on Howth Head, until he stayed low and outwitted whatever it was. Janet had no time to seek an opening, if one existed at all. Clenching the dagger in both hands, she slashed and chopped at the phantom wall. The pressure gave way so fast, she stumbled into the gloomy corridor.

She spotted a bank of light switches on the wall beside the staircase. A few quick flips and the hall lit up. She held her breath and listened, straining to hear above the pounding pulse in her ears.

Men's voices grumbled to her left. With the dagger firmly in her grasp, she ran toward them, calling Liam's name.

* * * * *

Liam rolled, barely avoiding the second attack. His back slammed into the wall. The move tortured his sprained arm, but a sprained arm wouldn't kill him.

Finvarra would.

Silently cursing his trembling hands and knees, Liam considered his options for escape. What a fool he'd been to forego the steel! Yet he drew hope from the frustration etched on Finvarra's face. If he could distract the featherbrained fairy, perhaps he could stall for time until someone came to his rescue.

"Don't you gougers ever think about consequences? My father will flatten your feckin' forts for this."

Finvarra's eyes narrowed with contempt. "Let him try. As for you, *Your Highness*, you spoiled my dance. You can't escape. You're mine."

"You're not my type, you and your magical muggery. Even with one arm, I'd throttle you in a fair fight."

"And with no arms?" Finvarra raised his hands again.

Liam tore the velvet case from his pocket and lobbed it. Good shot, he thought. He'd struck Finvarra's gut, if fairies had guts, and he hoped it hurt like hell.

A burst of white light incinerated the case and its contents.

Sorry, Mum.

He had to get into the chapel. Propelling himself to his knees, he staggered to his feet and leaned against the wall between the tapestry and the pewter font. Too bad it wasn't steel.

Prepared for another shock, he tore one-handed at the tapestry. Nothing zapped him. Tossing the case at Finvarra must have interfered with the spell he'd cast on the rug.

And the door was there. Liam nearly shouted for joy.

Behind him, Finvarra bellowed. An ominous sizzle followed the roar. Liam dropped an instant before a blinding fairy blast zapped the wall above him. He had to zap back, and fast. What else could he throw? He had no steel, no blackthorn stick, no four-leaf clovers...

Liam Conor Boru, you are a feckin' eejit!

His heart galloped. He'd need both hands. The sling was over his head and on the floor in seconds. His desperate grip on the holy water font triggered razor-sharp pains in his wrist. Waves of dizzying nausea nearly undid him, but somehow he wrenched the font from the wall. Aiming to kill, he hurled it as hard as he could.

The pewter missile struck Finvarra's chest, splashing him with holy water. His horrific howls echoed through the corridor.

As the fairy writhed in a ghastly dance, the hall regained its normal appearance. Finvarra became his aging, grizzle-faced self. The holy water had apparently crossed the wires that powered his glimmer.

"See you 'round, Finnie." Liam turned the latch on the door to the chapel.

It was locked.

The overhead lights in the hall came on.

"Liam! Liam, where are you?"

Janet!

She was barreling toward him, her face a furious mask at odds with her elegant ballroom gear. "Go back, Jan!" he shouted, his voice raw with fear for her safety. "Get out of here!" He ran toward her, thinking to protect her, for all the good he could do.

Finvarra tackled him to the ground. He landed on his injured arm and screamed.

* * * * *

Finvarra leapt and tackled Prince Liam. They grappled and rolled, and the prince cried out in pain at the blow to his damaged arm.

Finvarra's blazing wrath alone had dried his soaked attire, but the bite of the fiendish fluid lingered. What had possessed the insolent mortal to throw the priest-water at him? The boy should have sprinkled it on himself. Finvarra would have avoided him, at least until the wicked elixir evaporated. The mortals were such an inconsiderate lot. Barbarians at best.

Did Prince Liam really think he could simply run away? One good blast would mow him down, but Finvarra's battle frenzy induced him to fight hand to hand. He meant to savor the boy's distress at the imminent loss of his eyes.

"A fair fight, boy. That's what you said. Fight me now, if you dare."

"The devil swallow you sideways, fairy!"

For a mortal who wasn't a warrior, he put up a dandy fight. More than one of his desperate blows whacked Finvarra's shoulder and back. He began to enjoy the sport until a mortal knee painfully jammed his hip and reminded him of the vengeance he sought.

Invoking glimmer to increase his size and weight, he knelt on Liam's chest and made a "V" of his fingers. Liam Conor Boru wouldn't be the first mortal he'd blinded. "My face will be the last thing you see, pup."

"Leave him alone or I'll kill you!"

Finvarra sensed the presence of steel before he saw the dagger. He warily eyed the hellcat who'd pummeled him with the blackthorn stick. She held the knife awkwardly, clearly unused to wielding the weapon, though that didn't matter: even a nick would prove fatal to him.

He backed away from the gasping prince. "Your steel may keep me at bay, but it cannot stop my magic. I have you both now. Neither of you will leave this place until I settle the score."

"Settle this, pal!" Brandishing the dagger, the girl charged at him.

He quickly retreated into invisibility, sadly shouting, "I only wanted to dance!"

CHAPTER THIRTY-FOUR

Keeping one eye on the seemingly empty hallway, Janet knelt beside Liam. His contorted face and rapid breathing alarmed her. She should call for help, but she didn't know how. All she could do was try to protect him from further harm. Dagger in hand, she opened her purse, fished for the ring he'd given her, and slipped it on his finger.

His responding smile was more of a pitiful grimace, but his breathing slowed, and a tad of color returned to his cheeks. "Giving back my ring so soon? Was it my boorish behavior or the homicidal fairy chasing after me?"

"Joke later. We have to get out of here before he comes back. Can you get up?"

He surprised her with a quick twist and a powerful spring that had him standing over her. Like a bird of prey with a broken wing, he held his damaged arm to his side. His good arm reached for her. "I'm thinking I'll need a new rose for my lapel."

The struggle with Finvarra had left the poor white rose crushed beyond hope, but Liam's skewed arm concerned her more. She plucked the black sling from the floor. "You'll need this too," she said, taking the proffered hand that pulled her easily to her feet.

"Not as much as I need my eyes. They might not be perfect, but I'm fond of them." He swept her fingers to his lips. "Thanks, Jan."

She stood on her toes and kissed him. "Anytime. Come on, let's get that rose."

* * * * *

"Finvarra! Where have you been?" Oona whirled from the gilt-edged mirror in the outpost's private chamber. Her pouting lips and flashing eyes grew to enormous circles. "What happened to you?"

"Nothing a little glimmer won't fix." In no mood for questions, he stomped past her to a well-stocked table and poured himself a goblet of wine. One sip brightened his spirits. Two, and he sat in contented bliss. Three, and he nearly forgot Prince Liam Boru and his vixen.

Nearly.

Finvarra would let them think they'd escaped. Their false hope would make it all the sweeter when he caught them at last and trapped them forever in the castle cellars. "You look positively divine, Oona. You've applied your glimmer quite artfully."

"And you're a slick rogue. I haven't fixed my face yet. I just finished charming my hair."

Whatever she'd done, she looked younger. More like the Oona he saw in his mind when he thought of her. "Looking forward to dancing, pet?"

She glowed like a firefly. "Yes. I can't wait. It's been ages since we attended a mortal ball. I hear the contemporary men are quite handsome, and you'll enjoy the ladies, no doubt."

A fleeting image came to him of Treasa Boru laughing and spinning in his arms, her hair adorned with May flowers and bronzed by the light of a *Bealtaine* bonfire. Yes, he would dance with Princess Talty, the girl who so resembled Treasa, but he had business to finish first.

He drained his glass and conjured a change of clothing. "I'll meet you and the troop near the stairway, Oona. I must see to something before we go."

* * * * *

As he had in their mad dash beneath Howth Head, Liam held fast to Janet's hand. She matched his rapid pace this time, outrunning him twice in her press to escape the cellar. On guard for fairy traps, he pulled her back both times.

The corridor, bright in the overhead lights, appeared normal. The red exit sign glowed over the stairway as it should. Still, the closer they drew to the stairs, the more Liam worried. When they reached the lift, which had reappeared and looked as it always had, he stopped.

Janet yanked his hand. "You're not taking the elevator?!"

"I'm not going anywhere near it. I doubt I'll ever ride the dodgy old gouger again. I'm just wondering why no one is down here looking for us."

"Maybe they can't get through the barrier."

"That's my point, Jan. Why would a barrier still be in place if Finvarra is letting us go?"

Her face hardened. She raised the dagger. "This got me in. It will get us out. Come on."

Heartened by her confidence, and daring to hope they'd soon be free, Liam approached the stairs with her. A blast of hot air melted his hope, though it didn't surprise him.

He pulled her hand hard. "Stop, Jan."

"What's wrong?"

Before he could say he didn't know, flames engulfed the stairway.

"It's not real!" Janet cried. "It's not burning anything. We can run right through it!"

Liam snatched the sling from her and tossed it into the flames. The cloth ignited with a whoosh and disappeared in a flurry of sparks.

"Oh no! Oh, Liam, what will we do?"

Speed was their only chance. "Get to the kitchen, and fast!"

They ran past the Unicorn tapestry. The wine cellar should be just ahead.

It was. The door hung open, as it would during a party.

"You can't escape my magic…"

A ball of blue-white light whizzed past them. The corridor beyond them erupted in flames. Janet shrieked. Seeing no other way out, Liam tugged her into the wine cellar. They could reach the kitchen through the butler's pantry.

Breathing hard, she released his hand and turned toward the doorway, apparently inspecting it. Abruptly, she snarled like a cornered dog and stuck the dagger into the wooden doorjamb. "Stay away from us if you know what's good for you!" she shouted.

Despite their predicament, Liam grinned. "You're a fierce woman, Janet Gleason."

"Your sister told me to do that. I hope it works."

So did Liam.

The flames in the hall died away. As if in their stead, Finvarra appeared. "Mayhap I can't pass the dagger, but my magic can. I know how you love rats, boy. You and your hellcat will forever roam the walls of this wretched place as rats!"

Angry tongues of flame sparked from Finvarra's fingertips. He leveled his hands at the wine cellar.

They would never reach the door at the other end of the room in time. Liam hustled Janet to a spot between him and the wall and prayed that the knife and the ring on his finger would save them.

"Back off, or I'll blow a hole in you big enough to fit Knock Ma through!"

Kieran! Relief flooded through Liam, a torrential reprieve that nearly bowled him over. Janet's teeth chattered. Murmuring something senseless, he hugged her and then released her to peek around the door frame. He nearly whooped to see Kieran and Uncle Peadar scowling like demons, legs spread, the guns in their hands trained on Finvarra.

Similarly armed and nearly as menacing, Neil and Aidan rushed from behind the old fellas and took up positions effectively trapping the stunned fairy king. Of course, he could vanish, but Liam had a hunch that his pompous pride would make him stay.

"Liam!" Peadar's bone-rattling roar would have frozen a polar bear.

"We're all right!" The realization that the danger had truly passed left Liam trembling. The piercing throb in his wrist, which he'd forgotten during the last few desperate moments, felt like it would rupture his arm. Somehow he managed to smile for Janet. Her lips quivered valiantly back at him.

"Stay here till I call you." He bussed her forehead and stepped gingerly into the hall.

$$* \quad * \quad * \quad * \quad *$$

More curious than alarmed, Finvarra curbed the urge to strike Prince Liam down. The mortals who'd stormed the cellar clearly belonged to his clan. They seemed to think they could protect him. The bearded man, a hulking beast, exuded typical mortal belligerence. Finvarra dismissed him—until the gilded pin that marked the brute as a Fian warrior caught his eye.

The hawk-like mortal who'd issued the threat also wore the Fianna pin. A barbaric scar ran down his cheek, and he had the look of one who'd killed before and would do so again without hesitation. The two younger men sported no pins, but their unwavering stance and savage glares proclaimed them warriors too.

The presence of warriors didn't concern Finvarra. The presence of steel did. He sensed a lot of it, more than he could attribute to the paltry metal tubes these modern mortals wielded. He doubted such measly things could blow a hole in a house of sticks, let alone in the exalted King of the Fairies, but the steel troubled him.

He also sensed his troop's approach. Silently, he called to them, told them to hurry, that he was in danger. The mortals would flee when they saw a host of *sídhe* descending upon them.

Becula arrived first, her hideous form appearing right beside him. He savored the startled looks on the mortals' faces. Her repugnance came in handy now and then.

Beside him she might be, but with him, it seemed, she was not. "Yield, sire, I beg you. Their weapons are most lethal and will surely kill you!"

Disgusted by her treason, he peered down his nose at her. "Have you crept so long among them you've forgotten where your loyalty lies?"

"Never, sire. Please! Remember the legions of *sídhe* slaughtered at Slieve Mish and Taillten. Oh, do yield, sire. A battle here would surely be the end of us!"

"Listen to her," said the bearded giant. "We have no wish to harm you."

Finvarra glared. "I see no seeds of battle here. You're nothing more than an uncouth gang of ruffians. Your stunted cudgels are ludicrous at best."

Menace blazed in the scar-faced mortal's hawk-like eyes. He aimed his metal flute at an overhead light. "How about a little demonstration, bucko?"

Unsure what would happen, but sensing peril, Finvarra tensed. He shot a sideways glance at Becula. Her "I told you so" look enraged him. He would send her to live with her seal people friends after this.

"Now, Kieran, there's no need of that."

The newly-arrived man stopped beside the hawk. A handsome couple, both quite young, accompanied him. Finvarra barely noticed the dark-haired boy: the girl with Treasa's laugh-loving lips had transfixed him. She hastened to Prince Liam's side and asked after his health. His reply escaped Finvarra, so fixed was he upon the princess, who summoned the girl called Janet from the wine cellar in a pleasant and carefree tone.

"Welcome, dear friend," said the newcomer. "We are honored to have you visit Clontarf Castle again after all these years. Too much time has passed since you and yours have joined us for a dance or two."

Finvarra inspected the smiling speaker. His dark red hair and chestnut eyes proclaimed him a Boru. His attire resembled the other men's clothes, though beneath his black coat, a shiny gold sash crossed his shirt from shoulder to hip.

"Your attire is modern," Finvarra said, "but nonetheless kingly. Do I have the honor of addressing the High King of Ireland?"

"Technically, yes, though these days, I'm the only king." He held out his hand. "Brian Boru, sir. And you, I assume, are Finvarra, the King of the *Daoine Sídhe*."

Impressed, Finvarra moved to take King Brian's hand. The man called Kieran stiffened and raised his weapon.

Brian stayed his kinsman's arm. "It's all right, Kieran. Put the gun away." His commanding gaze encompassed each warrior in turn. "All of you."

Gun. So that's what they were. The leprechauns had told Finvarra of their capacity to inflict death. As he shook Brian's hand, he thought that perhaps he should listen to Becula more.

The air beside the old hag shimmered. Oona appeared with a bee-like buzz. Her huge round eyes, violet tonight, flared with alarm. "What's wrong, Fin?"

Wondering what was different about her, he shook his head. "Nothing is wrong, pet. An assemblage of wellborn mortals has come to welcome us to the ball."

Her head turned. The ends of her long blond hair brushed the floor. The slender form beneath her gossamer gown glowed with delight. "Why…it's the Boru clan!" she said in her tinkling trill. "At least you resemble the Borus I recall." Eyelids aflutter, her gaze homed in on Brian. "Ooh, so handsome!"

The mortal king smiled gallantly. "And you, madam, must be Queen Oona."

She giggled and nodded.

"Welcome back to Clontarf Castle."

A loud droning behind her announced the troop's arrival. The corridor teemed with *sídhe* whose party attire belied their somber faces. They'd received Finvarra's alert, then. Their presence fortified him, even as the lingering essence of deadly steel compelled him to raise a hand to keep them away. They stopped, awaiting his next command.

Unsure himself what that would be, he thrust his chin at Brian. "You welcome us, sir? You who have named your daughter after the terrible battle that saw the destruction of most of my tribe?"

Liam stepped forward, his face unreadable. "That isn't so. My sister's namesake is the Celtic Queen Taillte, who gave her name to that area long before the battle took place. She was the mortal foster mother of the Sun God, Lugh, an arrangement that proved the Celts and the Dananns could be friends."

"Just so!" Brian said cheerfully. "Friends who've lost touch. Shall we celebrate our reunion with a glass of champagne?"

Squeals of delight arose from the *sídhe*.

Finvarra tingled. The mortal king had granted him the dignity of friendship over the ignominy of defeat. The offer would have tempted him—hours had passed since his last sip of pilfered wine—but for the nearness of steel. Had the *sídhe* walked into a trap? If so, he would order the troop to retreat at once to a safer place, one from which they could freely destroy the mortals and their supposedly impregnable fortress.

"The steel, sir. Why do your people wear it if you come to us in friendship?"

"A precaution I trust is unnecessary now that we've met and talked. We both know we have no wish to be enemies."

The princess fussed with a belt at her waist. No, not a belt. A chain of steel from which hung a small scabbard. She tossed it into the wine cellar, pulled the dagger from the doorjamb, and threw that inside too.

"We'll put all our steel aside," she said, "but for the weapons the warriors must retain to protect my father."

"Hmmph," said Finvarra. "They may retain what they will. I won't be dancing with any warriors."

"I'm fine with that," Kieran said, returning his weapon to a scabbard inside his jacket.

Finvarra ignored him. "But you, fair princess. Will you reserve a waltz for me?"

"I'd be honored, sir."

"So you do believe in us?"

"They believe in you, sire," said Becula. "You wear no glimmer, yet you look as young as you did many mortal millennia ago."

Oona stared at his face. "Why, she's right, Fin! You do look handsome." She grinned playfully. "Maybe I should forbid you to dance with the mortal women tonight."

"Your appearance is indeed due to the mortals' belief," said Becula, "but only because we stand together in a contained space. Away from this place, belief in the *sídhe* will diminish."

"We can work to change that," Brian said. "We'll make the people believe in you again."

"How can you do this?" Finvarra asked.

"I can think of one way right off," the boy beside Brian said. "Liam is a fine storyteller, sir. No one can go back on old times the way he can. He'll tell everyone about your great feats."

The idea pleased Finvarra. "And those are many. Who are you, lad? You don't have the look of the Boru."

"I'm Kevin Boru, sir. My brother and I"—he glanced at one of the younger warriors—"take after our mother. There's no finer storyteller than Liam in all of Ireland. No one could do a better job of making the people believe."

Talty folded her arms and glared. "Maybe so, but my brother might not be inclined to help you after you injured him up on the cliffs."

Finvarra sighed deeply. "For the last time, I didn't do it. It was MacLir! Oh, for Danu's sake." He raised his hands. Before anyone could react, he cast a ball of healing light at Liam. The bruise on the boy's forehead disappeared. His arm would instantly heal as well. Even the rose on his lapel recovered. The smile of thanks on Talty's face had Finvarra suspecting she'd counted on his curative intervention.

He didn't mind. Not if the mortals could really help the *sídhe*.

Besides, he'd taken something in return for his seeming generosity.

"My arm's all right." Liam stretched his mortal limb, bending and twisting it every which way, staring in disbelief. "Thank you." He whipped his other arm protectively around Janet. "But that doesn't mean you can continue to kidnap our women!"

Finvarra rolled his eyes. "I only meant to borrow her," he fibbed, not wishing to derail the negotiations. "I really haven't invited all that many mortal women to live with me, you know. It only seems that way because too many deceitful girls have blamed me for stealing them to mask their own indiscretions," which wasn't a fib at all.

That's true," Oona sadly concurred. "The people began to despise us, and then they forgot all about us."

"You must let us help you," said Brian. "We want to share our bounty."

The King of the Fairies rejoiced. "Including your wine?"

"Absolutely. Why, I can have a keg of fine French burgundy delivered to Knock Ma once a month, if you like."

Finvarra's hands flew to his hips. "Every night!"

Brian scowled like a horse trader. "Once a week!"

Delighted, Finvarra grinned. "Done! And please throw in an occasional white. I do so love a good Pouilly-Fuissé!"

Laughing now, the kings shook hands.

"Join us upstairs, my friends," Brian said.

"We'll come up when the music starts," said Finvarra. "We must change our attire to blend in." He focused on the men's clothes. In seconds, he wore a similar outfit.

"Ooh," said Oona. "You look delicious dressed like that." Her gaze fell on Talty and Janet. Her dress didn't change, but her long blond hair flew into a coiffure much like theirs, complete with gold and ribbons. "The Celts always did have the most wonderfully elaborate hairstyles!"

"We'll see you later, then." Brian said, and he led his clan members from the cellar.

Before she left, Princess Talty recovered her dagger and sheath from the wine cellar. As the mortals ascended the staircase, the threat of the steel abated.

Becula vanished. So did the rest of the *sidhe*.

Oona glowed again. "I'm proud of you for helping Prince Liam, Fin. But it's not like you to give a boon without exacting payment."

"I exacted my payment, Oona." He took her arm, and they were back in their private chamber. "I reversed the dancing spell I placed on the girl. She'll be fine without it, I'm sure."

CHAPTER THIRTY-FIVE

Surrounded by the Borus and their Dacey cousins, Janet trudged up the stairs. She held her skirt to keep from stumbling, though Liam's grip on her arm would have prevented such a catastrophe. As they climbed, he lightheartedly summarized his chilling ordeal, from his denunciation of the devious elevator to his glowing appreciation of Janet's timely intervention.

"The rest you know," he said. "I'm thinking I'll be thinking twice before I slag you for wearing that gun again, Kieran."

Kieran responded with some sort of grunt, and they entered the room at the top of the stairs, the one Janet had been about to check out when she'd first met Liam's cousins. The switched-on lights and misaligned chairs made her think that the room had recently been in use.

King Brian told the men to empty their pockets. Prince Peadar cheerfully removed rings and a bracelet from his jacket and set them on the long oak table. Kieran Dacey followed suit. So did their gun-toting sons, Neil and Aidan, whose leisurely manner suggested they confronted hostile fairies every day. Kevin added a watch to the pile, Talty her priceless dagger and sheath.

"Neil," said the king, "go tell Eileen and the piper that despite the delay, the festivities will commence shortly. Aidan, get this stuff back to Liam's room."

The older boys scooped the pieces into a white pillow case that must have come from Liam's bed. They left the room while the king spoke quietly to the other men.

Then he addressed Janet. "Young lady, we haven't been properly introduced." He winked and smiled. "I'm Liam's father."

Awestruck and tongue-tied, she gawked at him. Liam's father. Liam's father was a king. A king in a gold sash. A real king, and he looked like one, so tall and trim with his dashing beard and his piercing x-ray eyes.

She remembered to smile. "I'm Janet Gleason, sir."

"Yes, I know." He squeezed her hand. "It's fine to meet you, Janet. Thank you for helping my son."

"That's one fierce lady you've got there, Li," Talty called from across the room.

Janet's cheeks burned. "I'm sorry I pushed you."

The princess grinned. "No harm, Janet. Needs must when the devil rides, eh?"

"Is that how you got the dagger, Jan?" Liam sounded impressed. "And the rest of the steel. Who raided my jewelry drawer?"

"I did," said Kevin. "It seemed like a good idea at the time. We all had your steel in our pockets, just in case. Except your father. Kieran and my father were looking out for him."

"I came this close to blowing that son of a—" Kieran caught himself. He looked about, as if some unseen creature might be listening. "That fairy gentleman away."

King Brian chuckled. "And I was ready to give you the nod if our negotiations failed, but what good would it have done? Even with Finvarra gone, the bitter feelings between *Them* and us would only have escalated. Best to remember that trouble hates nothing as much as a smile."

"That's the sort of strategy Declan wrote about in his diaries," said Liam.

His father nodded. "I should have read them years ago. They contain invaluable advice for dealing with the *sídhe*. Declan repeated often that we must be ever aware that we live in each other's shadows."

"It's hard to believe they'd quiet down for a dance and a glass of wine," said Kieran.

Peadar grunted. "Better wine than blood."

"I agree on both counts," said the king. "We must keep in mind that the *sídhe* aren't like us. They don't think the way we do. In fact, they hardly think at all. They run on intense, self-indulgent emotion. Whatever or whomever they love or despise, they do so with great passion. All they care about is the joy they can currently attain, even if they derive that joy from vengeance."

"So you sidetracked their vengeance with friendship," said Liam.

"Don't think it was easy for me, Li. I took one look at you coming out of that wine cellar and nearly throttled Finvarra myself. But amity is the best defense we can employ with the *sidhe*, even if we feel otherwise. They're ferocious enemies, but wonderful friends."

"Look how he healed your wrist," said Talty. "Now you can dance!"

Janet shuddered. Why should the mention of dancing upset her? She could waltz well enough, and Gramp had told her she could politely refuse the dances she didn't know. Her agitation eased when Liam's hand slid over hers.

"I'm looking forward to it now," he said, eyeing her with a fond look that suddenly turned to one of concern. He cocked his head. "Would you like some water or something, Jan?"

"No thanks, I'm fine. Just wondering what my grandparents will think of all this."

"It might be best if they hear it from me," said the king. "I'll speak to them after the dance. All right, everyone. Show time. Kevin, escort Janet to her grandparents before you join the head table. The rest of you come with me."

"Wait!" Talty pranced across the room. "We'd best check you for cobwebs." She frowned and brushed at Janet's sleeves and cheeks. "There. I think you'll do."

Her brisk tone held no grudge. Janet giggled with relief and thanked her. Encouraged by Liam's smile, she left the room with Kevin's gentle touch guiding her toward the great hall.

"Good on you for pulling Liam out of the fire, so to speak," he said.

Another wave of heat warmed her cheeks. "Is it always so crazy here?"

"A typical evening with the Borus? Hardly. This fairy stuff was a surprise for all of us."

The closer they drew to the great hall, the louder the buzz of collective conversation grew. Occasional flourishes of harp music rose above the din. The sound had unsettled Janet when she'd first arrived. Now it soothed her. The gloom that had lurked on the edge of her thoughts for days no longer pestered her.

She looked for Gram and Gramp but couldn't see over the heads of the guests. Kevin's greater height gave him an enviable view of the gathering.

"Your grandparents are over by the hearth." Fingers brushing her elbow, he ushered her through the crowd to the fireplace, exchanging polite pleasantries with the guests they passed.

Gram and Gramp were facing away from Janet, chatting with someone she couldn't see. They pivoted together at Kevin's "Ambassador Gleason?"

Gramp's smile glowed. "Ah, there's our Ladybug!"

Janet nearly shrieked when she saw who was behind them. Matti! Matti was here, all dressed up and looking gorgeous in a chocolate gown and a necklace of pink and brown gemstones. Behind her glasses, her made-up eyes squinted with humor. Rosy lipstick outlined her fiendish grin: she was clearly enjoying Janet's confusion.

"Hey, Jan. How's it going?"

Janet zoomed toward her. They hugged and laughed, and Janet asked who had sprung this very pleasant surprise. She eyed her grandparents suspiciously.

"Don't look at us," said Gramp. "We didn't know Miss Matti was here until a few minutes ago."

Kevin smiled smugly, the same way he had when he'd entered Talty's bedroom and admitted he knew about Janet. Apparently he was the culprit, or at least one of them.

Janet laughed again. "You're full of surprises tonight, Kevin. You too, Matti. I thought you were back in Boston. What on earth are you doing here?"

"I got arrested at the airport."

"You did not," Kevin said in a mock chiding tone.

"Okay, detained. By a dude with a scary scar on his face. He asked me all sorts of questions about you, Jan. Said I could come to the ball if I helped him find you. I told him to get lost, but Kevin came in and said it was okay." Cheeks pink, eyelids batting, she gushed the last part at Kevin, and this time he didn't seem to mind. "Kevin said the scary dude was his cousin Kieran. They told me who Liam really was. After I got the okay from my parents to stay until Sunday, the scary dude brought me to his house. I met his wife. A really nice lady named Breege. She's a real duchess! She called Louise at the dress shop, and the next thing I knew, I had tons of great dresses to try on."

Matti paused, and Gram laughed. "She's been telling us all about it while we waited for you, Janet. Where on earth have you been?"

"I've been showing her around the castle," Kevin said, "what with Liam tied up with his folks and all."

The sudden drone of bagpipes hushed every sound in the hall.

"What's that?" whispered Matti.

"Irish war pipes," Kevin replied. "As old as the Hag of Beara. The King's Piper is ready to lead the royal family to the gathering."

The guests who were seated rose. Everyone turned toward the wail of the pipes. Two lines of frosty-faced men in dress uniforms appeared in an enormous entrance across the room. The lines split right and left, and the soldiers formed an honor guard.

"The King's Rangers," Kevin said softly. "The piper is next. He'll be playing the Brian Boru March, nearly a thousand years old."

The growing racket chilled Janet. She loved it, loved the way the sound of the pipes vibrated up her spine and into her bones. Like a giant of yore, the piper marched in wearing a long black cape and a saffron kilt. The thick leather strap that supported his pipes crisscrossed a red sash on his chest. A huge black beret with a silver badge and a blue-green plume topped his outfit. He blew into a mouthpiece as he tramped, a different style of playing from the Irish elbow pipes Janet had seen.

And there was King Brian, holding the hand of a regal lady with upswept blond hair and a thin gold tiara. Liam's mother. The queen. A beautiful queen in a pearl-studded apricot gown that matched the rose in the king's lapel.

Side by side and no less regal, Liam and Talty followed their parents. They betrayed no hint of their recent adventures downstairs.

Cameras clicked and flashed. The piper stood at the end of the head table and played until the Borus reached their seats. Other members of the clan, including Prince Peadar, Kieran, and their wives and sons, took their places on either side of them.

"I have to run," Kevin said, tapping Matti's arm, and then Janet's. "Come find us after dinner." He slipped away and claimed a seat beside his lookalike brother.

At last, the thrilling caterwaul stopped; the piper stood at attention. Using a wireless microphone, King Brian welcomed everyone to Clontarf Castle and said he hoped the ambassadors and their families would always think of Ireland as their "home from home."

Dinner passed quickly. The pleasant wait staff served course after savory course. While her grandparents chatted with nearby dignitaries, Janet conversed with Matti about the food and Matti's adventures since Kieran Dacey whisked her away from the airport.

The harpist and pianist played until the last plate was cleared. Then two groups of musicians, all in formal attire, took their place. A man and two women arranged a cello and flute near the piano. A larger group with fiddles and other traditional Irish instruments began tuning up in a different corner. Gramp had said the waltzes would trade off with Irish set dancing.

King Brian stood and called for attention. The hall quieted instantly.

"Those of you who've done your diplomatic homework are familiar with the official motto of the Boru clan: 'The Strong Hand Rules.' We have several unofficial war cries too. One of our favorites is, 'When the belly is full, the bones like to stretch.' A fitting proverb after such a splendid dinner.

"Another saying we're fond of is, 'When cares overburden body and soul, dance.' That one harks back to the days when dancing masters roamed around Ireland teaching the people to kick up their heels. They wore silver buckles on their shoes, and when they showed off some of their fancier dance steps, their feet moved so fast, they were said to 'cover the buckle.'

"We don't expect you to cover the buckle tonight. After a short break to stretch our bones and let the ladies change into their dancing shoes, we'll take to the floor and start with a waltz or two. Later, we'll have a few set dances, which are easy to learn if you're so inclined.

"Before we break, I'd like to thank you all for joining our party tonight. May the hands you've stretched to us in friendship never be stretched in want. May this evening's fun in some small measure repay the generous gifts of time and good will you've given us tonight. And may the blessing of each day be the blessing you need most."

After a round of polite applause, the royal family dispersed. The guests mingled while the staff cleared and carried away the tables. Janet and Matti went to the ladies' room to freshen up. While Matti babbled away, Janet desperately tried to remember how to waltz.

* * * * *

Liam washed up and returned to the hall. His family had retired to their private lounge for a short break, and he was supposed to bring Janet there to present the necklace. He'd forgotten all about it until his mother mentioned it. No use for it but to tell her he'd lost it.

Janet and Matti were coming toward him. He couldn't get over how foxy Matti looked all dressed up, and Janet looked like a princess, one he meant to keep dancing in his two good arms all night.

Kevin suddenly appeared at his side and slipped a small black box into his hand. "Adam DeWitt just dropped this off. Said you might like to have it tonight."

It must be the keepsake Liam had asked him to find for Janet. Whatever had made him bring it tonight? Liam knew better than to question such coincidences. Holding his breath, he opened the box.

A necklace, not a locket—and no sapphires, thank heaven. After her experience with Becula's necklace, he doubted Janet would ever want to see sapphires again. She'd likely have hated the sapphire necklace his mother had chosen. Just as well he'd lost it.

Adam had written a note on the back of his business card:

> *Sir, The enclosed pendant is an amethyst from County Mayo. Amethysts are believed to offer powerful protection from harm, especially for travelers. This piece dates from the late nineteenth century and is appropriate for both casual and dress attire. If it is not to your liking, I will obtain a different item. Yours, A.*

The chain was gold, the setting classic. It was perfect. Liam sighed. He'd rather give it to Janet privately, as a special token of their friendship, but he saw no reason to disappoint his mother. Deciding he'd tell Janet the whole story later, he closed the box and tucked it in his pocket.

"Will you show Matti around a little, Kev? My mother wants to meet Janet."

Kevin's smile grew as the girls approached. "No better man, Li. Take your time."

✳ ✳ ✳ ✳ ✳

"Oh Fin, they're playing the first waltz! It's time to go up!"

"Hmm?" Finvarra frowned at his looking glass image. He didn't mind the modern dinner suit, but he despised wearing his hair so short. Oona had made him glimmer it off for the night, to fit in with the mortals' current styles. The rest of his appearance amazed him. He'd hardly had to alter his face and height at all. He looked young and tall without changing a thing.

"They believe in us, Oona."

She patted his arm. "Of course they do, sweet. They wouldn't have wielded such deadly weapons if they didn't. The troop is ready. They're getting antsy. Can we *please* go up now?"

Finvarra smiled at Oona's glimmer-free face, timeless and lovely again because of the mortals' renewed belief. At least the Borus believed. As for the rest of the Irish, he'd worry about them tomorrow. "Yes, pet. Let's dance."

CHAPTER THIRTY-SIX

Clontarf Castle's enchanting blend of medieval and modern decor flourished throughout the royal family's private lounge. Matching ivory couches and chairs infused the air with the rich scent of leather. Scattered around the room were bizarre bits of metal and wood, ancient furniture that intrigued Janet. She would definitely take Talty up on her offer to show her around the place.

Seated near the window, Talty waved when Janet and Liam came in. Gram and Gramp stood with King Brian and Queen Eileen near a small gas fireplace, all of them laughing and chatting away until they spotted the newcomers. Liam introduced Janet to his mother, who was warm and friendly. She flabbergasted Janet by asking Liam to give her a present from the royal family.

Fingers shaking, Janet opened the long black box Liam handed to her. It contained a beautiful amethyst necklace. Gram and the queen both seemed puzzled, but the queen recovered quickly and said, "Please consider it a small memento of your first visit to Ireland, Janet."

Too stunned to speak at first, Janet suddenly realized that Gram—and Louise—had known all along that the queen intended to give her the necklace. That's why she'd said no when Janet asked to borrow her sapphires! Janet wanted to hug her.

After she'd thanked the king and queen several times, she wondered what she was supposed to do. Should she wear the new necklace? Would she hurt Gram's feelings if she took off the topaz pendant?

Talty came to her rescue. "Janet's grandmother gave her the topaz especially for the ball, Mum. It matches her dress better than the amethyst. Perhaps she could wear that another time."

Smiling graciously, Queen Eileen said she hoped Janet would wear the amethyst to another royal function soon. Janet thought she'd enjoy that, as long as no fairies were involved. Feeling like a walking jewelry box, she put the amethyst into her purse beside her locket and left the lounge with Liam.

A waltz started up in the great hall. Her grip on his hand tightened. Why was she so afraid?

He released her hand and bowed like a gallant cavalier. "Fair Lady Janet, will you deign to grant me the supreme honor of this memorable evening's first waltz?"

She'd forgotten the steps! Waltzing with Gramp for practice had been easy, but this was for real, in front of people from all over the world. She couldn't do it!

Kevin and Matti were already dancing. Matti could barely waltz, yet she giggled and glided in Kevin's arms, the dance no more than a vehicle for her to be with him.

Liam clasped Janet's hand and drew her onto the dance floor and she panicked recalling the prom and her heels and tripping on the tablecloth and the dishes crashing, but Liam's touch erased all that. He put one hand on her back and clasped her hand in the other, and they joined the other waltzers. Secure in the refuge of his arms, her worries melted away.

"Hold me fast and fear not," he whispered in her ear.

She should have known he'd sense her anxiety. "What's that from?"

"What is now officially 'our song.' A Scottish ballad called 'Tam Lin.' It's about a girl who saved her fella from the fairies."

"I remember. The girl's name was Janet, and she picked an enchanted rose." Janet bobbed her head toward the off-white rose in Liam's lapel. "A hybrid tea named Alba?"

His vibrant laugh enfolded her like a mist full of rainbows. "Pretty *and* smart. I like you, Janet Gleason."

He whirled her in a circle, and she floated along with him, content to let him guide her through the growing throng of dancers. A stunning blonde dancing with Prince Peadar caught her attention. Or rather, the neon glow in the woman's violet eyes did.

"Speaking of the fairies, isn't that Queen Oona dancing with your uncle?"

Liam coolly inspected the dancers. His lips curved in amusement. "Yes, and there's old Finnie himself, waltzing with my sister and looking fine in his boy's regular haircut. Your friend Nora and her sapphire necklace are keeping Kieran on his toes. The room is alive with the feckin' things, though no one seems to notice that some of the guests are half a bubble off true. Ah well, we'll let them have their fun."

"Do you think he'll want to dance with me?"

"Finvarra? Why not? He said he only ever wanted to dance, and that's what he's doing. Would you mind if he asked you?"

"I guess not." Janet squeezed Liam's shoulder. "But I'd rather dance with you."

He spun her behind a column and stole a kiss.

* * * * *

Finvarra danced with all the Boru women: King Brian's elderly mother and aunt, his wife and good sisters, and yes, his bewitching daughter. He waltzed closely enough with Princess Talty to sense a warrior's soul poles apart from Treasa's gentle spirit. As much as he'd hoped she might be Treasa reborn, she wasn't. Nevertheless, Talty danced beautifully, gracing him with smile after welcoming smile.

"You cover the buckles well," she said.

Delighting in the compliment, he whirled and spun and laughed with her. He waltzed with Janet too, teaching her simple steps when the band played jigs and reels, no longer caring that he couldn't keep her. Thanks to King Brian's invitation, he'd have grippable girls aplenty whenever the mortals partied.

The warlike beat of a bodhran joined the primitive wail of the uilleann pipes. Despite the mortal years that had passed since Finvarra had last heard this particular pattern of music, the rhythm and notes remained the same. The drummer and piper were calling the Clan Boru to their distinctive clan dance: the venerable Siege of Dublin.

In droves they came, these handsome mortals whose noble lineage had guarded the kingdom for centuries. Those outside the clan who knew the dance joined them. Those who didn't split their ranks: some would watch; the rest would learn.

Finvarra rippled with pleasure. The Siege of Dublin, named for the action the Celts and their allies imposed upon Dublin's Vikings before the Battle of Clontarf, allowed a man to take hold of the waists of the ladies. He trawled about seeking an advantageous place in the forming lines. Off to the side, Prince Liam and his kinsman, Kevin, were teaching the steps to Janet and her buxom friend.

Liam spoke as he demonstrated. "It's easy. All you do is stand in your line holding hands with the fellas on either side of you. Three steps forward, three steps back, grab hold of the fella you're facing, swing around with him three times, move on to the next line, and do it all over again."

"I'm game!" said Janet's grippable friend.

Janet seemed unsure. "All right. I guess I can do it."

Finvarra meant to ensure that she could. "May I be of assistance?"

Liam smiled: no hard feelings. "Do you know the Siege of Dublin, sir?"

"Remember it? Why, I helped invent it! It's the greatest gripping dance of all time!"

A fiddle and a tin whistle joined in the primal pipe/drum mix. The drum beat louder. Hundreds of dancers stood waiting in dozens of lines to set the great hall shaking beneath their feet. At last, the piper hit the notes that signaled the start of the dance.

Finvarra took Janet's right hand, Liam her left. They coached her through the first swing, and she laughed at her success.

Sídhe and mortal alike stepped and swung, once, then twice. After the third line passed, Finvarra found himself face-to-face with Talty Boru.

He might have been back with Treasa, stomping the ground in the chill of a torchlit night. He gripped her and swung and moved on, and on and on, until the dance ended. Unthinkably heartsick, he alerted the *sídhe* and summoned Oona.

"We must leave," he told her. Ignoring her protests, he clasped her hand and sought King Brian, who mingled mirthfully with his guests.

When he was between groups, Finvarra engaged his attention. "Your Majesty, on behalf of the *Daoine Sídhe*, we thank you for most generously inviting us to your splendid *céilí*, but after the gathering comes the scattering." He held out his hand.

Brian clasped it tight. "Leaving so soon, my friend? It's hardly the tail of the day. The band is just warming up."

"We must return to Galway, sir. We wish to express our appreciation for your generous hospitality." Finvarra smiled. "And for your wine. I look forward to sampling a decent vintage or two."

"My pleasure, sir. Now that we've met, please don't be strangers. And don't hesitate to call upon us if you need anything. We'd be honored to help."

Oona's eyelids beat like a hummingbird's wings. "The locals of Tuam plan to pave over one of our favorite hurling grounds. We've tried stalling their machinery and untying their shoelaces, but they won't go away. Can you have them put their car park somewhere else?"

"I'll speak to the town council, madam. How can we reach you to let you know when we have our next dance?"

Finvarra thought for a moment. He doubted King Brian had a marble slab. "Email?"

Brian roared laughing. "Send an envoy to me at the King's Residence or Tara Hall, and we'll see what we can do."

"Thank you, sir. Good-bye." Finvarra raised his hand to signal the troop. One by one, the *sídhe* returned to their outpost beneath the castle.

Oona was pouting when she and Finvarra emerged in their private chamber. "Why did we have to leave? The dancing was far from over. I wanted to waltz with King Brian again. He's so handsome!"

"So you've said, but mind, pet. Silver already streaks King Brian's hair. They're mortals. We must leave them alone and keep to our own kind."

"But why can't we visit them now and then? We'd have food and drink and dancing all the time, just as we did when they first came to Ireland."

"When they first came to Ireland, we befriended them in truce and grew to enjoy their company. And then we attended their funerals. So many funerals, Oona. We not only lost many good friends to death, we lost the trust of those who came after them. I couldn't bear another mortal funeral."

"But we'd have these new friends for several of their years, at least."

"Short mortal years. Then they'll die, and their heirs will be wary of us. The cycle of mistrust and violence will start again."

"Please, Fin—"

"Enough, woman. Let's go home."

*****

The band announced the final waltz of the long, lovely evening. Pleasantly exhausted after dancing all night, mostly with Liam, Janet linked arms with him, and they made their way to the center of the dance floor.

Becula intercepted them, still in her Nora persona. "The others have already left, but I wanted a word before I go, if I may."

Liam stiffened and stepped in front of Janet. "And what might that be?"

Laughter rumbled in the old woman's throat. "I mean you no harm, sir. I never did. That's all I wanted to say. If you hadn't come after us up on Howth Hill, the king would have had his dance, and I'd have persuaded him to let your Janet go. She'd have remembered nothing. Finvarra only wanted to dance."

Amused by Liam's protectiveness, Janet stepped from behind him. "So everyone keeps saying. He and his wish to dance have caused a lot of trouble. You and your necklace have too."

Becula fingered the sapphire and sighed. "It's not the first time. I fear it won't be the last, though he won't get the urge to dance for a long mortal while now. Still, I regret the suffering you've endured. I wish to make amends. If either of you should ever be in need of help, call on old Becula. I'll hear you and do what I can."

"Thank you." Liam's tone implied that calling her would be the last thing he'd ever do, no matter how desperate he might be.

Janet couldn't fault him for his annoyance, but she felt sorry for Becula, forever tied to a selfish, juvenile king. "Yes, thank you. Good luck to you, Becula."

"And to the two of you. May fortune ever favor you." The air seemed to swallow her.

Liam huffed. "I'll never get used to the way they do that."

Janet thought it a great trick. She'd often wished she could simply vanish, or at least become another person, the way Becula turned into Nora. Not so much lately, however. Lately she liked the person she'd become since she'd moved to Ireland. She couldn't recall the last time she'd felt the need to be anyone but herself.

The lights dimmed. The music started, an easy air for the weary dancers. Liam found a spot on the floor, and they melded into the waltz position a heartbeat closer than usual.

And Janet danced.

ACKNOWLEDGMENTS

Sincere thanks to:

My daughter Bevin for her professional insight into Janet's theater background.

My Monday night writing group for their outstanding critiques and ongoing support.

My treasured aunts, Kathleen and Geraldine O'Brien, for so generously allowing me access to their incredible library of old Irish books. In one of these lovely antiques, I found "The Fairy Thorn," a poem written in the 1830s by Sir Samuel Ferguson. A phrase from this poem became the title of *Glancing Through the Glimmer*.

The postman my husband and I met near Knock Ma, County Galway, for his assurance that the fairies are still there.

ABOUT THE AUTHOR

Boston, Massachusetts native Pat McDermott writes romantic action/adventure stories set in Ireland. The Glimmer Books, *Glancing Through the Glimmer*, *Autumn Glimmer*, and *A Pot of Glimmer*, are young adult paranormal adventures starring Ireland's mischievous fairies and a royal family that might have been. The Glimmer Books are "prequels" to her popular Band of Roses Trilogy: *A Band of Roses*, *Fiery Roses*, and *Salty Roses*. Her contemporary romance, *The Rosewood Whistle*, features Ireland's music and myths. *Unholy Crossing* is her first ghost story.

Pat's favorite non-writing activities include cooking, hiking, reading, and traveling, especially to Ireland. She lives and writes in New Hampshire, USA.

For more information, or to contact Pat, visit her website:
http://www.patmcdermott.net

AUTUMN GLIMMER
The Glimmer Books / Book Two

Janet and Liam meet again for a Halloween weekend they'll never forget...

Fairies living beneath the lake on the King of Ireland's country estate? Janet Gleason isn't surprised. The American teen and her royal friend, Prince Liam Boru, have met the Good People before. Just before Halloween, three of the fairies, Blinn, Mell, and Lewy, leave their watery home to fill a magical bag with the flowers their queen requires to keep a hungry monster asleep. Blinn decides she'd like to see the mortal king's house. Lewy wants to taste oatcakes again, and Mell goes along on a tragic ride that leaves poor Lewy lost and alone. Can Liam and Janet help him find the flower bag before the monster awakens? Or will Lewy's misguided glimmer trap the young mortals forever in the palace beneath the lake?

Available in Print and eBook

A POT of GLIMMER
The Glimmer Books / Book Three

A leprechaun's feud with a Viking ghoul puts Liam and Janet in deadly danger...

Ireland, January 1014 - Fledgling leprechaun Awley O'Hay leads a raid on a Dublin mint. The mission: steal a shipment of coins to aid the High King, Brian Boru, in his war against the Vikings. Awley and his team plan the heist with commando precision, but they hit a glitch and only escape a bloodthirsty mob with the help of Hazel, the uncommon sister of one of the leprechauns. Yet the money master's vengeful ghost troubles Awley for centuries. So do Awley's forbidden feelings for Hazel.

Ireland, July 2015 - Janet Gleason has had her fill of fairies. They've not only plagued the American teen since she arrived in Dublin, they've also hindered her romance with her gallant friend, Prince Liam Boru. When Janet's grandfather, the U.S. Ambassador to Ireland, throws a Fourth of July celebration, Liam reluctantly attends with the rest of the royal family.

Also attending are several uninvited guests. A fairy witch named Becula arrives with Hazel, her clever and quirky protégée, to beg a favor of Janet. The unplanned appearance of Awley O'Hay and his leprechaun pals triggers a chilling visit from the money master, now an undead monster hungry for human flesh.

Liam and Janet fall into a nightmare that tests their courage in ways they never imagined. Nor did they imagine that real leprechauns are nothing like the "little men" of Irish lore.

Available in Print and eBook

Made in the USA
Lexington, KY
04 June 2019